RIVERBEND FRIENDS™

Running on Empty

RIVERBEND FRIENDS™

Jill Williamson

CREATED BY

Lissa Halls Johnson

A Focus on the Family resource
published by Tyndale House Publishers

Running on Empty
Copyright © 2024 by Focus on the Family.

A Focus on the Family book published by Tyndale House Publishers, Carol Stream, Illinois 60188

Focus on the Family and the accompanying logos and designs are federally registered trademarks and *Riverbend Friends* is a trademark of Focus on the Family, 8605 Explorer Drive, Colorado Springs, CO 80920.

Tyndale and Tyndale's quill logo are registered trademarks of Tyndale House Ministries.

Cover design by Mike Harrigan

All Scripture quotations, unless otherwise indicated, are taken from the Holy Bible, *New International Version,*® *NIV.*® Copyright © 1973, 1978, 1984, 2011 by Biblica, Inc.® Used by permission. All rights reserved worldwide.

The characters and events in this story are fictional. Any resemblance to actual persons or events is coincidental.

For information about special discounts for bulk purchases, please contact Tyndale House Publishers at csresponse@tyndale.com, or call 1-855-277-9400.

ISBN 978-1-64607-090-9

Printed in the United States of America

30	29	28	27	26	25	24
7	6	5	4	3	2	1

To Kaitlyn:

Thanks for inspiring Izzy's quirkiness, love of baking cupcakes, and wild leggings. She wouldn't exist without you.

Chapter 1

A GIRL COULD LEARN TO DO ANYTHING if she could find the right keywords.

I sat in the den at the family computer scrolling through a list of search results. I honestly doubted golfing would ever become my new fave, but I wanted to try my best.

My first search for "how to golf" brought up a host of tutorials, including several on mini golf. I added "-mini" to limit my search, and after browsing a few results, I learned that the first time a player hits the golf ball off the tee, they usually use a club called the driver.

So there are a lot of different kinds of golf clubs. Stars.

I refined my search by typing "how to use a driver in golf" and viewing the video results. This brought up a list of promising tutorials. With over 1.5 million views, "How to Hit the Golf Ball with Driver for Beginners" from the channel *Golf Guy* won out, and I watched the entire fifteen-and-a-half-minute video, taking as many mental notes as possible.

When that video ended, I moved the mouse to choose a similar video and accidentally jostled the desk. The sticky note I had placed over the webcam fluttered onto the keyboard. I picked it up and pressed it back over the camera, this time securing it with a piece of tape. I did not want anyone looking at me in my own home.

Paranoid? Maybe, but I'd learned the hard way to be careful about such things.

I was midway through learning how to putt when my cell phone played my custom text message alert: *"We love you, Miss Hannigan!"*

I glanced at the phone, which was lying face up to the right of the mouse pad.

Tessa: On my way.

I texted back: Shay's not coming, right?

I watched the words of my text sit on that white screen with the little *Delivered* notification underneath. When there was no sign of the three dots showing that Tessa was typing back, I squirmed in my chair, worried I'd annoyed her. I knew this thing between Shay and me was hard for Tessa and Amelia, but I just couldn't talk to Shay right now. I felt too . . . betrayed. Tessa and Amelia didn't understand, of course, but so far, they had tried to be supportive.

The problem? They were being supportive to both of us.

Not taking sides was likely the right thing for friends to do, but somehow, it didn't really feel like full support when I knew my friends were also supporting the person in the wrong.

"We love you, Miss Hannigan!"

I jumped. I'd zoned out while thinking about Shay, and Tessa had taken so long to reply that my phone had gone to sleep.

Tessa: No, she's not.

I breathed a sigh of relief. Of course Shay wouldn't be coming. This was *my* day. I had planned it with Tessa, and I had not invited Shay Mitchell.

I watched a few more videos. Golf sure seemed like an easy sport.

When I grew bored, I logged into my school account to see if our fall schedules had been posted yet. Still nothing. Ugh. I needed to know if Shay and I were in Baking and Pastry together or not. Baking and Pastry was a popular class, and I had been super excited to take it. Until the whole rift with Shay. Then I had called the office and put in a request for a new elective. I didn't really care which one I got. I just knew I couldn't handle spending so much time with Shay, especially when baking.

It would be *so great* if no one got their first choices. Then everyone would be disappointed, but no one would suspect I had changed my schedule. Then I wouldn't have to deal with it at all.

Please, God?

I heard the hum of the garage door rise and fall, then the inner door opened. "Isabella?"

"*Sí*, Papi?" I said.

Papi appeared in the hallway to the kitchen, and my brothers, Leo and Sebastian, were behind him. Leo, tall and skinny, stood a head taller than Papi, while Sebastian now matched Papi in height.

"Hello, Isabella Valadez," Sebastian said.

"You're still here," Leo added.

I checked my phone and shrugged. "Leaving any minute now, I'm sure. How was the car?"

Yesterday, Cody Nichols, my adorable neighbor, had bought himself a sports car. When Papi first heard about it, he said it was a street-racer. Papi and the boys had gone over to have a look, and I was quite curious about Cody's new wheels.

"Cody Nichols has a very fast car," Sebastian said, nodding as if to prove his point.

Papi smiled wistfully. "*Muy bonito.*"

"Papi's in love," Leo said.

"No," Papi said. "An Acura RSX is not classic enough for me, but it's a nice ride. Peppy engine with a slick manual shifter."

"He took you for a ride?" I asked.

Leo wiggled his eyebrows. "He let Papi drive it."

"Papi!" I couldn't believe my dad had driven Cody's new car.

"What?" Papi said, shrugging. "He offered. I just took it around the block."

I rolled my eyes, then asked Leo, "What did *you* think?"

"Oh, it's nice," Leo said. "It's fast, and the back seat is nearly useless, so he won't have to drive his friends everywhere. I'd take it in a heartbeat if he wanted to trade."

Leo drove a beat-up Honda Civic. All I knew about Cody's car was that it was small, sporty, and cobalt blue. The perfect color for Captain America, even though Papi had said the car was foreign.

"We love you, Miss Hannigan!"

I checked my phone.

Tessa: I'm here.

I closed the windows on the computer and jumped up from the chair. "Tessa is here," I said. "If you ever get your car finished, Papi, maybe you and Cody can race."

Since Leo was out of college for the summer, he and Papi had put in quite a few hours working on Papi's old '65 Ford Mustang in the garage.

"Oh, I wouldn't stand a chance," Papi said, tucking me under his arm in a side hug. "Have fun, *mija.*"

Leo snickered. "I kind of wish I could see you golf," he said. "Might be a good laugh."

"Estás pesado," I said, walking away. Leo could be pretty annoying sometimes.

At the door, I shoved my feet into my tennis shoes, grabbed my Captain Marvel baseball cap, and ran outside. Tessa's silver Camry looked small in my driveway. I hopped into the passenger's side and buckled my seat belt.

"You look adorable!" I said, admiring Tessa's royal-blue polo shirt tucked into a pleated white skirt, which she wore without leggings. I was taller than Tessa and had never been comfortable leaving my legs bare. I always covered them with leggings. Tessa also wore a white sun visor with her hair combed into a braided ponytail that fell over the top.

"Thanks," Tessa said. "So do you."

"*Pfft.* The whole golfing dress code had me worried for a while. I don't even own a collared shirt. Thankfully, Claire said I could borrow this." I glanced down at the words embroidered at the top left of my sister's polo shirt: *Riverbend Robotics Team 1015.*

"Alex and Amelia are both going to meet us there," Tessa said as she backed out onto the street.

I caught sight of Cody's car in his driveway. I wanted to tell Tessa that Papi had driven it, but I didn't want to give her anything that would add to her theory that Cody liked me—or that I liked him.

"How is your scarf coming along?" Tessa asked.

"Slowly." I hadn't touched it in over a week. "I'm not sure crocheting is my thing."

Over the past few months, I'd tried dozens of different activities. It was all part of my mission to discover the real Isabella Valadez. I got the idea from Zoe, one of the youth workers at the church Tessa and I attended, and so far, it had been a lot of fun.

In the arts, I'd tried calligraphy, candle making, origami, cross-stitching, and crocheting that scarf I'd all but abandoned. I'd also taken a painting class from Miss Carrie, Tessa's mom, and completed two whole paintings. *That* I had loved.

Leo had taught me how to play poker, cribbage, and blackjack. Papi had taught me how to play chess and do Sudoku puzzles.

I'd tried a lot of sports. My favorites were archery, tennis, and bowling. I had learned to juggle—I could do four balls! I'd also taken a line dancing class.

Since I'm from Mexico, I thought it would be fun to explore activities connected to my culture. So I learned some traditional Mexican dancing from watching YouTube, and I still wanted to take a class on *Jarabe Tapatío*, the traditional Mexican Hat Dance. I'd found a local class but couldn't bring myself to sign up because it would mean dancing with boys—boys I didn't even know—and I wasn't ready for that.

Once school was out, I'd gone hiking and camping with Leo and Papi. Leo also took me rock climbing and rappelling. My *abuelito* took me fishing. My neighbor, Mrs. Kirby, had been teaching me to garden and care for chickens. My friends and I even got to go horseback riding once—but that was before the fight.

Sadly, music, which I love, had been my most avoided category. I've always had a good singing voice, but I had no desire to again try the piano lessons I'd hated as a child. I thought it might be fun to learn the *vihuela Mexicana* so I could play some *mariachi*-style music, but Papi wouldn't buy me a guitar until I tried Leo's. So I'd played around with it and watched some online lessons, but it hurt my fingers so badly I quit.

Where would golfing end up on my list? Would it be another try and fail? Or would I discover a new interest that could change the course of my life?

Only one way to find out.

Tessa stopped at the gate of the Riverbend Country Club and gave her name to the security guy sitting in a little booth. He must have found her on his list because the bar across the driveway lifted, and he waved us through. I spotted Amelia sitting on a bench in a courtyard just off the parking lot. Her orange hair, which had grown out quite a bit since her *Peter Pan* haircut and looked super cute and wild now, was a beacon to the eye. Perhaps the new Izzy needed a short haircut? I had enough curls to pull off Amelia's look, but something told me short hair was not for me.

Tessa parked the car, and we headed over to Amelia, who was wearing a white polo shirt and what looked like a pair of men's pleat-front khaki shorts, along with blue-and-green argyle socks pulled up to her knees. She held a floppy straw hat in her hands. We were still at least ten steps away when Amelia started talking.

"You won't believe the week I've had," she said, standing to meet us. "We're going to do a play next Friday—they always do one at the end of camp. Guess what Jonathan put me in charge of? Managing the stage. Again. Can you believe it?"

"It's just because you're so good at it," Tessa said. "They don't dare trust anyone else."

"But this time I wanted to do casting, and when I asked Jonathan about it, he said Sophie always does casting. Always. Why do we all have to do the same jobs every time? Wouldn't we learn a lot more if we traded off and tried different things?"

"You totally would," I said, thinking of all I'd learned in the past few months.

"Did you tell him that?" Tessa asked.

"Um, *yes*! Do you think he listened, though? Of course he didn't. Because he has been in the organization two months longer than me, and that makes him an expert. And apparently that makes me forever a newbie. It's so annoying."

"That sounds really frustrating," Tessa said.

"That's not the half of it," Amelia said, then went into another story about how Sophie chose all the wrong students for the roles and the play was going to be an absolute disaster.

When Amelia finally paused for air, Tessa pulled out her cell phone and said, "Let me text Alex and see if he's close."

"I'm sure the play won't be a disaster with you running stage crew," I said.

Amelia sighed, gesturing at me with her hat. "I'm going to do everything in my power to help put on a good show, but I'm afraid it's going to be very juvenile."

"But it's a kids' camp, right?" I said. "It's for fun and learning. Plus, they *are* juveniles."

Amelia frowned. "I guess."

Tessa's phone chimed. "He's waiting for us in the pro shop. Let's go."

The pro shop was a golf store that sold clothing and all kinds of golfing accessories, like hats, sunglasses, shoes, and boxes of golf balls. Tessa spotted Alex standing between two displays, one for Oakley sunglasses and another for FootJoy, which according to the display were the best golfing shoes. We joined him there, and I picked up one of the golf shoes, curious.

"Why do you need a special shoe to golf?" I asked.

"They have spikes to help you keep your balance," Alex said.

I frowned and turned the shoe over, examining the spikes, which looked like little grabby stars. "Do a lot of people fall down while playing golf?"

Alex merely shrugged and followed Tessa through the store. Amelia and I trailed after the couple, who I noticed were now holding hands.

Ugh. I tried not to care or be jealous or judgy about Tessa and Alex, who seemed to have the perfect relationship. It was kind of hard, though. Merely looking at boys these days made me nervous. And while I'd just successfully spoken to Alex three seconds ago, now that he was holding hands with Tessa, calling attention to himself as a boy with romance on his mind, I suddenly needed to get away from him.

I paused, pretending to look at a rack of golf shirts. When I caught up with the group, I put myself on Amelia's other side, creating a nice, safe boy-buffer.

Tessa and Alex stopped at a counter where a man stood beside a computer. He wore a bright-yellow polo shirt with a gold name tag that read *Riverbend Country Club* and, beneath it, the name *Mike*.

"Hi," Tessa said. "We're here to golf under the name David Hart."

"Do you have a tee time?" Mike asked.

"Yes, one o'clock," Tessa said.

"We're drinking tea?" Amelia asked.

"Not T-E-A," I said. "T-E-E, like a golf tee."

"That makes much more sense," Amelia said.

"Okay, yeah," Mike said, concentrating on his computer screen. "I'll put you on the front nine. Let me just print your ticket." He fiddled with his computer, and a printer on the counter behind him began to hum. It spat out a small receipt, which Mike handed to Tessa.

"Here you are," he said. "Give this to the starter on the first hole." He glanced at the four of us. "Did you bring clubs?"

"No," Tessa said. "We need to rent four sets of clubs."

"Certainly," Mike said. "Shall I charge that to Mr. Hart's account?"

"Yes, please." Tessa raised her eyebrows at me and grinned.

I grinned back and sang, "Thank you, Mr. Hart!"

"You'll need some balls, too," Mike said. "Unless you brought some?"

"I brought one," Amelia said, setting on the counter a bright-green golf ball with one eye that looked like Mike Wazowski from the movie *Monsters, Inc.* "We've had it forever. I have no idea where we got it."

"You might not want to risk losing that one," Mike said.

"I guess you should throw in a dozen golf balls," Tessa said.

"For four of you?" Mike looked skeptical. "You might need two dozen."

Tessa glanced at Alex, who shrugged.

"Okay," she said. "Two dozen it is."

Mike typed a bit more on his computer, then set two boxes of Titleist Pro golf balls on the counter. "Here you are. I'll radio down to Dan. He'll get you set up."

"And where would we find Dan?" Tessa asked.

"Back out those doors and down the steps," Mike said. "You'll see the clubhouse and the golf cart parking lot. Dan will meet you on the lot with your carts and clubs."

"Our carts?" I asked, suddenly excited.

"It's a big golf course," Mike said. "You don't want to walk the whole way."

"Thank you!" I said, eager to get started. Eager to drive a golf cart!

Then Mike ended all my fun. "Only licensed drivers may drive the golf carts."

"Of course," Tessa said, and our foursome headed back outside. The sun shone bright and warm overhead, and I was glad to be wearing my cap. I sunburned easily, despite my brown skin.

"Did he give you a copy of the bill?" Alex asked.

"No," Tessa said. "I didn't think to ask. You think I should have?"

"Not necessarily," Alex said. "It just seemed like a lot."

"Was it?" A wrinkle formed between Tessa's brows. "Dad said not to worry about the cost."

"Two hundred and seventy-nine dollars and change," Alex said. "That's a week's pay for me during the school year."

"To golf?" Amelia said.

"It cost fifty each to rent the clubs," Alex said.

Guilt washed over me. "I had no idea golfing would be so expensive, Tessa," I said. "We should have borrowed someone's clubs."

"Doesn't your dad have some?" Amelia asked Tessa.

Tessa laughed dryly. "Dad does not want anyone touching his clubs. I didn't even ask Rebecca. Dad told me to rent them and said not to worry about the cost, so I said thank you and left it at that."

"Must be nice," Amelia muttered.

"Please thank him for me," I said. "Or even better, text me his mailing address, and I'll send him a card. I made some of my own when I tried papermaking a few months ago."

"He'd like that," Tessa said.

We walked down a set of cement stairs in silence, likely all pondering the cost of this sport. Down at the clubhouse, we approached a cluster of high school boys, all wearing the yellow polos of the Riverbend Country Club and beige chino shorts. Three boys were washing golf carts. Two others were lugging golf bags filled with clubs toward carts. The remaining boys were just standing there, chatting. They all looked clean-cut and sharp in their work uniforms.

"Look how *tan* they are," Amelia said. "All these boys in the sun all the time, washing those golf carts . . ."

Alex shot Amelia an amused look that turned her face nearly the color of her hair, and I felt a moment of regret that Claire had refused to come golfing with us. We couldn't be ourselves with Alex here. Still, Tessa's dad had insisted we needed two or four to golf, not three. This brought Shay to mind, but I doubted she would have liked golf anyway. Besides, my discomfort around Alex was nothing compared with how I would feel around Shay. If taking the lesser of two evils was the only way I'd get to try golf, this worked for me.

"Alex!" One of the yellow shirts peeled off from the cluster and approached us. I recognized that white-blond hair immediately. This was a Nichols boy, specifically Cody's brother Daniel. He had been one of the five seniors charged in the Dropbox scandal last spring, in which some guys had been sharing pictures of girls in an online folder. The scandal had also included my sort-of first boyfriend, Zac.

Daniel's frosty blue eyes panned over the four of us and stopped on me, sending a shiver up my arms.

Chapter
2

"HEY, DANNY," ALEX SAID as he and Daniel shook hands.

All three Nichols boys were tall, blond, and athletic. Gorgeous. While Cody was by far the cutest with his boyish face and bright smile, Daniel had a rugged, far-off look, like he was thinking about something very deep. He turned that bored gaze my way, and his lips curled into a knowing grin. "Izzah-belah," he said, pouring on a bad impression of a Mexican accent. "Long time no see." He winked, and I about died from the insinuation of what he had previously "seen."

Tessa handed Daniel the ticket and tucked her arm through mine. "The man inside said you would show us to our golf carts?" she said.

"Right this way, Miss Hart," he said. "I've prepared two fabulous rides for you, completely stocked with water, tees, and towels."

As we followed Daniel toward the golf carts, I hung back with Tessa, allowing Amelia to move ahead.

"How much do you get paid to work here?" she asked.

"A buck above minimum wage, plus tips," Daniel said.

"What do you do?" Amelia asked. "Is it hard?"

"Not hard, no," Daniel said. "We wash the carts, fetch lost balls from the range, mow the lawn. Stuff like that."

Amelia's eyes narrowed as she pursued him. "Do they only hire boys?"

"Dunno." Daniel stopped and placed his hand on the top of a golf cart. "I doubt it, but I haven't seen any girls working here. It's a very physical job, so you have to be in good shape. Plus, they want the help to look good in their uniforms."

Amelia's mouth gaped, but before she could respond to Daniel's veiled insult, he rushed on. "This is your cart, along with that one." He pointed to the cart on the left. "Your clubs are already loaded in the back. Keys are in the ignition, and your scorecards are on the steering wheel. Take your ticket up to the first hole. The starter will meet you there."

Starter? Stars. Golfing had so much special lingo.

I walked to the second golf cart—the one farthest away from Daniel. "Look how cute!" I said, examining the colored scorecard attached to a clip in the center of the steering wheel. "It even has a place to hold the little pencil."

"Yamaha," Alex read aloud the brand name logo on the clipboard. "Nice."

In a little dashboard-like console jutting out from the windshield, four cup holders held four water bottles still dripping with condensation. There was also a pack of four plastic golf tees.

Tessa picked up the package. "Ooh, look! They gave us some tees."

"Whoa," Amelia said from the back of the cart. "That's a lot of clubs."

I joined her, surprised at the size of the golf bags and their contents. Plus, hanging from each bag by a grommet and hook was a yellow-, white-, and green-striped towel with the Riverbend Country Club logo. "What's with the towel?" I asked.

"To keep the balls, clubheads, grips, and tees clean and dry," Daniel said.

I realized then that I knew nothing about this game. Even after watching thirteen YouTube videos this morning, it had somehow not occurred to me that there were quite so many clubs—and other paraphernalia—for golfing.

"I know you need a driver to start," I said, eyeing the clubs to try to guess which one it was. "But I don't know what the rest of these are for."

"This isn't like mini golf, where you each get one ball and one club," Daniel said. "With pro golf, there are different clubs for different shots."

Nervous about speaking to Daniel, I directed my next question to Alex. "What kinds of clubs are there besides the driver?" I asked. "The putter?"

"You use the putter on the green," Alex said.

"Okay, that's two," Amelia said. "There are . . ." She lowered her voice to a whisper and counted, landing on "twelve more."

I didn't like how complicated this was getting, and we hadn't even started.

Alex pawed through the clubs in one bag. "The biggest one is the driver," he said. "It's classified as a wood. So are these smaller ones that have the same shape. You use them to hit long shots on the fairway without a tee." Then he pulled out a club that looked just like the driver and the other woods but was a little smaller. "This is a hybrid. It looks like a wood, but it hits like a long iron. And these are the irons." He tapped the heads of several clubs that all looked the same. "Use these when hitting toward the green. Low-numbered irons are for longer shots, and high-numbered irons are for shorter shots. The wedges are for hitting short, high shots from near the green or if you end up in a sand trap. And the putter is for hitting ground balls on the green."

Daniel laughed. "Dude! You should apply to work here. I'm sure it's a lot easier than being a waiter."

Alex grimaced. "I'm good."

"Well, have fun, man. I'll see you later." Daniel strode away.

"Glad he's gone," Tessa mumbled. She placed one box of golf balls in the back of each cart, then said, "Who is riding with me?"

"I am!" Amelia said before I could even think.

I gaped at Alex, my eyes so wide the air tickled them. I didn't want to ride with a boy all day!

Tessa had already climbed into the driver's seat of one of the golf carts, so I ran over to her and said, "Let me drive, then you can ride with Alex."

"You have to be licensed to drive," Tessa said. "That's why I brought Alex instead of Lauren."

Lauren was in our grade and went to our church. She would have been a much better choice! But I supposed Tessa was right. I didn't have my license yet. My parents never found time to let me drive the car because they worked so much. My older sister and brother got their licenses before we moved to Riverbend, but life in the city was a lot busier than life in the country had been. I was starting to wonder if I would ever get behind the wheel of an actual car.

"But I really want to try it as part of my experiment!" I said. "Maybe I'll be good at it. Maybe I could get a job here. Wear a yellow polo." Never in a million years would I take a job with Daniel as a coworker, but Tessa didn't have to know that.

"We should both apply here," Amelia said from the passenger's seat of Tessa's cart. "I bet if we went back and mentioned affirmative action to Mike, we'd be hired by the end of the week."

"Please?" I said to Tessa. "Just one time? Pretty please with peanut butter frosting?"

Tessa sighed, but she was smiling. "I'll think about it. Maybe we can wait until hole six or something where we're so far away that no one can see us."

"I'm pretty sure they have cameras all over," Alex said from the driver's seat of the other cart. *My* cart.

"Really?" Tessa frowned. "Then maybe we shouldn't . . ."

"But they also probably won't be able to tell you and Izzy apart from a distance," Alex added. "Plus, the whole driver thing is more of an honor system. Trevor's mom has been letting him drive her around the course since he was ten."

"All right," Tessa said. "Later. For now, let's go."

I squealed, awkwardly hugged Tessa in the driver's seat, and then reluctantly got into the other cart with Alex.

"You lead the way," Tessa told him. Alex pressed the accelerator, and we were off, rolling smoothly down the narrow, paved, tree-lined trail. I couldn't even hear the engine.

"These don't take gas?" I asked.

"Some golf carts do," Alex said, "but the ones at this club are electric."

"Huh. That's cool."

Alex laughed, which eased my nervousness a bit.

The little tree-lined road was shaded from the sun, and the air felt cool as we zipped along. At the sign for the first hole, Alex pulled off the road. An elderly man was sitting on a bench, one foot crossed over his other knee, his arms stretched along the back of the bench. He had white hair and was wearing the yellow polo shirt of the Riverbend Country Club.

Alex and Tessa parked the golf carts. Everyone got out and approached the starter.

"Why's he called a starter?" I asked.

"Because it's his job to tell us when to start."

My expression must have conveyed my confusion because Alex continued, "You know how in mini golf, sometimes multiple groups get bunched up at one hole? The starter makes sure that doesn't happen here. Our tee time is one o'clock, and we can't start before then. Otherwise, we might catch up to another group."

"You *should* work here," I told him. "You know a lot about golf."

"Alex knows a lot about every sport," Tessa said, grinning at him.

The starter introduced himself as Roger. As soon as he saw how clueless we were, he sent us back to the carts for our scorecards. He then explained how the scoring and penalties worked, and what all the different markings on the course meant.

"Every hole has a par number," Roger said. "That's the number of strokes an experienced player should require to complete that hole, although new players often go over that number. Hole one is a par four. You're playing the front nine today, so at the end of the nine holes, the golfer with the fewest strokes wins." He checked his watch. "Go ahead and get started."

"Izzy, you go first," Tessa said. "This day was your idea."

"Okay." I walked back to the cart and frowned into the mess of clubs, trying to spot the biggest one. "I start with the driver."

"That's right," Roger said. "You need to hit the ball over the wetlands to the green. See that striped pole out there? In the distance beyond it there is a red flag. That marks the hole. Hit your ball near either of those, and you'll be in good shape."

I pulled out the longest club and recalled that Golf Guy had said in his YouTube video that the driver isn't an easy club for anyone, let alone a beginner. I stuck my tee into the ground and balanced the ball on top. I tried a slow-motion swing, rotating back and then forward through the swing, imagining the head of the club making a big, even smiley face around my body. I took a few practice swings and concentrated, trying to come at the side rather than the top, just like Golf Guy had said. This was going to be easy.

I relaxed and hit the ball.

It shot away, crooked, going off to the left.

"That's not bad," Roger said.

"It's not?"

"You got it across the marsh," he said. "Some struggle to do that on their first try."

Pleased, I grabbed my tee and let Tessa take my place.

Tessa's ball went straighter than mine, but not quite as far. It did make it across the marsh.

Amelia missed her first two shots. I pulled out my phone to take a picture. "Come on, Amelia. You got this!"

"Is that a new phone case?" Tessa asked.

I snapped a shot of Amelia swinging—another miss—then held up my phone to Tessa. "Yes, it's called an EyePatch Case. It has a little door to cover up the camera." I flicked the switch to show her how it worked. "It covers the camera on both sides."

Amelia propped her hand on her hip. "Well, it's much better than the Band-Aid you had on your last one. Or the stickers."

I heard the sarcasm in her tone. She obviously didn't understand. "I don't like the idea that someone could be watching me through the cameras on my devices. The EyePatch Case means I no longer have to worry about losing stickers."

"Anything that keeps you from having to worry is worth the cost, in my opinion," Tessa said. "I'm all about making life easier."

Amelia swung again, this time hitting the ball, but it went almost straight up into the air. Tessa and I screamed and ran over by a tree. The ball finally plopped onto the grass about three yards away.

I couldn't help it. I started laughing.

"It's not funny," Amelia said.

"Sorry. I just thought it was going to hit us," I said.

Two more golf carts arrived and parked beside ours.

"You're going to have to keep moving, kids," Roger said. "Another foursome is about to start in five minutes."

"I can't hit it!" Amelia said.

"The maximum number of hits you can take is double par," Roger said. "This is a par-four course, so if you reach eight here, you're done. Double par is our max."

"I don't know what that means," Amelia said.

"How many swings have you taken?" Alex asked.

"Four."

"Then take a two-point penalty and drive over to the green," Roger said. "Then you'll have two chances to make the shot."

Amelia snatched up her ball and tee. "Fine."

Alex took his turn from the blue tee box. His driver made a powerful *crack* as it struck the ball. His tee spun out of the ground while the ball shot out over the marsh. It looked like it landed right by the red flag.

"Figures," Amelia said. "He did better than all of us."

Tessa tucked her arm into Amelia's. "That's just because Alex loves sports. I guarantee you that if you and Alex were on a stage together, you would put him to shame."

"You don't think I can act?" Alex asked as we headed for our golf carts.

"I know you can't," Tessa said, kissing his cheek in a rare public display of affection.

"Hmph," he said, his nose tilted in the air like he was trying to be angry, yet he was grinning.

We girls all started laughing, which made Alex blush. Then I had to get in the golf cart with him again.

"I can't play poker, either," he told me.

"Bluffing is overrated in poker," I said, remembering what I'd learned from my brother. "The best players spend time observing their opponents to study what they do. You don't have to bluff often, but it's important that the other players believe you're capable of bluffing."

Alex steered the golf cart onto the road. "How come?"

"Well, if you don't ever bluff—if you only bet when you have a good hand—then you'll be predictable and everyone will fold, and you won't win as much."

"How do you know so much about cards?" he asked.

"Leo taught me to play."

"Part of your experiment?"

"Yep."

"Does this experiment have an end in sight?"

"I don't know. Maybe. Maybe not. I mean, there's so much out there in the world. It could take a lifetime to try everything."

"That's likely true."

It was also true that this whole thing had left me a bit weary. I mean, it was fun to try new things, but after months of it, I didn't feel like I knew myself any better than when I'd started.

—⚡—

At the second hole, Alex and I met Tessa by the boxes. Amelia was still sitting in the cart.

"Is Amelia upset?" I asked.

"I think she's embarrassed." Tessa swatted Alex's arm. "Did you have to get a birdie on your first hole?"

He grinned. "What can I say? I'm awesome."

"Maybe be slightly less awesome?" Tessa suggested.

"Hey, your dad paid good money for this day," he said. "I just want to make the most of it."

"How about if we aren't so strict about how to keep score?" I said.

Alex shot me a look like I had blown out the candles on his birthday cake.

"You can keep your score however you want," I told him. "But let's not be so strict on the double par thing. Or maybe we only count the strokes where we actually hit the ball."

"That sounds good," Tessa said. "And no penalties either."

"Perfect," I said.

"I'm taking a penalty if I need to," Alex said.

"But you don't care how *we* play, right?" Tessa asked.

"You girls do what you have to do," he said, then grinned evilly at the golf course. "And so will I."

Tessa giggled. I left the couple there and joined Amelia at the cart. "New rules," I said, and once I had explained everything, Amelia was ready to play again.

Alex focused on his game, but now that the pressure of keeping score was gone, we girls had a good time playing just for laughs. When Amelia hit the ball into the weeds, she fetched it and brought it back to the green. No more drama.

After hole three, Tessa let me drive, and my anxiousness disappeared completely.

As Alex went up to the tee box to take his turn at hole five, Amelia said, "I know we're supposed to hate Daniel, but that guy is unfairly handsome."

"I'm just glad he's graduated and I don't have to see him at school," I said. "Zac, too."

"I agree," Tessa said, swatting at a small cloud of gnats.

"You know, Izzy," Amelia said, "for your next experiment, I think you should go out for the cross-country team."

"Running is boring," I said.

"Not when you're running with a cute guy," Amelia said. "Cody is on the team."

Fire sizzled through my veins. "I've already told you. I'm not interested in Cody. We're just friends. In fact, let me make something very clear." Hands on my hips, I glared—first at Amelia, then at Tessa. "I am never dating again. Guys only want one thing. I can't trust them. Maybe when I'm older, I'll meet someone more mature, but high school boys are all the same. And I want nothing to do with them."

"What about high school boys?" Alex said, walking toward us.

"My turn!" I said, pulling the driver from my bag. I ran past Alex before he had time to ask his question again. If the girls wanted to tell him what I'd said, that was fine. I hoped it didn't offend him, but I also hoped it made it clear that I was watching him. He'd better not break Tessa's heart by being stupid.

Instead of answering Alex, Tessa started talking about an event at Booked Up, the bookstore owned by Shay's aunt. I pressed my tee into the grass and set up my ball.

"I still can't believe how well it went," I heard Amelia say. "Maybe it will draw more famous authors to Riverbend."

"I hope so too," Tessa said. "Laura is so good at what she does. She deserves all the success."

"I'm sorry I missed it," Alex said. "Sounds like it was cool."

I hit my ball, and it sailed away, not going nearly as far as Alex's had, but at least it reached the fairway. I pulled my tee out of the grass and skipped back to the girls. "What did you miss?" I asked.

Tessa and Amelia exchanged wary glances.

"What?" I asked.

"My turn," Amelia said, striding toward the tee box.

I turned to Tessa. "Tessa?"

"There was a signing at the bookstore," she said. "Shay asked us to help because the author was kind of famous, though I'd never heard of her."

"Who was it?"

"Gwen Wilson. I guess she writes graphic novels."

"The G. Willow Wilson who wrote *Ms. Marvel*?" I asked, shocked that someone like that had come through Riverbend. "She only ever appears at big conventions. Why didn't someone tell me?"

"Well, it was kind of last-minute," Tessa said.

Heat rushed through me and pimpled my arms. I couldn't believe this. "But you know how obsessed I am with Marvel. My family would've wanted to come. We have the whole series. Even Bash read them."

Tessa looked ashamed. "I guess I didn't realize that. I mean, I know you all like the Marvel movies, but I didn't think this was related. Shay did suggest inviting you, but Amelia and I talked her out of it."

"Why? I can't believe G. Willow Wilson was in town. I could've met her."

"You said you needed space," Tessa pointed out.

Alex was just standing there, picking at a stray thread on his shirt.

"But it was a signing," I said. "My family would have stood in line with, like, two hundred other people. We wouldn't have had to talk to Shay. It would have meant so much to Sebastian."

"I'm sorry," Tessa said. "I really am."

"Well, I'm not," Amelia said, returning from her shot, which I hadn't even seen. "If you would talk to Shay, everything would go back to normal. You're just being stubborn."

"That's not fair!" How could Amelia say such a thing?

I knew why, really. It was because she had no idea. Tessa, either. They were both so naive, and I was glad for them. I wished I could be innocent like that again. Unfortunately, too often that sort of naiveté made people ignorant and judgmental.

In the distance, two golf carts were arriving.

I was not about to let us get passed. I strode toward my golf cart and got in. "Let's just go," I said, eager for a reason to change the subject.

But my dark mood continued, and at hole six, I hit my ball into a water hazard. As I stormed across the grass to fetch it, I was glad for a chance to get away from the others and let a few tears escape. This had been a bad idea. Why was I still trying new things? You'd think that after three months I'd have figured out who I was, but I just kept flailing about like a fish out of water. I'd never felt more discouraged about life. Why did everything have to be so hard?

I reached the water hazard, which was a small pond lying in

a depression. I spotted my ball sitting in the shallow water at the edge. I didn't think it was against the rules to hit the ball from there. Not that it mattered, since we'd thrown out the rules. So I stepped past the yellow stakes and walked carefully down the steep bank. I positioned myself with my right foot on the edge of the water, pointing my club back toward the others. I'd have to hit the ball up the bank, which was about two feet high. I tried to think about what Amelia had been doing wrong to get her ball to go so high in the air. Hit the ball lower down, maybe?

From my precarious position, I'd be lucky to hit the ball at all. I rotated my club back, then swung as hard as I could. The ball went flying. Unfortunately, so did I. My right heel twisted and skidded in the mud beneath the grass. My foot shot out. I lost my balance, then fell.

Right into the water.

I gasped at the coldness, a mistake that rewarded me with a mouthful of slimy water. I gagged and panicked, flailing my arms until I managed to get my feet beneath me and stand. My lungs fought to expel the water, which left me standing there dripping, shivering, hunched, pathetic—there weren't enough adjectives to describe my state.

"Izzy! Oh my goodness, are you okay?" Tessa asked.

I pushed my sopping hair out of my eyes and found her standing at the top of the ridge, Alex beside her, both of them staring at me in horror.

I answered with spine-wracking coughs but managed to take a few robot-like steps toward the shore.

Amelia arrived. She gasped, then burst into laughter. "Oh, Izzy! You are amazing and completely reckless. You don't do anything halfway. I love that about you."

I begrudgingly sifted her words for the compliments tucked in around the mocking criticism and tried to hold on to the former. I didn't want to fight anymore. I just wanted to go home.

When I reached the shore, Alex and Tessa each extended a hand and pulled me up the steep bank. The sound of a cell phone camera jerked my gaze back to Amelia, who lowered her phone and grinned.

"Classic."

"That better not show up online," I said, my teeth starting to chatter.

"It won't," she said. "I promise."

I growled, grateful I had left my cell phone in the cart rather than taking it for a swim.

"I'm going to sit in the cart," I said. "The rest of you can finish the game, but I'm done. Golfing is not for me."

Chapter
3

TESSA DROPPED ME OFF AT HOME, but before I could go inside, I saw Harland, one of Mrs. Kirby's chickens, rambling around my yard. *That bird!* The side gate to Mrs. Kirby's backyard was closed, but that never stopped Harland, who had a gift for escaping. I approached her carefully, knowing that when she saw me, she would run. I was about two yards away when I stepped on a twig. The crack sent Harland's neck wobbling around, her bitty eyes fixed on me. Then she squawked and took off.

I gave chase. First Harland ran out to the street and around the post of our mailbox. She stopped to peck at a worm in the dirt, but as I got close, she shot away toward Mamá's flowerbeds. Harland's fat body seemed to glide over the dirt, leaving almost no marks. She wove around Mamá's rosebushes and blue sage, then disappeared between the black-eyed Susans and the silvery foliage of the artemisia bush.

I preferred her there, actually. The angel hair on the artemisia bush was so soft I sometimes liked to pet it, and I would much rather have to reach through it than the thorny rosebushes while trying to grab that stubborn hen. I faked going around the front, stomping a foot out in front of me on the ground as a decoy. As I expected, Harland darted back the other way, where I was waiting.

Mrs. Kirby had long ago taught me how to pick up a chicken. There's an art to it, and Harland had been in my yard enough times that I had it down pat. I used both hands to pin down Harland's wings so she couldn't flap. Then I lifted her. I threaded the fingers of one hand between her legs, locking them into place, and used my other hand to clutch her to my stomach.

"Got you," I said. "This is not your playground. You know better than to come over here uninvited. What would Mrs. Kirby say?"

I carried the chicken across my yard and through Mrs. Kirby's side gate. She was on a monthlong cruise to Australia with a friend, and I was responsible for feeding and caring for her animals while she was away. I carried Harland toward the coop, but before I could manage to get the door open, the chicken pecked me so hard I dropped her, and she ran through a crack in the garden fence.

Aha! So *that* was how she always got out. I ran out the gate, leaving it open this time so I could chase Harland back through. What followed was another awkward chase, this time through the wilds behind Mrs. Kirby's property. I finally managed to tackle the chicken by diving on top of her and catching her in a pile of old grass clippings between Mrs. Kirby's two compost piles. Just as I sat up and tucked Harland close, a burst of grass rained down on my head. I screamed and again lost Harland to the weeds. I was still wet from my fall in the water hazard at the golf course, so the fresh grass stuck to me. I looked like a St. Patrick's Day donut with sprinkles.

Perplexed, I glanced up in time to see Cody peeking over the fence, his eyes wide.

Oh my stars.

"Sorry!" he said. "I didn't know you were here."

I have never been one for fashion, and—outside a small stint of madness when I was stupidly dating Zac Lloyd last spring—I've always been about as low-maintenance as a girl could get. But right now, even I knew I looked ridiculous.

Cody disappeared, but I could hear him coming around through the gate. I readied myself for another interaction with my adorable neighbor, but he walked straight up to Harland. He picked up the chicken as if it were nothing more than a stray ball that had been lobbed over the fence.

I glared at the chicken, annoyed that Cody had made that look so easy. Even with grass clippings and dirt on his pants and sporting work gloves that reached to his elbows, my neighbor still looked like Captain America personified. With his wavy blond hair, brown eyes, and smile that had the power to render a girl speechless, he could easily grace the cover of a teen magazine. He flashed that smile at me then, locking me frozen and completely horrified.

I reminded myself that boys were humans, and that I no longer responded to the feelings they sometimes stirred in my stomach.

"What happened to you?" he asked.

"There was an incident at the golf course."

He chuckled. "Sorry I missed it."

I wasn't. It was bad enough having one boy witness my blunder, but if Cody had been there—this boy I was trying desperately hard not to crush on—I might have passed out. Time to change the subject before I did just that.

"Are you doing yard work for Mrs. Kirby?" I asked.

"Yeah. She hired me to take care of her lawn and compost piles while she's gone."

Ugh. I should have seen this coming. "I'm feeding her chickens and cats."

Cody lit up, but inside, I panicked. I could not be spending time over here every day with Cody Nichols. Though we were friends, he was far too cute to have to see on a regular basis. For months, I had been stuffing any romantic inclinations that might creep up on me when coming into the proximity of a cute boy. Cody Nichols always made that extremely difficult. I didn't trust myself around him, and I certainly didn't trust him with that smile, which he was giving me again. I fixed my eyes just to the right of his head, looking at the leaves of an oak tree behind him rather than that hypnotic face.

Oak trees were much safer.

"Papi and my brothers liked your car," I said.

"I wanted a red one," he said, "but Dad talked me into blue. He said red cars get pulled over more often."

"You *do* like revving the engine." The entire block had likely heard Cody driving that car around the other day.

Again with the cute grinning. "It's a nice engine, but I'm responsible. I drive safely. It's just fun to throw into corners."

"That sounds dangerous."

"Nah. I'm careful. Anyway, I guess with both of us working here, we'll be seeing a lot of each other this month."

I think I said, "Yeah," but my mind was tumbling with anxiety over this prospect. Tessa thought Cody had a crush on me. Could she be right? Six months ago, that would've been a dream come true. But I'm sadder and wiser now. I frowned, not liking how that thought made me feel like the girls that con man Harold Hill and his friend Marcellus sang about in *The Music Man*. I supposed if I made another mistake like I had made with Zac, that's exactly the path I would end up on.

Still tucked in Cody's arms, Harland squawked, pulling me out of my daze. I scrambled to my feet. "Thanks for catching Harland," I said. "I have to go."

And before Cody could get in another word or hypnotic smile, I ran home.

—∿—

The brush with Cody sent me on a mission of high-level impor-
tance. I showered, changed into some clean clothes, then got right
to work. I found Claire in her room, reading some ancient novel.
The overachiever was taking four AP classes this fall, one of which
required her to read six books this summer.

"Want to make a few extra bucks?" I asked.

Claire looked up from her book. "Doing what?"

"Feeding Mrs. Kirby's animals until she gets back from her
cruise."

"That's your job. Why can't you do it?"

If I told Claire the true reason, she'd laugh at me. "I was thinking of finding a real summer job. Something full-time."

"Feeding Mrs. Kirby's animals takes you, like, a half hour a day.
It's not that big of a deal. Even if you were working forty hours a
week, you'd still be able to squeeze it in."

"Yeah, but I don't want to fill every minute of my day with
work. It's good to have balance in your life, you know? I don't
wanna end up like Mamá."

To be fair, Mamá was doing much better. She had quit managing the urgent care and usually only worked about forty-five hours
a week. That was a vast improvement from the sixty-plus hours she
had been working before.

"And what makes you think I want to fill every minute of *my*
day with work?" Claire asked.

"You've always loved working and making money," I said.

"The amount of money I'd get for feeding Mrs. Kirby's animals
isn't worth it to me. Just do it yourself." She went back to reading.

I knew better than to beg. That would only make Claire dig
in her heels more.

Plan B was to text my friends. When I sent the proposal over
the group chat, Amelia replied almost instantly.

Amelia: Can't. I have theater camp.

Me: Yeah, but it will only take a half hour every day. You could squeeze that in.

Amelia: I'd have to ask my mom for a ride. She'd never agree. She's all for me getting a job, but not when it would drain her gas tank unnecessarily, and your place is too far to walk.

Ugh. Two down. I had little hope Tessa would agree. I wished Shay could do it—she loved animals—but I still wasn't talking to her.

I *couldn't* talk to her.

Two hours passed before Tessa finally replied. As I had predicted, she just made things more difficult.

Tessa: Why can't you do it? You were so excited about it.

Here goes nothing.

Me: She hired Cody to take care of her lawn. I can't work with Cody every day!

Tessa: ?

Amelia: Why not?

I hadn't explained to my friends my newfound aversion to romance. Before Zac, I had been a clichéd, drooling, boy-crazy teenage girl.

In other words, I had been a fool. I would not put myself in a position to be a fool again. And while the odds were not high that Cody and I would show up at Mrs. Kirby's at the same time each day, the mere possibility made me anxious.

Me: I'm worried I'll accidentally give him the wrong idea.

Tessa: You finally agree that he likes you?

No, I did not. Someone like Cody could never choose someone like me as more than a friend, but saying that would not get me out of this commitment.

Me: Maybe.

Amelia: If he likes you, what's the problem?

Me: I have a lot going on right now. I don't have time for boys.

Amelia: It's summer. And you don't have a job. You don't even have to watch your brother anymore. You have nothing but time.

Me: I don't like Cody that way. I don't want to hurt his feelings.

Amelia: Umm . . . It's OBVIOUS you like him that way.

Me: How? What have I done lately to make this so obvious?

The word *lately* in that last message was paramount, because in the past I had been extremely obvious about my former crush on Cody.

Amelia: I don't even know what to say to you right now.

Tessa: Isn't Mrs. Kirby already gone?

Me: Yeah.

Tessa: Well, it would be one thing to have a friend sub for you in an emergency, but you gave her your word that you would take care of her pets. I think you need to honor that commitment.

Ugh. Couldn't my friends at least *try* to see this from my point of view? I had no response to Tessa's final argument, so I just abandoned the chat. I was meeting with Zoe tomorrow. I'd ask her how to get out of it.

—⟋⟋⟍—

The Valadez family had been having a Marvel movie marathon this summer. Tonight's selection was *Captain America: Civil War*. It was one of my favorites.

Mamá brought home pizzas, and we all ate in the living room in front of the TV. All except Sebastian, who didn't like changes to his routine. But Papi had fed him early at the table, and now he happily sat in his chair, watching the movie while the rest of us ate. Oh, and Leo wasn't with us either, since he lived in an apartment near the college with his friends.

In *Captain America: Civil War*, the world's governments decided that the Avengers' heroics needed to be regulated, which caused a rift among the superheroes. Captain America believed they should have free agency, while Iron Man wanted to accept government oversight. Eventually, things escalated into an all-out war between the two sides.

When I first saw this movie, Iron Man's behavior really annoyed me, but after my experience with Zac and Sebastian last year, I kind of understood where he was coming from. Iron Man felt immense guilt for all the damage that had been caused by superheroes—for the many lives lost—and he was tired of being responsible for saving the world. I felt that way last year when Sebastian was picked up by the police for attacking Zac.

Plus, I understood why Iron Man felt betrayed by Cap when he found out that Cap had known all along who killed his parents. Shay knew what I'd been through with Zac and the Dropbox scandal, yet she had still chosen pornography over being friends with me.

That might sound a little dramatic, but that's how I saw it.

Iron Man took things too far, of course. He was so blinded by his anger that he couldn't be rational and tried to kill Cap.

I couldn't stop thinking about this, so when the movie ended, I posed a question to my family. "If this situation were real, whose side would you be on?"

"Captain America," Mamá said. "No question."

"I'm going to disagree and go with Iron Man," Claire said. "I mean, if all the Avengers were as loyal and true as Captain America, then maybe they could succeed without regulation. But they're not. Too many vigilantes in the kitchen makes for a big old mess. I'd hate to be a police officer in the Marvel Universe."

"Sebastian?" I asked. "Which Avenger is right in *Civil War?*"

"Captain America, Isabella Valadez. Captain America is always right."

"I agree," I said. "But I also see where Claire is coming from. Iron Man made some good points until he let his rage blind him."

"Yeah, he went a little nuts," Claire said. "So, who do you pick?"

I thought about it, then smiled when the answer came to me. "Not that he was trying to win people to his side," I said, "but I pick T'Challa."

"T'Challa is the Black Panther," Sebastian said.

"Right," I said. "I like how he was able to remain rational when Iron Man couldn't. He hated that Zemo's actions had killed his father, but when he learned the truth, he gave up his quest for vengeance. He recognized that it wasn't his place to punish the man. And he knew revenge wouldn't make him feel better."

Mamá patted my leg. "That is very wise, Isabella. I change my answer to Black Panther."

I smiled and leaned my head against Mamá's shoulder. "What about you, Papi?" I asked.

Papi hummed and rubbed his chin. "Black Widow."

"What?" I said. "She never even picked a side!"

"I know," Papi said. "She tried to support both her friends, no matter how they treated her. She wanted them to stay rational—to work it out without fighting. Of course, there are times when two people will never agree."

I thought of Shay and me. "That doesn't mean they're both right," I said. "That's why I admire what T'Challa did. I don't think he personally forgave Zemo. Some people don't deserve forgiveness. Not until they've changed, anyway. But T'Challa chose not to actively take revenge."

"He saw what hatred was doing to Iron Man," Mamá said. "He didn't want that for himself."

"*Sí*," Papi said. "Letting go of his anger allowed him to extend grace to Zemo. Forgiveness did not condone Zemo's actions, but it set Black Panther free from carrying around that bitterness."

—⟊—

That night while I was lying in bed, not sleeping, I thought about our little family discussion. Several parallels between the Avengers and the situation with Shay jumped out at me. Both Iron Man and T'Challa sought revenge for the deaths of their loved ones. Iron Man sought to kill Bucky, and while T'Challa started out on the same path, he instead offered forgiveness to Zemo.

Did I like that Shay had been looking at pornography? No.

Did I think she needed to get help? Absolutely.

Did I think she owed me an apology? Yes.

But I wanted to be a T'Challa in this situation, not an Iron Man.

I didn't want to get revenge or even to pursue justice. I wanted my friend back. I just wasn't sure what that looked like.

Papi said that forgiveness didn't condone the actions of another but set the victim free from anger and bitterness. I wanted that. And, honestly, I knew I could forgive Shay for what she had done. But did I have to tell her? Or could I just hold the forgiveness in my heart until she came to me and apologized?

I liked that second plan better.

If Shay asked, I would forgive her for what she'd done—and might still be doing. But until she admitted she was wrong and got help, I couldn't be her friend anymore.

Chapter
4

SATURDAY AFTERNOON, I went down to Grounds and Rounds to meet with Zoe. When my friends and I had enacted Operation Encouragement to cheer up the girls in the *Peter Pan* play who had been victims of the Dropbox scandal, we had invited them to meet with Zoe at Booked Up so they could get some encouragement from a caring adult. Ever since that night, I had been meeting weekly with Zoe. My friends didn't know how badly it hurt my feelings that they had not included me among the girls receiving care from Operation Encouragement. I considered myself a victim of the Dropbox scandal, but apparently my friends did not. This was why I couldn't talk to them about boys. They were just not capable of understanding what I'd been through.

Zoe and I hadn't talked about the Dropbox situation in a while. These days, we kind of just talked about whatever was on my mind, which lately had been Shay. Today, I needed to talk about the situation with Cody. Hopefully, Zoe would have some ideas about how I could get out of working with him for the next four weeks.

I entered the coffee shop, greeted by a host of tantalizing smells and the chilled hug of air conditioning, and there sat the very boy I'd been trying to avoid, at a table with Zoe. *My* Zoe.

What in the world?

He must have come in for coffee, seen Zoe waiting, and sat down to say hi. That made sense.

I got in line, ordered my drink, then tried to decide if I should interrupt so Zoe knew I was here. This was the one drawback of meeting at a coffee shop. Such a public location hindered confidential discussions. Too many people could come in and talk to us. Yet Zoe had always been intentional about sitting at the table in the far corner, which afforded the most privacy. That was where she and Cody were sitting now.

The barista handed me my drink, so I had no more excuses to linger on this side of the shop. Nothing left to do but walk over there and interrupt. I did have an appointment, after all.

I wove around the tables, and when I got close, Cody looked up. He met my gaze, and his cheeks turned pink. His cuteness hit me like an *oomph* to the stomach. He swung those big brown eyes back to Zoe, who checked the time on her phone.

"Sorry about that," she said. "Looks like we went over. See you next week?"

Cody's eyes rolled this way and that, looking at everything but me. "Sure, bye," he said, then slipped away like someone who'd been caught picking his nose.

I lowered myself into Cody's abandoned chair, trying not to notice how nice and warm he had left it. "Why are you meeting with Cody?" I asked. "His family doesn't go to our church."

Zoe flashed me a wide smile. "I claim all Riverbend as my mission field. The more involved I get at the high schools, the more students I meet. I try to make time for everyone."

Yeah, but Cody?

"How have you been?" Zoe asked.

"Horrible." I told her all about the golf disaster, fully ready to roll right into the Cody calamity, but Zoe cut me off.

"You know, you've tried so many different activities over the past few months. Maybe you should look for some that combine multiple interests."

I frowned. "What do you mean?"

"Well, if you like swimming and you like aerobics, try water aerobics. Things like that. It might be time to narrow down your interests and choose a couple to stick with for a while."

That seemed the opposite of trying all the things I could, but in all honesty, I had grown a bit weary of doing that anyway. "I'll think about it," I said, not really wanting to waste my time with her talking about my floundering mission to discover the real me. "I have a problem and need your advice."

Zoe folded her hands on the table. "I'll do my best."

"I need someone to take over feeding Mrs. Kirby's animals."

Zoe frowned and leaned forward. "Didn't you squeal like you'd won the lottery when she asked you to take care of her pets?"

"Yes, but that was before."

"Before what?"

I inhaled a deep breath. "Well, it turns out she's paying Cody to take care of her yard."

Zoe's brow crinkled. "And that's a problem *why?*"

My phone chimed. I ignored it and thought about her question. Could Zoe not see the problem? After all our meetings? "I just don't think it's wise, us spending time together alone."

My phone sounded again. Twice.

"Why not?" Zoe asked.

Seriously? I couldn't bring myself to tell her that the mere idea of getting into a relationship with a boy gave me nightmares. My friendship with Cody might not survive drama like that. "I don't want to give him the wrong idea."

My phoned played its song a few more times, and Zoe laughed. "My, you're popular today. Go ahead and check it. Just in case it's something important."

I turned over my phone. I had seventeen text notifications! My heart leaped, wondering if something bad had happened. Then I saw it was our group chat—the old group chat with me, Tessa, Amelia, and Shay.

Tessa: School schedules are up!

Amelia: They must have posted them yesterday afternoon because I checked in the morning and they weren't up yet. What did you get?

Tessa: Looking now.

Shay: Where do I log in again?

I flipped my phone face down on the table. "It's nothing," I told Zoe, though my stomach was churning at the thought that I'd finally know if I had any classes with Shay. "Just the girls talking about their school schedules."

"Oh, good," Zoe said. "Well, as far as your concerns about Cody, don't worry about it. He's a trustworthy guy. Besides, you'll be outside. Next door to your house. Nothing to worry about."

Just like that, I was out of options. I reluctantly agreed to continue helping Mrs. Kirby. I had to go over twice a day, once in the morning and once in the evening, and Cody would only be there once a day. I would just have to make sure I wasn't there when Cody was. I lived next door. How hard could it be to wait until he left to go over and feed the animals?

—⟋⟍—

When Zoe and I finished our meeting, I checked my phone. I had fifty-three text notifications now! I stared at that little white number in the bright red box, trying to decide if I wanted spoilers or not. I had no way to check my school schedule on my phone, so I wouldn't know what classes I had until I got home.

But I could at least get answers about the Baking and Pastry class.

I pulled up the text thread and scrolled past several texts of Tessa giving Shay instructions on how to log in to the school site to access her schedule.

Tessa: I have Baking!

Tessa: I also have Creative Writing I and French I.

Amelia: I have Drama I and II and Theater Dance. It counts for a PE credit and a theater credit. Since I still needed a PE class, it's perfect.

Tessa: That's so fun, Amelia. I didn't know there were options besides regular PE.

Amelia: Sure there are! You can take tennis or cross-country or several different sports. I forget all the options. What do you have first hour?

Tessa: Here's my schedule: Chemistry, AP Comp, French I, Baking and Pastry, lunch, Creative Writing I, US History, Algebra II.

Amelia: We have Creative Writing I and Alg II together. Why are you taking two Eng classes?

Tessa: Creative Writing is an elective for me.

Amelia: Smarty pants.

Shay: Ok, I'm logged in. Where do I go?

Tessa: Click on your student ID number, then on the word "schedule" under your name.

Shay: I see it.

Amelia: Click on schedule and it will come up.

Amelia: Srry. I'm too slow.

Amelia: Here is my schedule: Theater Dance, US History, Chem, Drama I, lunch, Creative Writing I, Drama II, and

Alg II. What a way to end the day. At least I'll have Tessa to keep me sane.

Shay: I have Baking class too. Izzy will be so happy. We're going to learn to bake, Tessa!

Tessa: And Izzy will outshine us both. Don't we get to be in groups of four? We'll need to find one more person for our group.

Shay: Too bad Amelia isn't baking with us.

Amelia: I'll like being Ms. Larkin's TA for Drama I. I can't wait to hear what the fall play will be.

Tessa: Izzy? Where are you? Schedules are up. We are baking this year!

Amelia: Post your whole schedule, Shay.

Shay: Chemistry, French I, study hall, Baking and Pastry, lunch, Creative Writing I, US History, and Algebra II.

Amelia: Ooh! We all have Creative Writing I and Alg II together! And I think I'll have Chemistry with Izzy.

Tessa: Hooray!

Shay: Yay! And Tessa, Izzy, and I will have Baking and Pastry too!

Tessa: That will be so fun.

Actually, no. That would not be fun. Not with things as they were between Shay and me. And why were Shay and Amelia taking Creative Writing? I thought that was something only Tessa and I were doing. I don't even remember saying anything to Amelia about it.

I put my phone in my pocket and climbed onto my bike. I rode home, stewing over what I'd do if the school hadn't moved me out of the Baking and Pastry class.

This whole thing was super annoying because I would normally love to take a class like Baking and Pastry. But I had no desire to put myself in a position where I'd be miserable all semester. Zoe had taught me that I was the best person to act in my own interests. Too often, if I didn't speak up, nothing would change because no one would know I was unhappy. When I'd changed my schedule, I'd been trying to be proactive. To advocate for myself. Even if I was the only one who knew it.

I got home and, thankfully, didn't have to kick anyone off the computer. I logged in to my school account and pulled up my schedule.

Algebra II
US History
Chemistry
Computer Programming
Lunch
Creative Writing I
Drama II
Concert Choir

Computer Programming? Claire, maybe. But me? No thank you. I was going to have to call the office or go in on the first day. I did not want to take Computer Programming. Ever.

But the four of us girls all had Creative Writing together. I supposed I had Tessa to thank for my one class with Shay Mitchell this fall.

I went upstairs to change into my paint shirt, then looked out my parents' window to see if Cody was in Mrs. Kirby's backyard. I didn't see him, so I went over and fed the animals.

By the time I got back, Sebastian was home from school. He was standing in the kitchen, book open on the counter, cookie in hand. The lid to the cookie jar sat on the counter beside his book.

"*Hola*, Sebastian," I said, joining him in the kitchen.

"*Hola*, Isabella Valadez."

I set about washing my hands in the sink. "What are you reading?"

"The Menagerie, book two, *Dragon on Trial* by Tui T. Sutherland," he said.

"Is that a new series?" My brother was obsessed with Sutherland's Wings of Fire series.

"Not new, just different." He took a bite of his cookie and turned the page.

I texted Mamá to see what the plan was for dinner, and she asked me to pull the *chile relleno* casserole from the freezer and get it warming in the Crock-Pot.

Only after I had done that did I pull up the text thread with the girls. Shay had last texted a picture of her pets, Stanley the greyhound and Matilda the cat, curled up together on a chair in her living room.

Shay: Izzy, look. ♥

Gah! They were the sweetest. I missed them so much. But how dare Shay use her animals to try and get in good with me? That was a low move.

I purposely didn't give her picture a heart, even though it deserved twelve hearts for adorableness alone. Instead, I just texted the facts.

Me: Something is messed up with my schedule. I have Computer Programming fourth hour.

Tessa: What? That's ridiculous.

Me: I know, right? Doesn't that sound like torture? Why would I ever take that class? It wasn't on my list of options.

At least I wasn't lying about that.

Amelia: Post your whole schedule, Izzy. We must have something together.

Me: We have some, yes. Just a sec.

I sent a screenshot of my schedule.

Tessa: We all have Creative Writing. Hopefully that will be fun!

Shay: I can't believe we are in Baking without Izzy.

Me:

Me: I'm going to talk to the office and see what they can do. I do not want to be in a programming class.

Amelia: We have three classes together, Izzy! All fun ones too. That's awesome.

Amelia: And you girls can still try out for whatever play Ms. Larkin chooses, even though you're not taking Drama II.

Tessa: No thanks!

Shay: Yeah, I'm good.

Me: I'm in!

Especially if Shay wasn't.

—⋙—

At church on Sunday, I sat with Tessa in the section where most of the teens usually sat.

"There's a cross-country meet at home tomorrow," she said. "I'm going to go watch Alex. You want to come?"

"I don't even like watching popular sports," I said. "How could it be fun to watch people run cross-country?"

"You cheer them on at the start and the finish line," Tessa said.

"Is this about Cody?"

"You guys are friends. I think he'd like to hear you cheering for him."

I narrowed my eyes. "Did you not hear me when I said I'm never dating again and want nothing to do with guys? Did you miss how desperately I tried to find a sub for feeding Mrs. Kirby's animals?"

"Okay, okay," Tessa said. "I just miss hanging out with you. There's never much time at church."

"You want to come to lunch with us after church? My grandparents will be there, but you and your mom are welcome to join us."

"Thanks, but we have plans. We're meeting Phil and Kayleigh at the park for a picnic."

"That sounds serious."

"Mom says it's not, but I don't believe her."

Another couple. I found this news a little depressing. Tessa had thought her parents were so in love, but then her dad left her mom for another woman. Apparently, not even marriage could keep a girl safe from a broken heart. What was the point of even trying to find love?

After church, we went out to lunch with Nana and Tata, Papi's parents. They were a good example of a relationship that looked like it was going to last. They'd been married forever, and they were still pretty cute. Mamá's parents had also been married a long time, but they were consistently grumpy. Sometimes I wondered if they even liked each other.

Not so with Nana and Tata. Tata still opened the door for Nana and pulled out her chair. And she always laid her hand on his whenever anyone prayed. In fact, they were always holding hands. It was adorable.

It was Sebastian's turn to choose the restaurant, so we ended up at the Peachtree. I ordered a cheeseburger and fries.

"Claire, how goes the college search?" Tata asked.

"Good," she said.

"She hasn't even applied to one school yet," Mamá said.

"The early admission deadlines aren't until November first," Claire said. "I have time."

"The earlier you apply, the better chance you have," Mamá said.

"That's not how it works," Claire said.

"Oh, I suppose you've been to college and med school, so you know all about it," Mamá said.

"What schools are you looking at, Claire?" Nana asked.

"Luddy, of course, and Purdue. I'm also applying to Ivy Tech since it's close to home and less expensive. But I'm going to be applying for a lot of scholarships through robotics."

"She hasn't filled out any scholarship applications yet either," Mamá said.

"That's not my fault!" Claire said. "They're not even accepting applications yet."

Thankfully, the waiter arrived with our drinks and distracted everyone from the tension between Mamá and Claire.

"Izzy, guess what?" Nana said after the waiter walked away. "I'm all set to launch the new Bible study. We start next Saturday. It'll be once a week at my house for six sessions. Starts at two o'clock. You're still going to come?"

"Oh," I said, a little taken off guard. "That's great."

Back when I first started trying new things, Nana had invited me to join her Bible study when she started up again in the fall. That was months ago, and I had said yes, not really thinking about how busy I might be with school. But I could do anything once a week for six weeks.

"What is the study about?" I asked.

"King David," she said. "It's going to be wonderful."

My heart sank. It might sound weird, but I'd never liked David. How could such a person be a man after God's own heart? Sure, he started out really good, but then he kept killing people and getting married, after he already had plenty of wives. And it only got worse from there.

I didn't say any of that to my nana, though. Instead, I said, "Can't wait!"

Her Bible study was the same day and time that I met with Zoe, though, so I'd have to reschedule or take a break for a few weeks. With all the teens she was apparently meeting with these days, I hoped Zoe had room in her schedule to fit me in at another time. I didn't think I could do without her.

—⟋⟋⟍—

On Monday, the last day of summer before school started, I was bored out of my mind. Not so bored that I wanted to go to the cross-country meet at our school, though. A little part of my brain that was still addicted to my cell phone kept trying to convince me to pull it out and check Tessa's social media to see if she had posted any pictures of a certain adorable cross-country runner.

I refused to yield to such demands.

Instead, I happily took my time next door, feeding Mrs. Kirby's pets without fear that Cody would show up. I wondered if Cody was good at cross-country. How did someone excel at a sport like that? Was it just timed distance running? Did they run as far as a marathon?

"We love you, Miss Hannigan!" my phone sang, which made the chickens scatter.

I pulled it out and saw that Shay had texted me a picture of Matilda sleeping on top of the DVD player, her head upside down and hanging over the side.

"Awwrgggg." In the space of that non-word, my emotions went from elated by adora-cuteness to completely annoyed that Shay thought she could patch things up by sending pictures of her pets. What about the porn? And what about Gwen Wilson? Had Shay been asleep when I forced her to watch the first season of the *Ms. Marvel* TV show? Did she really just forget that I would want to meet the author of the comic at Booked Up? Shay couldn't just be friends with me when she wanted to. She needed to stop playing games and deal with the real problems going on between us.

After I fed the animals, I went home and picked out what I was going to wear for the first day of school. This used to be more exciting to me, but after the whole Dropbox fiasco, I approached the task with a great deal of caution. I loved wearing leggings with fun prints, and that hadn't changed, but I now felt it necessary to always layer. I chose my watermelon leggings along with a black knit skirt, a kelly-green tank top, a fuzzy black cardigan, and black high-top Converse shoes. Cute and in no way revealing any part or shape of my body.

What I couldn't control was how the students would react when they saw me. Would they remember all that went on last spring? Or would they have forgotten? That night, as I tried to go to sleep, I prayed for two things: one, the ability to get out of Computer Programming, and two, a student body with short memories.

Chapter
5

THE MORNING OF THE FIRST DAY OF SCHOOL, Claire agreed to drive in a little early so I could get my schedule changed.

"It's only because the idea of you programming anything terrifies me," she said as she backed out of the driveway.

"Thanks a lot," I said, but not even Claire's insults could provoke me to anger. I needed her that much.

"I also wanted to leave the house before Mamá could question my life choices," she added.

"I'm sorry she's being so hard on you lately," I said.

"She's just worried about me going away to college."

It seemed like more than that to me. "But she wasn't like this with Leo."

"Leo's a boy," Claire said. "I know she wants the best for me, but she's also terrified that I'm going to come home for Thanksgiving break tattooed, pierced, and pregnant."

I laughed. "That doesn't sound like the Claire I know. Mamá should trust you."

"Why are you being so nice to me? Are you going to ask to leave early for school every day?" Claire slowed to drive around a sharp bend in the road. "You didn't take jazz choir, did you?"

"No," I said, "though jazz choir would be fun. I was trying to tell you how I really feel."

"Well, thanks," Claire said. "Just don't do that too often. It's weird."

"No problem," I said.

When we got to school, Claire parked in the senior lot. I couldn't believe this was my sister's last year of high school. It would be strange next year with her in college. I wondered if I should try to get my license this year. It seemed like a lot of work when my bike got me most places I needed to go, but biking to school was kind of a long ride so early in the mornings, plus I couldn't ride my bike in winter.

Claire headed off to the senior lockers, and I got in line at the office. When my turn came, I shared with Mrs. James, the school receptionist, my mortification at having Computer Programming on my schedule.

"What are my options?" I asked.

"I suppose that depends on what class you want," she said.

"What else is offered for fourth period? Electives, I mean." I didn't want to take any AP classes as electives. I wasn't Tessa.

"Well, let's see," Mrs. James said. "There is Debate."

"No, thank you," I said, thinking of how I'd been avoiding Shay rather than confronting her. I could imagine myself trying to argue with people for a grade by saying nothing.

She chuckled. "Okay, how about Fire Science?" She glanced up and, at the expression on my face, said, "That looks like a *no*. I also see Woodworking, JROTC, Auto Repair, Astronomy, and Spanish I. Would you like to take a foreign language?"

"I already speak Spanish," I said.

"Oh. Good for you," she said. "How about Sociology or Civics?"

"Are there no art classes left?" I asked.

Mrs. James shook her head. "You could put your name on a waiting list and see if anyone drops the class."

Ugh. All this to avoid Shay. I was pathetic. An idea came to me. "What about business classes? Are there any of those?"

"Let me take a look . . ." Mrs. James clicked around on her computer. "Intro to Business is fourth hour, and there is room in the class. What do you say? That would count for an elective."

"Perfect," I said. "Sign me up for Intro to Business." I would be taking Zoe's advice. She said I should try to combine interests. I liked to bake and post pictures of my food on Instagram, so perhaps a business class would help me learn how to do both better. And if I hated it, I could always switch next semester.

And best of all, I wouldn't be forced to bake with Shay five days a week.

Mrs. James printed out my new schedule, and I headed toward the junior hallway to find my locker. The first day of school was usually one of my favorites. Being a people person, I always found summertime far too isolating. Yet I hadn't walked the halls of Northside High School for two minutes before I heard someone say the word *Dropbox*.

I couldn't tell who said it, and it didn't look like anyone was staring at me. Yet whenever I made eye contact with someone, I swore they glanced away. When people looked at me, did they see the fake topless picture Zac had posted to my Snapchat?

My anxiety spiked. I was likely overreacting, but I couldn't shake the memory. I mean, sometimes when I thought about Zac, I remembered the picture he had sent me. I didn't *want* to remember that picture. It just popped into my head—burned onto my brain. If I remembered it so clearly, others likely did too—especially the male population.

My hands started to shake. *It's all good*, I told myself. *Zac isn't here. The Dropbox scandal is long over.*

I desperately wished I could go back in time and never speak to Zac Lloyd. That boy had ruined my thoughts forever.

Pornography was evil. How could Shay fill her mind with those kinds of images on purpose? The two I had seen had nearly driven me insane.

I found my locker, right across the hall from the boys' bathroom. Great. Just where I needed to be. Grumbling to myself about that non-perk, I fumbled with my combination. Even with my shaking hands, I managed to open it on my first try. This lifted my mood for a millisecond.

"*Hola*, Isabella," a guy said, a few lockers down. "*¿Cómo te ha ido?*"

The male voice made me jump. It was only Michael Torres. He was a friend of Cody's and was on Claire's robotics team. We'd had PE together last year. We occasionally practiced our Spanish with each other, but I wasn't sure it was wise to keep that up. I didn't want to give him the wrong impression.

Unfortunately, I also couldn't think of anything to say that wouldn't sound terribly rude, so I said, "*Ahí vamos*," which meant I was going through it. Then I grabbed an empty notebook and a pencil and shut my locker. I added a quick "Got to go!" and then took off in the opposite direction before he could respond.

I didn't slow until I reached the stairwell. For some reason, the canyon-like enclosure felt safer than the open hallways. I took my time climbing the stairs, and by the time I reached the second floor, I had calmed down. The upstairs hallway seemed less crowded.

I walked into Mrs. McLeod's Algebra II classroom and scanned the scattered students for a familiar face. Amelia didn't like the idea of ending her day with math, but I felt like that was better than starting the day with it.

"Hey!" Dev said, pointing at me. "You look like someone I know. Can you take off your shirt so I can be sure?"

Beside him, Dev's best friend, Hayden, laughed. "I don't recognize her with her clothes on."

Tingles ran over my body as every face in the room turned and fixed their eyes on me. I wanted to say something, but my brain had abandoned me. Why wasn't I saying anything? What *could* I say?

Cody Nichols appeared. He stepped between the statue of me and where Dev and Hayden were still laughing. "Shut up," he said. "How did the two of you manage to pass Geometry, anyway?"

As Cody absorbed the attention of the room, I came back to myself. I was grateful to have Cody go all Captain America in my defense. I wanted to hug him. The very thought brought on a rush of shame. Imagine what Dev would say then! Plus, I shouldn't be touching any boys. Especially not Cody.

My adorable neighbor turned and looked at me, those brown eyes of his too perfect to be legal. "Probably best to sit on the other side of the room," he said.

I'm pretty sure I nodded. Everything seemed blurry. I did walk across the classroom and choose a seat, though. Cody parked himself on my left like some kind of military-trained bodyguard, putting himself between me and the threat. That made it extra hard not to let my mind fawn all over him.

No, Isabella, I told myself. *You cannot think about Cody in that way.*

This gave me the urge to whine inwardly like a puppy.

I thought back to last year, when I was drooling over Zac from afar. Tessa had told me no, and from that moment on, I had started whining like a puppy every time Tessa and I saw Zac. The memory made me smile.

"You okay?" Cody asked.

My breath caught. I glanced at him, careful not to look too long. "Yeah. Thanks."

"They're jerks."

"Yeah."

Wow. I was sounding like some kind of foreign exchange student who only spoke two words of English. I wanted to say something to make Cody laugh, but that wouldn't be wise. I let the moment pass, eager for Mrs. McLeod to start class and save me from having to think.

Speaking of which . . . what was going on in my brain? I was sixteen years old. I'd never had a problem defending myself in the past. I shouldn't need rescue now. Not from a boy. Not from anyone. Why couldn't I speak up now?

"I'm going to fix the hole in the fence. After school."

Cody. Talking again. To me. "Mrs. Kirby's fence?" I asked.

He smiled. "Unless you like chasing Harland around?"

No smiling back, I told myself. *No smiling. No!*

I smiled back. "Chasing Harland *is* my daily cardio. If he stops getting out of the pen, I might have to take up a sport."

"You could do cross-country," Cody said. "I'm in the—part of cross-country. On the team."

Did Cody just jumble his words awkwardly? To me? Stars, he was so cute.

Must end conversation before I drown in handsome-boy aura.

"Running is boring," I said.

"Not if you run with friends," he shot back.

Thankfully, Mrs. McLeod finally decided to earn her wages and start class, thus ending my dangerously-close-to-flirtatious conversation with Cody Nichols. Sitting by him every day in this class was going to make avoiding him impossible.

After math, I filed out into the hall with the mob and started making my way to my second-period class, US History. I had Mr. Lucas again this year, which made me happy. He was a fun teacher and one of Claire's robotics coaches.

The whole time I was inching along in the crowded hallway,

Cody inched along beside me, chatting away about how he liked that Mrs. McLeod weighted homework equally against tests. Where was he going? Was he following me?

He stayed with me all the way to Mr. Lucas's classroom.

"You have US History now?" I asked.

His grin attacked my senses. "Yep," he said.

"Yo, Cody," a deep male voice said.

A group of basketball players were already seated in the middle of the room. I recognized Trevor Mercado and Jeremy Jenkins, among others. Cody walked toward them, and I seized that moment to look for a desk far away from all that testosterone.

"Izzy!" In the front row, Amelia waved at me.

Thank you, Jesus. I joined her there, grateful to sit with a girl.

Amelia leaned in close and lowered her voice. "I see you and Cody arrived together. Avoiding him going that well, huh?"

"No," I said. "He just keeps showing up."

"How very interesting," she said, smirking.

Ugh. That girl would never take my side on this. "I hope these are the only two classes he and I have together."

But when Amelia and I got to Mrs. Parks's third-period chemistry class, there was Cody. His friends were in this class too, including Alex, so he sat with them, and I sat with Amelia again, but this was starting to get weird.

What really threw me over the edge, though, was when that boy fell into the chair beside mine in Intro to Business.

"Are you following me?" he asked.

His clean Cody smell gusted over me, but I managed to say, "I was here first."

He grinned, and I swear a dimple appeared in his cheek, even though I knew the boy didn't have dimples. Was it the way he was turning his head to look at me? Why wouldn't he stop looking at me?

"Hmm, I suppose that's true," he said.

I looked around us. There were several students I knew in this class. Ryan, Luke, and Kyle were all seniors on the robotics team. Chad had been in my Drama I class last year, and Maddy had helped choreograph *Peter Pan*. And then Cody.

"I didn't know you were interested in business," I said to him.

"I've learned a lot working at Paprika's," he said. "I've been thinking I might want to start my own sporting goods store someday. What about you? I never would have pictured you in this class."

"I thought I might learn how to turn baking cupcakes into a business."

He beamed knowingly. "That fits. Brilliant idea, you going into the cupcake business. I almost couldn't make myself eat the cupcakes you brought me for my birthday. They were so amazingly decorated that I didn't want to ruin them by eating them. But then I did, and they tasted even better than they looked."

My stomach warmed at Cody's praise. I had made him some Diary of a Wimpy Kid cupcakes for his birthday since that book series had been a favorite of his in middle school.

Cody leaned to one side of his desk as he talked to me about some new cupcake-shaped cookie cutters he had unboxed at Paprika's, telling me that he thought I might need them. His hair was so golden. His eyes were so brown. His lips . . . *No.* I was not allowed to look at Cody's lips. In fact, why was I looking at him at all? Why had I asked him about being in this class? Had I no self-control? I was supposed to be avoiding him!

"Good morning, my young entrepreneurs," said a man standing at the front of the class. He was tall and slender and wore a sleek gray suit and a bright-purple necktie. "My name is Mario Federici. Welcome to Introduction to Starting a Business. I know that's not what it says on your schedules, but that's what I call this class. I hope you'll find it both educational and interesting." He walked to the whiteboard, which had a simple equation written on it:

Business = $

He tapped the whiteboard with two fingers. "Business equals money. How many of you think that's true? Let's see a show of hands."

I raised my hand, glancing around the room to see who else agreed. Most of us did, Cody included.

"I thought so," Mr. Federici said, "and that's okay. It's not uncommon for people to assume the main reason you start a business is to make money. But it's not the truth. In fact, it's dead wrong. What business really equals is making people happy." He erased the dollar sign and changed it to a happy face. "This is what business is all about. When you create a product or a service that makes people's lives better—more productive, happier—that will, in turn, make you a lot of money. Capiche?"

The class uttered affirmative agreement.

"Statistics show that fifty percent of all businesses fail in the first five years," Mr. Federici said. "That's a hard truth. Failure hurts. Failure is not fun, especially after dedicating five years of your life to something. And life after failure is hard. Life after a bankruptcy is especially difficult and painful. What we want to do in this class is identify the most common forms of failure so that we can design a business the right way from day one. This will put you ahead of the game and set you up for success. So tell me, my young entrepreneurs, what do you think are the most common reasons businesses fail? Shout them out."

"Not enough money to invest," Ryan said.

"Good," Mr. Federici said, writing it on the board.

"Spending money on the wrong things," said a guy I didn't know. "Like buying too much inventory that no one wants or not having enough of the things people do want."

"Sure, sure," Mr. Federici said, jotting it under Ryan's answer.

"The owner gets in over their head and doesn't know what they're doing," Maddy said.

"Okay, yes." Mr. Federici wrote that down as well. "Keep them coming. Faster."

I wanted to answer and wracked my brain to think of something to contribute.

"Not enough advertising," Luke said.

"Their expenses continually exceed their profit," Cody said.

"They don't know how to find customers," I blurted out.

Ryan answered again with "They can't do the work and can't afford to hire help."

"They don't communicate with customers. Or at least not effectively," Kyle said.

"They refuse to use technology," Chad said.

"They won't spend money on marketing or advertising," Ryan said, answering a third time. "Maybe they don't have it, or they're too cheap to spend money, or they think they'd be wasting it."

"A lot of thoughtful ideas here," Mr. Federici said, having scribbled everyone's answers on the whiteboard. "Good stuff. Let me tell you my reasons. You might want to write these down."

Papers rustled as everyone pulled out notebooks or turned to clean pages.

"First, this is the biggest reason businesses fail: They don't understand their customer." Mr. Federici wrote *Don't know customer* on the whiteboard. "You need to know who your customer is," he said. "You need to know what they want. What are their buying habits in regard to your product or service? Second, the proprietor doesn't communicate their value proposition to the customer." This he wrote on the whiteboard as well. "Why should the customer choose you over the competition? How are you different? What does the customer gain from doing business with you that your competitor isn't already offering?"

I took notes as quickly as I could, wondering who my customer was if I was just posting photos and videos on my Instagram. Was that even a business?

Mr. Federici continued to write as he lectured. "Third, their business model does not work. They fail to make a profit. There could be a lot of reasons for that, but they don't bother to figure them out. And the fourth most common reason businesses fail is that the owner is a poor leader who makes bad decisions." He capped the marker and tossed it onto the tray beneath the whiteboard. "In this class, we're going to learn what that looks like and make a plan to do the opposite. Capiche?"

"Capiche," a handful of us parroted back.

I caught myself smiling. I liked this guy and was glad to be in his class.

Chapter
6

"THAT WAS GREAT," Cody said as we left the business classroom and headed toward the cafeteria.

"It was," I said, surprised by how much I had enjoyed a class that wasn't part of the arts. "Mr. Federici's brusque Italian style is kind of delightful."

Cody laughed. "Yeah, he's pretty cool."

As we entered the open cafeteria, the cluster of students thinned. Cody and I got in line, and by the time I got my tray of food, Tessa and Amelia were already seated. With Shay.

The tingles attacked me again. As I watched the trio from afar, I started to recognize the feeling as anxiety.

What could I do? Why hadn't I foreseen this possibility? Or made a plan in advance? Because I wasn't the type to make plans, that's why! Why hadn't Tessa foreseen this and made a plan? Or at least warned me?

Because Tessa didn't care. She liked Shay better. I noticed how the two of them were talking right now. Tessa was probably on Shay's side. None of them understood what it was like to have their naked picture—even a fake one—shown all over school on Snapchat. None of them had to deal with the kinds of comments Dev and Hayden had made this morning in math class.

I suddenly sensed pulsing anger taking over me, which brought on a quick flood of shame. The truth? I was glad my friends didn't understand. Having everyone in school see that picture had been a horror I wouldn't wish on my worst enemy. Even Shay.

I hoped Shay wasn't sending anyone pictures.

I suddenly felt compelled to run across the cafeteria and ask Shay that very question. Shake her a little bit and warn her of the consequences. But that was silly. Shay knew better, just like Zac had known better. They both chose porn anyway. They thought it was harmless. They didn't care that it objectified people. They didn't care who it hurt. They liked it, apparently.

But was I any better? My eyes roamed over the boys sitting at a nearby table, taking in the broadness of their shoulders and the muscles in their arms. I used to say boys were hunky when I noticed such things. Was that any different? Was noticing a boy's muscles similar to looking at pictures of naked boys? It sure seemed different to me.

What might Zoe say to that?

"What are you doing?"

Cody. Standing beside me, holding a tray.

I had been standing in the middle of the cafeteria, lost in my reverie. For how long?

Before I thought it through, I said, "I can't sit with Shay right now. We're having a fight."

"What about?"

I shook my head. I was *not* talking to Cody about *that* topic. Stars.

When I didn't answer, Cody said, "Want to sit with me?"

Oh. Oh no. Sit with Cody? That violated my plan to avoid him—though my school schedule had already thwarted that resolution big time. Perhaps it was the lesser of two evils. I certainly couldn't eat standing in the middle of the cafeteria. What was the matter with me, anyway?

I nodded dumbly and followed Captain America to a table filled with cross-country runners. It felt weird not to sit with my friends. It felt even stranger to sit at a table filled with muscled boys, the very creatures I most wanted to avoid. They had grown over the summer. I felt dwarfed beside them. Nervous. Vulnerable.

Cody asked me something, but I had no idea what he said. "Huh?" I responded, brilliantly.

"If you joined cross-country, these would be your teammates."

All the more reason to never join cross-country. "That's true," I managed to say, then I stuffed my face with a huge bite of pizza.

Classy.

But maybe I was on to something here. If I made myself completely ridiculous, perhaps Cody would distance himself from me. The idea had merit. I would have to think on it more.

Somehow, I survived lunch and made it to fifth period, Creative Writing I. And guess what? Cody had that class as well, so we walked there together.

What is going on here, God? Is this your idea of a joke?

How could I possibly shake this boy if he was in so many of my classes? Honestly, he was just so nice, I was starting to doubt whether I wanted to shake him. Which was exactly how things had started with Zac. *I must shake Cody! I must be wise and protect us both from what could turn into another bad situation.*

As I was arguing with myself, we entered Mrs. Lopez's classroom. I already knew Shay would be there with Tessa and Amelia, but I was dismayed to see them all sitting together at the front of the classroom.

Just being in the same room as Shay sent a surge of anger through me. I didn't like feeling this way. Hadn't I put on my Black Panther awesomeness and forgiven her? Why was this so hard?

Tessa and Amelia were in the front row, and Lauren, who went to my church, was on Tessa's left. Shay sat behind Amelia. Cody sat behind Tessa, creating a nice buffer for me. Suddenly, I found myself grateful to have Cody by my side so that I wasn't facing Shay and my friends alone.

I sat beside him, behind Lauren and kitty-corner with Tessa, which was far enough away from Shay that I might actually survive the hour.

"Izzy!" Amelia said, her eyes bulging with some hidden thrill. "I told the others at lunch, and Ms. Larkin will announce it again, but I thought you'd want to know right away."

"Know what?" I asked.

"Our big fall play is going to be *A Christmas Carol.* Isn't that awesome? I would love to be the Ghost of Christmas Present. Are you going to try out?"

"When are tryouts?"

"Not until later this fall. And there will still be One Acts for Drama I, which we're allowed to try out for if we want, but it would be a lot to have a part in a One Act and then turn around and have a part in *A Christmas Carol.* I'm probably going to do it anyway, though."

"I'm sure I'll try out for the play," I said, "but I don't know about the One Acts."

"I guess you couldn't get into Baking and Pastry," Tessa the Traitor said, abruptly changing the subject.

"Nope," I said, pulling a sad face. "Taking a business class instead."

"Oh," Tessa said. "Well, we missed you at lunch."

"Really? I didn't see where you were sitting." Wow. Blatant lies. This was new for me.

Tessa tipped her head to the side, not buying my fib for a moment. She leaned close and lowered her voice. "I'm sure we can work out something for lunches."

"I think you already did," I murmured back, feeling bold about my answer. Perhaps it was the Iron Man within me, wanting to fire off some insults to make myself feel better.

"*Izzy*," Tessa said, clearly disappointed. "Why don't the four of us get together and talk?"

The tingles attacked then. I wanted to bite back again or—even better—say something coherent and wise, but who would listen? None of these people understood what I was going through, and telling them was far too risky. I had put myself out there enough times, and I was tired of being hurt.

This line of thought only frustrated me more. How could I go from Iron Man bold to Nebula insecure in a breath? Maybe I was a distant relative of the Hulk. Snarky when mad but quiet when confronted.

"Good afternoon," Mrs. Lopez said, walking to the front of the class. She handed a stack of papers to each student in the front row. "Please take a class syllabus and pass them back."

In front of me, Lauren handed back a grip of floppy papers. I took one stapled set and passed the rest behind me.

Mrs. Lopez began to go over the syllabus. There would be no tests in this class. Our entire grade was based on writing assignments, oral presentation, small group participation, and one special project.

"The first assignment of the year is called 'Who Am I?'" Mrs. Lopez said. "This has two parts. First, you will build a diorama that reflects your personal identity. I realize this might seem like more of an art project than a creative writing assignment, but the process of creative writing is more than just putting words on paper. I want you to dig deeply into yourself. I want you to engage the five senses. Building a diorama will not only help you do that, but finding physical items to represent you will also give you something tangible to write about.

"Which brings me to the second part of this assignment. You will write a piece that explains your diorama. You will read your piece aloud as you share your diorama with the class. As creators, we must know ourselves. Discovering who we are helps us see how we are similar to and different from others. When we create stories about people in our writing, we want to be able to portray them realistically, humanly, and powerfully."

She walked to her desk and brought forward an example in a cardboard box. She held up the box on its side, displaying a collage of pictures, fabric flowers, some papers, a toy car—all kinds of things. It reminded me of my *abuelita*'s home altar.

"This is my diorama," she said. "I made it in my master's program. I filled it with things that are important to me or have greatly impacted my life. Pictures of my family and friends, flowers from my wedding dress, some excerpts of my writing, and a miniature of my first car, which was the first thing I paid for all by myself as an adult. This project changed me—it so powerfully impacted me that I have required all my creative writing classes to begin with this assignment.

"If the project sounds intimidating, don't fret. Over the next few weeks, you will be working in small groups where you will answer questions that dig into your lives to help you discover who you are. Then you'll write short pieces that you'll be able to use in a final writing project.

"Creative writing is a bit like making pottery. You rarely get it right on the first try. You create drafts, edit those drafts, and refine until you are satisfied with the results."

She went on to talk about the other, more typical writing assignments we'd be completing that semester, but I was stuck on the diorama.

I didn't want to do it, plain and simple, which seemed strange because I had been working with Zoe on this very topic for the past few months.

It was one thing to explore my personal identity. It was another thing to have to talk about it with other students. Possibly with Shay. Or Cody. And present it to the whole class. Besides, even after all the work I had done these past months, exploring so many new things to figure out who I was, I still didn't know. How could I put my failure on display like that?

I frowned at Mrs. Lopez's diorama. Now that I had studied it longer, it looked more like the *ofrendas* some people of Mexican heritage use to celebrate the Day of the Dead than it did a Catholic home altar. Mamá had been raised Catholic and started attending an evangelical church while in college. She now had issues with *ofrendas* and felt the *altarista* in Abuelita's house was pagan too. Abuelita called it a prayer altar, but Mamá thought it was a way to communicate with the dead. It was one of the many things they argued about, along with praying to the saints, the concept of purgatory, and how to make authentic *pozole*.

After class, I approached Mrs. Lopez at her desk, hoping to find a way out of doing this assignment.

"Mrs. Lopez? I'm concerned about the diorama assignment," I said.

"How so?"

"My family is Mexican American, but we're also Christians. I mean, Protestants. My Mamá used to be Catholic, and she is not going to like how these dioramas look like *ofrendas* from the Day of the Dead. Mamá says *ofrendas* are pagan."

"Well, Izzy, you can make your diorama look however you want," Mrs. Lopez said. "It doesn't have to resemble an *ofrenda*. It doesn't even have to be three dimensional. Make a poster or decorate a jacket. You could make a painting or a drawing."

Her flexibility was not helping me weasel my way out of this expose-my-soul project. "I'm still not sure Mamá will feel comfortable with me putting so many images together. It will still look like an altar."

Mrs. Lopez picked up a pen and a sticky note. "How about you give me your mother's phone number, and I'll give her a call and explain the assignment?"

"Sure," I said, reluctant but seeing no way around it at this point. I pulled out my phone and read Mamá's number to Mrs. Lopez.

I left class feeling wary that my plan to get out of this assignment had failed. I could think about little else in Drama II. Not even the excitement of seeing Ms. Larkin again and watching her energy while officially announcing *A Christmas Carol* could pull me out of my funk.

As Ms. Larkin shifted to discussing the Drama II syllabus, Amelia, who I thought had been jotting down notes in her binder, ripped out the sheet of paper she'd been writing on and passed it to me.

It wasn't notes at all.

These are the roles I think you'd be great for: Belle, Fan, Mrs. Cratchit, or Martha Cratchit.

I pulled out my pen, circled Martha Cratchit, and wrote, *Who is this?*

Amelia reached over and wrote her answer right beneath my question. *Bob Cratchit's oldest daughter. She works in a hat shop.*

I didn't remember that from the movie versions I'd seen. I read Amelia's list again, thought it over, and shrugged. I could play any of those roles, but the ghosts would be more fun. I didn't dare tell Amelia I wanted to be a ghost when I already knew she wanted to be a ghost. Could you imagine if Ms. Larkin cast me in a part Amelia wanted? Yikes. I couldn't stand to lose any more friends at the moment, so I decided to keep my interest in playing a ghost to myself for now.

My last class was Concert Choir, and I was grateful to be ending my days with such a familiar and stress-free class. Mr. Tam felt like an old friend, as did the other students in choir. This was the only class I had with Lilliesha and Hyun Ki this semester, which didn't seem fair, but I was grateful to have some friends to talk to outside my regular squad.

How long would this conflict with Shay go on? Was I going to have to find a new squad?

I honestly hoped not.

At home later that night, when Mamá came in from work, I was all set to tell her how Mrs. Lopez was forcing everyone to make *ofrendas* in class.

Unfortunately, Mamá broached the topic before I could. "Mrs. Lopez called me today," she said.

"Oh?" I said, trying to sound innocent.

"You're going to do the assignment, Isabella," Mamá said. "After all the experimenting you've done, it should be easy."

One would think. Yet after three months of experimenting, I felt as lost as ever.

I opened my mouth to argue with Mamá, but the look on her face kept the words from materializing. "Yes, Mamá," I said, wondering how I could possibly get through such a presentation without sounding like a fool or breaking down in tears.

Chapter

7

IN BUSINESS CLASS THE NEXT DAY, Mr. Federici sat on the front edge of his desk and pointed around the room, asking everyone what types of business interested them.

"Baking," I said when my turn came. "Specifically cupcakes."

"There's a lot of money to be made in desserts and pastries," Mr. Federici said, his Italian accent thick. "We humans like sugar. Next!" He pointed at Cody, who again sat beside me.

"I'd like to own my own store," he said. "Sell sporting goods."

"How many stores in Riverbend sell sporting goods?" Mr. Federici asked.

"Uh, one?" Cody said. "Three if you count Walmart and Target."

"I do count them because customers are going to count them. What does that tell you?"

"People like sports?" Cody said.

"That's true," Mr. Federici said. "Plenty of interest in sports in this town. The trick is to figure out if a new store can take some of that business. Usually—but not always—it's the new guy who goes out of business. Next!"

Around the room he went. A lot of students said they wanted to work in technology, engineering, or computers. Kyle Dodson said film, and Luke Williamson said video games. Maddy Ross said fashion, and the class laughed.

"What's funny about fashion?" Mr. Federici asked. "Everybody here is wearing clothes today. That's big business. Let's keep it moving. Ms. Packer?"

"I don't want to own a business or even work in a particular industry," Sophie said. "I just want to work in management."

"That's good," Mr. Federici said. "Management can be tough, but every business needs management. But every business also needs receptionists, accountants, salespeople, an office manager, someone in public relations, someone in marketing, someone in human resources, someone in finance doing the budgets. If you work for a big company, those are going to be salaried positions. If you work for yourself like Mr. Nichols over here with his shiny new sporting goods store, you're going to do most of that yourself."

Mr. Federici went up to the whiteboard. "Now I want you all to brainstorm what you think are the top industries in the country. What do you think?"

People said computers, cars, food, insurance, and entertainment, like video games and movies. Someone said tourism. Mr. Federici wrote them all in a list on the board.

"Okay, not bad," he said when we finished. "You got some of them, but I think you'll be surprised when I tell you what the research says. First, what's the biggest industry in the United States—the one that brings in more money than any other? Software. Second is computers and computer accessories. So software is a bigger business than the device you use it on. Number three? Pharmaceuticals. That's big business. Might be number one someday. Number four is the oil and gas industry. Again, no surprise. How many of you own a car?"

Seven hands shot up.

"In five years, it'll be all but one of you. And cars always need more fuel. Number five is a surprise. Household products. Americans like to be clean and look nice. Six is software entertainment, which means what?"

"Video games?" Luke said.

"You got it. Americans spend a lot of dough on this one. And speaking of dough, are you surprised we haven't seen food yet? Look at how much money Americans spend on things we don't really need! Number seven is computer services."

"What is computer services?" Luke asked.

"Computer services is made up of network support, internet service, IT, cloud computing—things like that. Number eight is health care. Big business in this country, health care. Number nine: life insurance. And number ten is one you've probably never heard of: semiconductors. I know what you're thinking: *Mr. Federici, what's a semiconductor?* Anyone know?"

"It conducts electricity in electronics," Ryan said.

"Ten points for Mr. Gorman. It's all those flat little boxes on a circuit board. Almost all electrical devices need semiconductors, and somebody's got to make them. That's big business."

Mr. Federici paused for a moment, as if collecting his thoughts. "A couple more things," he continued. "Remember how I mentioned that Americans spend a lot of money on things we don't really need? Well, here we finally arrive at food and beverages. How's that grab you?"

He waited for us to react, then went on. "Ms. Ross," he said to Maddy, "your fashion industry didn't make the top twenty, though some clothing falls under the online retail industry—people shopping on the internet. What are they buying? Just about everything, and they're probably buying it from Amazon.com. What does this list tell you about Americans and what we value?"

"Comfort," Ryan said. "We want to eat and entertain ourselves."

"While we're on our computers," Luke added.

"We want modern conveniences," Cody said. "Electronics and shopping from home."

"A lot of people aren't exercising," a kid named Marcus said.

"Sitting at all those computers, working, playing video games, and shopping, right?" Federici said. "What else?"

"People have to get clean," I said. "Wash themselves, their clothing and bedding and towels, and their dishes and floors. Groom themselves and wear makeup and perfume."

"Americans like to look good and smell good," Federici said.

"What about the pornography industry?" Cody asked. "Where does it fall on your list?"

My cheeks warmed at the mention of that topic. The room fell silent, and all I could hear was the air conditioning blowing through the vent above the door. Then a few kids snickered, and Marcus barked a laugh.

Mr. Federici's eyebrows curved up like the McDonald's arches. "Well, Mr. Nichols, the porn industry was not on this list because it's not regulated and monitored the same way as many of these other products. My research on that industry puts its revenue in the billions, though. Why do you think that is?"

"Because chicks are hot," Marcus said.

Several kids laughed.

Mr. Federici tipped his head from side to side. "That's a surface-level answer. Dig deeper, Mr. Cole. Why do people spend money on pornography?"

Marcus's cheeks had flushed now. "Because they want to see it?"

"Okay, better," Mr. Federici said. "Do porn customers buy once, and then they're happy?"

"No," several in the class chorused, including me.

"Right," Mr. Federici said. "It's an industry with recurring revenue. Anyone know what that means?"

"Repeat customers," Ryan said.

"Exactly. It's addictive," Mr. Federici said. "Like cigarettes or coffee or gambling or vaping. You get hooked, you come back for more. That's a strong business model, even if it's sometimes unethical."

A moment of silence washed over the class, and then Mr. Federici said, "All right. Good talk. Now I want everyone to grab a textbook off the shelf and turn to chapter one. We're going to read through this together and learn all about economic systems and business. Sounds delightful, doesn't it? I'll do my best to make it interesting."

As class went on, I couldn't stop wondering why Cody had asked about pornography. That couldn't be why he was meeting with Zoe, could it?

I certainly hoped not.

After lunch, in creative writing class, Mrs. Lopez divided us into small groups, which put me with Tessa, Cody, and—much to my frustration—Shay.

"I've put a list of tasks on the board," Mrs. Lopez said. "Everyone needs to complete each task. First, record your answers in your journals, then go around the circle and share the answers with your group. You'll turn in your journals at the end of class for me to check your answers, so make sure you write them down."

I read over the tasks on the whiteboard:

1. Write ten statements answering the question "Who am I?"

2. Write down five groups you are a part of and rank them from 1 to 5, with 1 being the most important to you. (Think gender, race, class, social groups, etc.)

3. One at a time, share your answers with your group. Once you've shared, the other group members must each ask you a question to get to know you better. (Make sure the questions are different!)

I opened my notebook to a blank page and numbered it to ten. At least the first two tasks on Mrs. Lopez's list weren't terribly difficult. I wrote:

Who am I?
    1. I am Isabella Valadez.
    2. I am a daughter.
    3. I am a sister.
    4. I am a friend.
    5. I am Mexican American.
    6. I am a Christian.
    7. I am a teenager.
    8. I am a baker.
    9. I am an actor.
    10. I am a singer.

Groups I'm part of:
    1. Female
    2. Mexican American
    3. Middle class
    4. Drama
    5. Choir

The dark thought crossed my mind that I should add *Dropbox Girl* to the list of groups I was part of. Ugh. I really hated this class. How was this creative writing? I wanted to write stories and poems and songs, not further torture my already tortured soul.

After everyone had finished making their lists, we went around the circle to share and ask questions.

Tessa volunteered to go first. She twisted the end of her ponytail and shared about being both an only child *and* a big sister, which was new. Her adorable half brother was about six months old. She talked about being a swimmer and a Christian and a girlfriend to Alex.

Gag.

She also put down *abandoned* because of what had happened with her dad and the divorce. I thought that was really brave of her to say, but then I realized she'd set a vulnerability precedent for us, which annoyed me. I hadn't gone deep like that with my answers, and I had no desire to.

"How long can you hold your breath?" Cody asked, starting us off on the question round.

"I'm not sure," Tessa said. "If I'm just streamlining, I could last around twenty-five or thirty meters in the pool. That's probably close to ninety seconds."

"Nice," Cody said.

"Attention, please!" Mrs. Lopez called from where she was standing beside a group that included Chad and Hayden. "Please keep your questions respectful and not too personal. This is a get-to-know-you exercise, not truth or dare."

"We were only doing the truth part," Hayden said to Mrs. Lopez.

She shot him a look. "Keep it PG. These should be questions you'd ask me or your mother." She walked on from Hayden and Chad's group, and I turned my attention back to our circle.

"What do you want to do for a job someday?" Shay asked Tessa.

Tessa's smile faded, and she folded her arms. "I don't know, actually, which is frustrating sometimes."

More vulnerability. I thought up something silly to lighten the mood. "If you had to wear a pair of wacky leggings with pictures on them, what image would you choose?"

Tessa chuckled. "Hearts, I guess. Tiny ones."

"No," I said. "They'll be big, gaudy, hot-pink and lime-green ones."

"Oh, gosh," she said. "I hope I'm wearing these as pajama pants."

Shay looked reluctant to share her responses. She was a shy person, so I knew this would be hard for her. She mumbled her answers, and there were a few I couldn't hear. Her first answer was *loved*, which she didn't explain, though I figured it had to do with her aunt and her birth mom. Her second one was *adopted*. She also said she was an animal lover and talked about her job at her aunt's bookstore. She listed *adopted* and *Second Chance Farm* as some of her groups.

"What is your favorite book?" Tessa asked.

Shay twisted her lips. "*Little Women*, maybe?"

Tessa lit up. "That's one of my favorites too! I love all the sisters and the family stuff."

"Me too," Shay said, and Tessa reached out and touched her arm.

I felt my eyes mist a bit and blinked it away, trying to think of something to ask Shay that wasn't *"Are you still looking at porn online?"*

"If you could live in a world with only one animal, which type of animal would you choose?" Cody asked.

"I don't want to live in that world!" Shay said.

I wanted to say "Me neither," but I held my tongue.

"Uh, I don't know," Shay said. "That's a really hard question. I love horses, but you can't bring a horse into the house with you! But I think I'd have to pick horses anyway."

That led to my turn. Animals was a safe topic, so I took Cody's lead. "If you could own any kind of horse, which kind would you choose? Or what would it look like?"

"I'd want a quarter horse," Shay said. "They're strong and steady and not too crazy. Usually."

Nice! I'd survived one interaction with Shay Mitchell. Score one for me.

We all looked to Cody, who was next. "Okay, so, I did this a little different," he said. "I wrote down names people call me?" It wasn't really a question, but his lilting tone revealed his uncertainty. "I put *Cody Nichols, son, brother, grandson, cousin.* Then I put *Cubby,* which is a nickname my mom gave me that annoyingly stuck for way too many years."

Everyone chuckled, and I fought against his adorable magnetism that was trying to pull me in.

"Then I wrote *friend,*" he said, "*teammate, student,* and *believer*—because I'm a Christian. My groups were *male,* uh, *basketball, cross-country, track, ASB.* And I also put *Paprika's,* since I spend a lot of time there." He sat back and flicked his brown-eyed gaze to me.

"I kind of want to know more about the nickname Cubby," Tessa said.

"It's just what my mom called me when I was little. Please don't call me Cubby, though," he said, his voice a near whisper. "I don't want that getting out."

Tessa winced. "I can see how that could be bad for an athlete."

"Yeeahhh," he said. "Anyway, we're running out of time. It's Izzy's turn."

I began reading my lists. When I was halfway through, Mrs. Lopez wandered over and stood on the outside of our circle, observing.

"Okay, question time," Tessa said when I finished.

"I have a question," Mrs. Lopez said. "What is your favorite thing to bake?"

Before I could answer, everyone in the circle said "Cupcakes" at once, and we all laughed.

"Wow. Looks like this group knows you well," Mrs. Lopez said.

"Izzy, you'll have to make Mrs. Lopez a cupcake sometime this year," Tessa said.

"What's your favorite kind of cake?" I asked her.

"*Tres leches*," Mrs. Lopez said.

"Good choice," I said. "I've never tried to make *tres leches* cupcakes, though. This will be fun!"

"I want one when you make them," Cody said.

"Me too," Tessa said.

"And me," Shay added.

"Okay," I said. "I'll work on it."

"I look forward to it," Mrs. Lopez said, walking away.

"My turn," Tessa said. "My question is, if you could only pick one dessert to eat for the rest of your life, what would it be?"

"Oh!" I said. "What is this cruel world you and Cody have devised, with one animal and one dessert?"

"It's no place I'd want to live," Shay said.

"Answer," Tessa said, grinning.

I thought about it. *Really* thought about it. "I'm going to go with French silk pie because it's fudge-like but also pie-like, and it comes with whipped cream. My recipe uses chocolate cookie crust."

"I approve of this choice," Tessa said. "Shay?"

"If you could have any superpower, what would you want?"

I liked that question and already knew my answer. "The ability to talk to animals," I said.

"I'd like that one too," Shay said, smiling at me.

For some reason, it felt painful to accept her smile, so I shifted my gaze to Cody, whose eyes were already fixed on mine. "What's your biggest fear?" he asked.

"Yikes!" Tessa said. "You ask hard questions."

Shay laughed, and Cody grinned, looking quite pleased with himself.

Honestly? My greatest fear was that the picture Zac had photoshopped of me would start circulating again. I knew it was out there—that some people likely still had it saved on their phones. It had been screenshotted 164 times, after all. But I wasn't going to say that. Not here.

"Spiders," I said, wrinkling my nose.

Blessedly, the bell rang then. I jumped up from my desk and headed for the door, needing to get out of that room. I felt conflicted because some of this was fun, but I couldn't forget my anger toward Shay. Just because we had an assignment together didn't mean everything was back to normal.

"Izzy?" I heard Shay's voice. "Izzy, hold on a minute. I have a video of Matilda I want to show you."

Ugh. Of course she did. I poured on the speed, pretending not to hear.

"Izzy!" Amelia this time.

I didn't stop for Amelia, either. I saw the bathroom, and the thought crossed my mind that I should go in there. Then it would make sense why I might be hurrying away.

But they might follow me in, and then I'd be trapped.

So I bypassed the bathroom and darted down the stairs, heading toward the multipurpose room where Ms. Larkin taught drama classes.

I entered an empty room and slowed to a stop, wondering if class was elsewhere today.

"Hello, Izzy," Ms. Larkin called from her desk. "Phones in the shoe organizer, please."

Right. I turned back to the door. Mounted on the wall beside the entrance, the shoe organizer had see-through pockets. As I was slipping my phone inside one, the door banged open, and Amelia barreled inside.

"Izzy!" she said. "What is the matter with you?"

"Me?" I asked, playing dumb.

"Why were you running down the hallway?"

"I wasn't running," I said.

She narrowed her eyes at me, and her freckles looked more orange than ever.

"Did you need something?" I asked.

"You know what? No, I don't." She reached past me, tucked her phone into the shoe organizer, then walked deeper into the room. "I'm good."

Chapter

8

SOMEHOW, I MADE IT THROUGH THE FIRST WEEK OF SCHOOL and survived several face-to-face encounters with Shay. She even texted me a video of Matilda getting caught opening a cupboard. So cute. I wished I had a cat that opened cupboards.

I wished I had *any* cat.

Saturday afternoon, I pulled on my TARDIS hoodie and rode my bike to Grounds and Rounds to meet with Zoe. When I walked inside, I found her sitting with Cody. Again.

What on earth? I could easily brush off him meeting with her once, but two weeks in a row felt suspicious to me. Were they meeting regularly? Why?

Panic shot through me as I remembered Cody's question about pornography in business class. What if he had been looking at the pictures on Dropbox too? Maybe he was getting help for that.

What a terrible thought! Cody wouldn't do that.

Would he?

I ordered my coffee and decided to use the restroom while I

waited. I didn't want Cody to catch me staring. When I finally stopped worrying about why Cody might be meeting with Zoe, I started worrying about what he might think if he saw *me* there a second week in a row and wondered why *I* was meeting with Zoe.

Thankfully, Cody was gone when I came out. I grabbed my coffee and sat down at the table.

"Hi, Izzy," Zoe said, smiling brightly.

"I saw you with Cody again," I blurted out. "Do you guys meet every week too?"

"I can't really talk to you about my conversations with Cody," she said.

"Why not?"

"Well, it's just not right for me to say anything."

Oh.

"How did your first week at school go?" Zoe asked.

Shame about being nosy threatened to pull me under, but I took the branch Zoe offered and dived into telling her about my week. I mostly focused on how everybody seemed to be staring, and how I could swear people were talking about me and the Dropbox scandal. Besides Dev and Hayden, two other boys had spoken to me rudely this past week, and I told Zoe what they had said.

"How did that make you feel?" she asked.

"Gross," I said. "Embarrassed."

"Did you reply to any of these comments?"

"No. I just ignored them." The thought popped into my head that I should tell her how Cody had defended me, but I was still smarting from being told it wasn't my business to ask about him. I decided she didn't deserve to know.

"I imagine that's hard to do," Zoe said about my ignoring the rude boys.

"I guess."

"Am I wrong?" she asked. "Is ignoring them easier or more difficult than engaging in conversation?"

"Easier, I suppose," I said. "But I haven't been able to speak at all. I kind of just space out. Freeze."

"I'm sorry, Izzy. That sounds extremely difficult." Zoe took a sip of her drink. "You know, it might help you to speak to a professional about all this."

Tessa had a counselor she talked with about her parents' divorce. "A shrink?"

"A professional counselor. Someone trained in trauma and post-traumatic stress."

The words surprised me. "You think I have post-traumatic stress? I thought that was just for soldiers."

"I don't want to make any kind of diagnosis," Zoe said. "I'm not qualified to, and I don't mean to scare you. But lots of people get forms of post-traumatic stress from situations that have caused any level of trauma in their lives. What you went through was harrowing and continues to be, though in a different way from a soldier's experience. I don't think it feels small to you at all."

It certainly didn't, but PTSD? "I don't want to talk to anyone but you," I said.

"I just want you to think about it. That's all. And I'm happy to keep talking with you. I do have a minor in counseling, but I'm not licensed as a certified therapist. So I can listen and give you advice, but I am not a professional."

"I don't think I need a professional," I said, willing myself to believe it. "I just need more time."

"All right." Zoe took another drink. "What bothers you the most about being at school?"

I didn't even have to think about it. "I feel like my mere existence in that place bothers people. The way the picture Zac sent of himself bothers me."

"Remember, you didn't do anything wrong."

"I know. But I can't stop seeing that picture. So it stands to reason that it pops into other people's heads too. The moment I walk by or sit next to them in class, they see it. I remind them of it. People can't look at me and think about anything else."

"I understand why you feel that way," Zoe said, "but lately you seem to be wired to think the worst of everyone. Honestly, with the exception of the boys who spoke to you, you can't know what anyone else is thinking. I want you to remember that. When you catch yourself assuming that someone is thinking bad thoughts about you, stop yourself and imagine that this person is thinking about other things. Their own problems, for example. Their own assignments. The challenging relationships in their own lives. People tend to be overwhelmed by their own junk. We're all mostly thinking about ourselves. Too much." She grinned. "But when you go through trauma, it's common to feel like the spotlight is always on you. Yet that is often not the case. Could you practice that for me?"

"I'll try," I said, though I wasn't sure I believed her.

"Some days, trying is all any of us can do. Just remember, you don't have to do this alone. God is with you. Pray to Him for strength. Pray for Him to remind you that other people are occupied with their own lives. It also might help to pray for those people, whether they're saying cruel things to you or you're just worried they might be thinking ill of you. Pray God's blessings upon their day. It's hard to be angry at others when we are praying for them. But if you ever feel bullied or in danger, find a teacher you trust and tell them. Don't take abuse from anyone."

"I won't." I didn't want it to happen again, but if it did, I hoped I wouldn't freeze up.

—m—

When my meeting with Zoe ended, I got up to leave the café and saw Tessa and Alex sitting at a table near the window. I headed toward them.

"Hi, Izzy," Tessa said.

"Hey," Alex said.

"Hi." I stopped at the end of their table. "Did you guys see Cody in here?"

"Yes, he was here," Tessa said.

"About an hour ago," Alex added.

"He was meeting with Zoe," I said. "You guys know why?"

"No clue," Alex said.

I bit the inside of my cheek, unsure if I wanted to open this can of worms. "You don't think he was involved in the Dropbox thing, do you?"

"No way!" Alex said. "Cody isn't like that. He doesn't even date."

Everybody knew that, but suddenly I was curious. "Do you know why?" I asked.

Alex was giving me a look similar to the one Cody had given Dev and Hayden. "If you want to know about Cody's business, ask Cody," he said.

Shame gripped me in its talons again. I had annoyed Alex and apparently insulted Cody's honor or something. I wanted to fix it, but I was also hurt that Alex had snapped at me. "Fine," I said. "I will."

I left feeling frustrated and embarrassed to have been lectured by Alex. Did that mean he and I weren't friends anymore? Alex and I had never really been friends in the first place, but I didn't like the possibility that we were *less* than friends now.

As I unlocked my bike from the rack, I reminded myself that I was supposed to give Alex the benefit of the doubt. He could have a headache, and maybe that's why he snapped at me. However, the annoyed look on his face—that was now burned into my brain—made that difficult to believe.

God, please bless Alex. Give him a wonderful day.

I jumped onto my bike and rode toward home, continuing to

pray for Alex. It was a bitter pill at first, to pray for someone I was
annoyed with, but I kept praying as I pedaled. Somewhere along
the way, I stopped being mad at Alex and started wondering about
what Zoe had said.

PTSD.

The thing is, back in April, I thought I was okay. I really did.
The girls and I had worked together to switch Zac's phone with
Amelia's to help Deputy Packard get the evidence he needed to
press charges. I'd made peace with my parents and talked to Zoe.
I even had to make several official statements at the courthouse.

Yet as time went on, I had a few weird spells. I would be fine,
and then out of nowhere something would remind me of Zac or
porn or the Dropbox thing. I'd start thinking about it, replay-
ing certain conversations in my mind, repeating them, creating
imaginary conversations about things I should have said to Zac. I
would rant. Thoughts would spin. And I'd get myself all worked
up, sometimes to the point of tears.

I figured this was normal. I'd been through something pretty
horrible, and being mad about it seemed like a natural reaction.

But then we started rehearsing for *Peter Pan*, and someone
made a flyer that said "PETER PAN FEATURES THE DROPBOX GIRLS."
It had six names on it, all girls who had a role in *Peter Pan* and who
were also linked to the Dropbox scandal, including me. That flyer
pushed everything to the surface again, and my angry daydreams
increased. I felt angry all the time.

Then my friends had come up with the idea of Operation
Encouragement to support the girls mentioned on the flyer. I
didn't realize it at first, but as we started divvying up the names
and giving the girls surprise gifts and encouraging notes, it became
clear that no one was giving me anything. When my squad had
conceived the idea for Operation Encouragement, they weren't
thinking of me as one of the Dropbox girls, even though my name
was on that flyer. My friends meant for Operation Encouragement

to be for all the girls *but* me. Amelia, who'd been stage manager on *Peter Pan*, went all mama bird over the other five girls whose names were on the flyer, watching them every minute to make sure they were okay.

She never worried about me. At all.

I had pushed aside my hurt and slapped on a smile, told myself that what I had been through wasn't the same as the others. Those five girls really had been naked in their pictures, but the picture Zac posted of me had been faked with Photoshop. What right did I have to be upset? I had brought all this on myself anyway. How many people had tried to warn me about Zac? Sooo many. But would I listen? Nope. I had wanted a boyfriend more than I had cared to listen to common sense.

What Zac did was awful. Although the whole school still thought that picture was real, my friends and I knew the truth. Back then, I had to give my friends grace. Tessa was going through real problems with her stepmom. And Shay was dealing with her grandma. Plus, Amelia had created the Wall of Fame for the *Peter Pan* company, and people had written some kind things about me there. That, and the arrival of Tessa's baby brother, Logan, had been enough to distract me from my hurt feelings. Additionally, we were making tons of cupcakes to fundraise for the *Peter Pan* flying apparatus, and I'd always found baking therapeutic.

So I put on my happy face—faked it like a true thespian—and no one ever knew how alone I felt.

I almost told Tessa. She was the one person who asked me how I was doing right after the flyers started popping up around school.

But I lied and told her I was fine.

I needed to be fine. The thing had gone on long enough.

Tessa had hugged me and said she was praying for me. Then she never brought it up again. And why should she? I said I was fine.

But maybe I wasn't so fine after all.

—ഘ—

An hour later, I was looking out the window of my parents' room and watching Cody work in Mrs. Kirby's backyard when my phone sang, *"We love you, Miss Hannigan!"*

I pulled the cell from my pocket and looked at the text message.

Tessa: Hey, I just wanted to apologize for today at the coffee shop. I think Alex overreacted. He's normally not like that.

Me: No worries. It's okay.

Tessa: I tried to find out why Cody doesn't date, but Alex totally shut me out. I think he's onto me. He just kept saying, "Cody doesn't date." Which we already know.

I watched Cody maneuver the push lawn mower around the oak tree in Mrs. Kirby's backyard. He had earbuds in, and I wondered what he was listening to.

Me: It's okay. You don't have to try to find out anything.

Though I secretly really wanted to know.

Tessa: I've known Cody even longer than I've known Alex. He had a girlfriend in sixth grade, for like a week. And he dated another girl at the beginning of seventh grade. That was it. No one else that I remember. Maybe you should just ask him.

Me: Ask him why he doesn't date or why he's meeting with Zoe?

Tessa: Both.

I pondered this as I watched Cody remove the grass bag from the lawn mower and dump it over the back fence into the compost pile.

"If you want to know about Cody's business, ask Cody," Alex had said.

And I'd said, *"Fine. I will."*

It was one thing to say that to Alex to salvage my wounded

pride. It was another thing to actually do it. How did a girl ask a guy such a thing without sounding interested in him? And why did I care so much? I didn't want to date anyone either.

I figured I was just curious to know what would cause a guy to make that kind of decision. I respected it. I wanted to understand it too.

Chapter
9

MONDAY MORNING, I CAME UP WITH A NEW WAY TO AVOID SHAY: Always be talking to someone. Unfortunately, the only person always willing to talk to me was Cody. Out of sheer lack of options, I found myself walking the halls with that beautiful boy far more often than was normal for a nonromantic friendship.

Those hallways were quickly becoming dangerous ground.

To make matters worse, in business class Mr. Federici was absent. Our substitute teacher passed out a worksheet and told us we could work in pairs to fill it out. Cody scooted his desk beside mine.

"Let's do this," he said.

"Okay," I said, frustrated by the way my stomach zinged anytime that boy moved.

We worked together to fill out the worksheet, which was about economic terminology, and had it completed in fifteen minutes. Then Cody doodled a basketball on his notebook. He followed this up with a sketch of an ice cream sundae, then drew a tic-tac-toe board.

He pushed his notebook to me. "You first," he said.

I drew a smiley face in the center.

As we played, it crossed my mind to ask him why he didn't date, but I couldn't think of a good way to bring it up. After winning the third game of tic-tac-toe in a row, an idea occurred to me.

"Do you know how to play questions?" I asked him.

His gaze flicked to meet mine, his eyelashes dark despite his golden hair. "What's questions?"

I grinned. "So you do know how to play, don't you?"

He raised his eyebrows. "Do I?"

"Don't you?"

He twisted his lips. "What's your favorite color?"

I thought about it. "Do you think I might like purple?"

He shrugged. "How should I know?"

I tapped my chin. "Who is someone you could ask who might be able to tell you?"

"Hmm, is Tessa someone who might know?"

I scoffed. "Why would she know?"

"Is there someone better to ask?"

"Couldn't you ask me?"

He fell silent, and I thought I might have beaten him already, but then he said, "When didn't I ask you?"

I giggled. "Are you just teasing me?"

"Does that sound like something I would do?"

"Don't your brothers tease you a lot?"

A grimace pinched his face. "Why else would I have been born?"

Aww. "Didn't your dad teach you about the birds and the bees?"

His jaw dropped.

Yeah . . . I couldn't believe I said that one either. He exaggerated his shock, which made my face burn. I laughed so hard,

I had to cover my face to mute my guffawing—and hide my embarrassment.

"Keep it down, please," the substitute teacher said. "Other students are still working."

I glanced around. "Who else is still working?" I whispered, hoping I might catch Cody off guard.

"Who cares?" he said.

So the game was still on, was it? I fought back my smile and decided to ask some questions that would hopefully lead to the one I wanted answered. "Have you ever had a girlfriend?"

He frowned. "Why are you asking?"

"Don't you remember if you had a girlfriend?"

"How could I forget?"

"Was she *that* memorable?"

"Don't you know that memorable isn't always a good thing?"

Now we were getting somewhere. "How old were you?"

He tipped his head to the side. "What is that grade between sixth and eighth?"

Okay, so seventh grade, which matched what Tessa had shared. "Why don't you date now?"

He fixed his stare on me, and my cheeks blazed again. Oh, stars. Had I made a mistake?

"What are you doing Friday?" he asked.

My eyes bulged. Yep. Total mistake. "Are you changing your mind about dating?"

"How do you know I *don't* date?"

Again, I tapped my chin as I scrambled for the right question. "What friend do you have who might have let that slip?"

He grunted. "Why would I pick such a poor friend?"

Elbow on my desk, I propped my head on my fist. "Why won't you just answer the question?"

He seemed to squirm a little, which made a combo of regret and excitement sweep over me.

"Why are *you* changing the game?" he asked.

"Who says I'm changing it?"

He shook his head. "Not here."

I beamed, my mouth wide like a character from the Muppets. "That's not a question. I win!"

"Volume!" The substitute teacher shot me the crook eye.

"Sorry!" I said, wincing at her.

Cody turned in his desk, his gaze on his notebook. "You win," he said softly.

Now what? The game was over, but I still didn't know anything. *Not here*, he had said. What had he meant by that?

The bell rang. Cody grabbed his books and stood.

"Wait!" I said, popping to my feet so fast that my desk scraped over the floor. "If not here, where?"

He studied me. "You really want to know?"

I nodded.

"Why?"

That was the real question. "I know why I don't date," I said carefully. "I'm curious why you made the same choice."

"All right," he said. "Let's grab lunch. Then we'll go outside and find somewhere quiet."

I gathered my things and followed him out the door, feeling like I was walking on thin ice. As we walked toward the cafeteria, the energy between us changed. During the game of questions, it had been delightfully thrilling. Now it was mysteriously tense. Several times as we squished close to weave through the crowded hallway, my arm touched his, which sent tingles of electricity through me.

I replayed parts of the questions game in my head. Had he meant to ask me out on Friday? Or was he just being silly? A niggling feeling inside told me I was playing with fire. I didn't want to give Cody the wrong idea, yet I was pretty sure I had spent the last hour flirting with him. I hadn't meant to. It just sort of happened.

I should run away, and fast—tell him I forgot I had to meet Claire, or something.

But I didn't. My traitorous feet moved parallel to his as we entered the cafeteria, waited in the food line, then carried our lunch outside to the lawn.

Through all of this, we didn't speak one word to each other.

Talk about nerve-racking.

Cody found a spot under a shady oak tree and sat down. I made my first wise decision of the day and sat across from him rather than beside him. I instantly regretted that, since now I had nowhere to look but right at him!

"When I was in seventh grade, my brothers were in ninth and tenth," he said. "They had friends over all the time, but they didn't like me hanging around them. I still tried. I thought my brothers were awesome, and I'd been following them around since I could walk. They thought I was a pest. To them, I've always been a pest."

"You are the most un-pest-like person I know," I said.

"I appreciate that," he said. "But everything is different with siblings."

"True," I said.

"So, like I said, I followed my brothers everywhere. In seventh grade, I got a crush on one of their friends. Ellie. Whenever Ellie was around, I tried to talk to her. At first, she just teased me to make my brothers laugh. Then one day, she started talking to me for real. She would come over to our house and talk to me first. If I wasn't downstairs, she'd come looking for me. I knew she liked me. I was positive. Until the day I heard them all laughing about me in the backyard. Turns out my brothers had talked her into pretending to like me. As a prank. She was just messing around."

"That's so mean!" I said, shocked a girl my age would do that. Cody had been Sebastian's age at the time.

"Yeah, it was cold," Cody said, "and it killed me. I was humiliated. I swore off evil females until I was old enough to be able to tell, for certain, whether a girl really liked me."

"Can anybody ever really know that?" I asked, thinking how Zac had played me.

"I think so," Cody said. "For most high schoolers, dating is shallow. It's all about who's more popular and who you might be seen with. Or about who is available, like just anyone will do."

I winced inside, remembering how excited I'd been for people to see me with Zac. "When I was . . . hanging out with Zac . . ." Stars, was I really going to talk about Zac with Cody? I pressed on. "I thought it was real. But for him, it wasn't even shallow. It was a scam."

"I'm sorry about that, Izzy," Cody said. "I should have said something sooner."

"I wouldn't have listened. So many people tried to warn me, but I was too caught up in the dream. It never occurred to me that a person would do what he did. Just like you probably never thought Ellie would do what she did."

"True, but don't compare them. Ellie and my brothers were mean. Cruel, even. Zac was a predator—a felon now."

I didn't like the word *felon*. "A con man," I said.

Cody nodded and took a bite of his hamburger.

"What about Tessa and Alex?" I asked. "As a couple, I mean."

Cody swallowed his bite. "They're different."

"Why?"

He shrugged. "They don't play games."

Shame washed over me. I hoped Cody wasn't referring to how I'd used the questions game to get to this conversation. "Thanks for sharing your story," I said. "I hate that it happened to you, but I'm glad you told me." Plus, it also kind of made me feel a little better that I wasn't the only far-too-trusting person out there.

"Sure," he said.

We ate in silence for a few minutes. It was awkward eating across from someone, so I started watching a group of kids hit a volleyball back and forth near the front of the school.

Cody broke the silence. "My boss is hiring."

I turned back to him. "At Paprika's?"

He nodded. "I get a 10 percent discount on everything in the store."

Goosebumps prickled my arms. "No need to brag."

He chuckled. "Anyway, they want someone for weekdays after school from three to five to cover for me. I thought you might be perfect for the job, though you'd have to be careful not to spend everything you made."

"You're quitting?" I couldn't imagine not seeing Cody in his blue Paprika's apron when I went into the store.

"No," he said, "I have cross-country practice. I'll still work from five to seven. But since you refuse to join the team, I thought you might like the job."

"You really think they'd hire me?"

"They love you."

"As a babysitter." The people who owned Paprika's were Mrs. Kirby's daughter and son-in-law. They had three adorable children that I watched whenever they needed a night out.

"Every employer wants someone they trust handling their money," Cody said. "You should apply."

I wasn't sure that was a good idea. I'd already crossed every single Cody boundary I'd set. Apparently I couldn't control my behavior around this boy. Yet with Cody at cross-country practice, I wouldn't be working with him. That made the offer extremely tempting.

"I'll ask my parents and pray about it," I told him.

"Cool" was all he said.

—m—

In creative writing class, Tessa and Amelia caught me by the door while Cody went inside and sat behind Shay.

"Well?" Tessa said.

"Well what?" I asked.

"You ate lunch with Cody outside," Amelia said. "We saw you."

"We had to finish a conversation we started in business class."

"You guys are working on a project?" Tessa asked.

"Sort of." I needed to change the subject before I got caught liking Cody when I was working very hard *not* to like Cody. "He told me Paprika's is hiring someone to cover his shift while he's at cross-country practice."

"Ooh," Tessa said. "I can't think of a better place for you to work."

I beamed. "I know, right?"

"Are you going to apply for the job?" Amelia asked.

"I'm going to ask my parents first," I said. "Cody said I'd get a 10 percent discount."

"Don't even try telling me that's the only reason you'd want the job," Amelia said.

"That and working with all that kitchen stuff," I said.

"And working with a cute guy," Amelia said.

"Nope," I said, a little too smugly. "We wouldn't be working the same hours. I'd be covering for him when he's gone."

"*Izzy*," Tessa said. "It's okay to like him."

I watched him from across the room and thought about what his brothers had done to him. About how he didn't date because he'd been hurt. "I do like him," I said. "As a friend."

My. How adept I had become at lying these days.

Chapter
10

WHILE MY FAMILY GATHERED AROUND THE TABLE for a dinner of fried chicken and rice, I patiently waited for my chance to broach the topic of a job at Paprika's.

"How was robotics practice, Sebastian?" Mamá asked.

My brother was not one to talk while he was eating, but Mamá always tried anyway.

"They learned some Java programming basics," Papi said. "Sebastian prefers the engineering side of robotics over programming, though."

"That's not a surprise," Claire said. "Programming can be super boring."

"Sebastian can do anything he sets his mind to do," Mamá said.

"It's not a question of *can* he do it," Claire said. "I know he can. I just think he'd be bored doing it."

"Did you get the email I sent you today?" Mamá asked Claire.

Here we go.

"*Sí*, Mamá," Claire said, "but I don't qualify for that scholarship since I'm not going into a medical field."

"It was an engineering scholarship," Mamá said.

"Biomedical engineering," Claire said. "That's not what I want to do."

"Claire wants to do mechanical engineering," Papi said. "Maybe design."

"Probably design," Claire said. "Bash and I have that in common." She nudged our brother's arm as he sat reading his latest Tui T. Sutherland book at the dinner table. His eyes never left the book as he jerked away from her, then slowly settled back into position.

Before Mamá could find a new angle to interrogate Claire, I jumped in. "Something happened today," I said. "I'm pretty excited about it, but I need to make sure it's okay."

"What happened?" Papi asked.

"I kind of got offered a job at Paprika's."

"Were Nicole and Robert at the high school today?" Mamá asked.

"No," I said. "Cody told me they're looking for someone, and he seems to think I'll get the job if I apply." My parents' stares compelled me to continue before they started listing reasons to say no. "It's very part-time. Only two hours a day, and it might only last a few months while Cody is in cross-country. They need someone to cover while he's at practice. Think it would be okay?"

"How would you get there?" Mamá asked. "And home?"

"I figured I could put my bike in the back of Claire's truck on the way to school, then ride there after school, then home after my shift."

"That's a long bike ride after working on your feet," Papi said.

"I thought about that," I said, "but it's only a two-hour shift, so I think it would be okay. I'd like to try it, anyway."

"You know for sure that the Bellangers want to hire you?" Mamá asked.

"No," I said. "I thought I should make sure it was okay with you before I went into the store and interviewed."

"That was wise, *mija*," Papi said, which made me smile.

"But it might not work out," Mamá said. "Don't get your hopes up."

Ugh. Always so negative. "It might not," I agreed. "I've never had a job interview before. I might bomb it."

"It's easy," Claire said. "Just tell them what they want to hear."

"No," Mamá snapped. "You tell the truth. If you have the qualifications they are looking for and are the best one for the job, they will hire you. Lying is not the way."

Claire's eyes widened, like she was fighting the urge to roll them. She took a bite of her dinner and set about chewing thoroughly.

I moved ahead to seal the deal. "Cody said—if you're okay with it—I should drop by tomorrow after school."

Mamá exchanged a look with Papi.

"It's a good opportunity," he said. "Babysitting and feeding chickens are not like a real job. It's time you took on that kind of responsibility."

Mamá nodded. "I agree. Make sure you dress appropriately. No panda bear pants and T-shirts with silly sayings on them. Understand?"

"Yes, Mamá. I promise I'll wear something nice."

—⁓—

Wednesday night was the reboot of youth group after taking a break for the summer. Tessa had said she would start trying to bring Shay, though, so I volunteered in the nursery to help with the little ones whose parents were at the church for a Bible study. I doubted I would get away with this for too long, but for now, it was the perfect fix. I saw Tessa from afar, but no sign of Shay. She was probably late. Instead of feeling awkward sitting by myself or with Lauren, I got to feel joy playing with babies.

No better feeling than that, if you asked me.

The next day for school, I dressed for my interview in a white blouse, black jeans—because they were the closest thing I had to slacks, and I couldn't very well ride my bike in a skirt—and my fuzzy black cardigan. The moment Cody saw me walk into Algebra II, he grinned.

"Your parents said yes."

I propped a hand on one hip and struck a pose. "How did you guess?"

"Your outfit doesn't look like everyday-Izzy wear."

He was right about that. "Any tips for my interview?"

"Nah," he said. "Just be yourself. They already love you."

It tickled me to hear Cody say this. What made him say such a thing? Did the Bellangers mention me often to Cody?

I tried to concentrate on math, but I was too excited about my interview. Unfortunately, whenever I was excited, time seemed to crawl. So Algebra II felt like the longest hour of my life. When the bell rang and Cody and I headed out of our classroom, I almost ran straight into Amelia, Tessa, and Shay, who were waiting outside.

"There you are," Tessa said. "We have a proposition for you."

"Okay . . ." I said slowly.

"After school, my house," Tessa said. "You teach us to make *tres leches* cupcakes. If you text me the ingredients, my mom already said she would pick up anything we need. She was so excited when I told her our plan. She misses you."

Normally, this kind of proposition would have made me squeal. And while I did miss Tessa's mom, whom I'd taken a painting class from earlier this summer, I sensed a hidden ambush in this plan. Tessa thought if she could get me and Shay together, we would work everything out. She didn't realize how complicated the whole mess really was.

Thanks to Cody, I now had an out. "That sounds so fun," I said. "But I can't. I have my job interview after school today."

The girls' gazes took in my outfit.

"At Paprika's. Right," Amelia said. "Are you nervous?"

"A little," I said, which was true.

"And you made this happen?" Amelia asked Cody.

"The Bellangers need someone while I'm at cross-country practice," he said, "and I know how much Izzy loves the store."

Tessa's eyes flicked between us, and she smiled knowingly. "That was thoughtful."

"It really was," I said to Cody. "I'll see you girls in Creative Writing."

"What about tomorrow after school?" Amelia asked.

"I guess that depends on how my interview goes," I said, walking away with Cody toward our US History classroom.

"See you guys later," Tessa called.

"Bye," Shay added.

"Bye!" I used as friendly a tone as possible, but I didn't look back.

Amelia kept pace beside Cody and me. "Listen," she said, "if we can't all get together in the afternoons, how about a sleepover? Or we could get together on Saturday sometime?"

I frowned at her persistence. "Maybe, but I think Papi needs me to watch Sebastian on Saturday." It was a complete lie, but Amelia would never know that.

"Ugh, I so get that," she said. "It's nice that your parents give you some warning when they want you to babysit. My parents just spring it on me. All the time."

"That stinks," I said as we walked into history class.

"Later," Cody said, joining his friends on the far side of the classroom.

"I'm used to it," Amelia said as we made our way to the front. "But we have to get together soon. We all miss you."

"I'm sure we'll figure it out," I said. As soon as Shay got her life together.

Amelia started talking about a family she babysat for once a week, but all I could think about was how much I needed this job. The girls were not going to give up on their plan to trick me into fixing things with Shay. Having a ready excuse to say no to their schemes would be a huge relief.

—m—

When I walked inside Paprika's, the bell over the door tinkled. I loved the smell of this place—bamboo salad bowls, bulk spices, and a wide variety of scented candles. That, and all the colors of kitchen accessories, thrilled my senses. I looked for Mr. Bellanger. Movement by the glassware caught my eye, but that was just a customer. I made my way toward the register in the center of the store and waited about two minutes before Mr. Bellanger poked his head out from the office door in the back.

"Izzy!" He approached the counter, folded back a table leaf, and walked inside the little island-like space. He leaned onto one elbow, grinning at me. "I hear you'd like to work here a few hours a week."

"I would!" I said, beaming.

He chuckled. "Well, we'd love to have you."

"That's it?"

"That's it!" he said.

"If only all interviews were that easy," I said.

"Then you'd leave us! Let me show you around." The counter was still folded back, and he exited the register island and waved at me to follow.

"How is Mrs. Kirby doing?" I asked. "Have you heard from her?"

"She's been having a grand adventure," Mr. Bellanger said. "She called from a port in Tokyo. She and Corrine were just about to have lunch at a Japanese teahouse. I told her that her garden and pets were in excellent hands."

"They are," I said.

Mr. Bellanger showed me his office and the small room beside it, which served as the employee break room. A small rack on the wall held employee time cards.

"You'll start a new card each Monday," he said. "Write down the time you arrive and the time you leave. If you're working more than six hours, you need to sign out for a half-hour lunch. Otherwise, you get a fifteen-minute break every four hours. You don't sign out for breaks. You take those on the clock."

Mr. Bellanger showed me the stockroom. Boxes, crates, and shelves with merchandise filled the space. A garage door covered the back wall. "We always try to put out new merchandise right away," he said. "What you see on the shelves over there"—he pointed to a rack on the side wall—"are the customer holds."

"Got it," I said.

"Your job is primarily to work the counter and help customers," Mr. Bellanger continued. "You don't have to worry about receiving merchandise, since that usually happens before eleven o'clock each morning. If things are slow, come back here and open any stock that might be waiting." He gestured to the center of the space. "Sometimes we get an afternoon delivery, and if no one answers in back, they'll come around the front and ask at the counter. If someone does come with freight, the garage door button is here." He motioned to a button mounted on the wall just inside the door that led back inside.

He then took me to the register and showed me how to ring up merchandise. While we were working, the customer in glassware came to the counter with a pitcher she wanted to buy. Mr. Bellanger had me ring up the purchase under his guidance, and I did it! It was so fun. Then he showed me where the paper was, and I wrapped up the glass pitcher and placed it into a Paprika's shopping bag.

I had this down already.

"If you don't have plans for Labor Day, we're going to be open," Mr. Bellanger said. "I'd love to have you work from, say, eleven to seven? You'd get a full day's pay. If you can't, that's all right."

I was employed. At a cooking store. How amazing was that?

"I'll be here," I said, my eyes scanning the merchandise for my first employee-discount purchase.

—⟨⟩—

Later that night, Tessa texted on our old group chat—the one *with* Shay in it.

Tessa: Well, Izzy? How did the interview go?

Me: I got the job!

Tessa: Congratulations!

Amelia: Whoo hoo!

Shay: I knew U would! UR perfect for Paprika's!

Tessa: We'll just have to find another time to get together.

Amelia: What about Monday? It's a holiday.

Me: Mr. Bellanger asked me to work that day.

Tessa: ☹ Okay, we'll figure it out.

Tessa: Hey, I made us a Google Drive folder to upload any pictures of us so we could have access to them for the diorama project.

Amelia: Good idea!

Shay: THX!

I didn't like the sound of that.

Me: Pictures?

Tessa: I want to put a picture of us in my diorama. Shay's aunt took a great one at your birthday party, Iz. Shay said she would have her aunt upload it to the drive.

Shay: Yep. I'd be happy to.

Me: I don't want anyone uploading pictures of me to the internet.

Tessa: Google Drive isn't really the internet. It's a private folder.

Me: Don't upload pictures of me anywhere! I'm serious! Don't!

Amelia: Yikes! Calm down, Izzy.

Nobody ever calmed down because someone told them to.

Me: No one has my permission to upload my picture. Please tell me you understand what I'm saying.

Tessa: I think you're overreacting a bit. No one can get access but us.

Amelia: We can text them instead. Why not post them here in the group chat?

Me: Please don't text pictures of me either. If you want one in your diorama, print it out.

I didn't want pictures of me sent by any digital means. Period.

Shay: Izzy should get to decide what happens with pictures of her. I won't upload anything, Izzy.

Tessa: Fine.

Amelia: I wasn't going to put pictures in my diorama anyway. I'm coming at the project from a completely different angle. You're going to love it.

I was relieved to know that no one would be uploading pictures of me but annoyed that Shay had been the one to stand up for me. I supposed she felt she owed it to me. Did that mean we were even? In what? I honestly didn't know how to interact with Shay. All I knew was that I couldn't be around her without wanting to yell, and I didn't like yelling.

Best to keep my distance until I was able to be calm and cool, like the Black Panther.

Chapter

11

SATURDAY, I RODE MY BIKE TO NANA AND TATA'S HOUSE for my first Bible study with Nana's friends. I parked my bike in the backyard and entered through the kitchen door, where Nana greeted me with a hug. Her kitchen smelled of freshly baked cookies.

"*Hola, mi vida*," Nana said. "How was your day?"

"Good," I said. "I got a job at Paprika's."

"That's wonderful! Would you like something to drink? I have coffee and juice."

"Coffee, please," I said. "Where are the cookies? I can smell them."

"In the living room." Nana poured me a mug and pushed the sugar and cream my way. "You didn't bring your Bible."

"I have one on my phone," I said as I set about perfecting my brew. "It's kind of awkward to carry one on a bike."

"I suppose that will have to do. Come and meet the ladies." She led me into the living room, where three women had already made themselves comfortable.

"This is my granddaughter Isabella," Nana said. "Isabella, these are my dearest friends. This is Carmen." She pointed to the woman in Tata's recliner. She had a wide, dimpled smile and wavy black hair streaked with silver. "She has twelve grandchildren and makes the best fried ice cream."

"No-fry fried ice cream, actually," Carmen said. "All of the yum with none of the oily mess. It's lovely to meet you, Isabella."

"Please, call me Izzy," I said.

Nana gestured to the first of two women seated on the couch. She was as small as most sixth-grade girls, had deep wrinkles and a pixie haircut, and wore more rings than a jewelry store. "This is Elizaveta," Nana said. "She owns Bellegente, the salon on Cherry Street, just off Main."

"I know that place," I said. "My friend Tessa and her mom get their nails done there."

"You have gorgeous hair," Elizaveta said, admiring my wild curls.

"Thanks," I said, pleased a beautician thought my hair looked nice even when windblown.

"And this is Felisa," Nana said, gesturing to the woman sharing the couch with Elizaveta. She had a round face hugged by a bob of fine, copper-toned hair.

Felisa offered a shy smile in greeting.

I sat beside my nana on the love seat, and she asked for prayer requests. Carmen wanted prayer for her infant granddaughter Carrie, who had been sick with pneumonia, and for the baby's mother, Susan, who was exhausted.

"If she's not better by Sunday night," Carmen said, "I'm going over there to give her a break first thing Monday morning after Mateo leaves for work."

"Please keep Eliana in your prayers," Felisa said of her adult daughter. "Last night she went on her third date with Jacob."

"Is this the man she met online?" Nana asked.

"Yes," Felisa said. "He's an engineer."

"That's a good, stable job," Elizaveta said.

"Yes, but he's been divorced twice," Felisa said. "So I worry." To me, she added, "Eliana's first husband left when the kids were just babies. I don't want her to get hurt again."

I nodded, grieved to hear about a man leaving his family and about another who'd been twice divorced. "How old are her kids now?" I asked.

"Samuel is seven, and Hannah is nine," Felisa said. "I take care of them when their mamá is at work."

"Eliana is a nurse," Nana added.

"She has worked so hard to put her life back together," Felisa said. "I don't want anything to ruin that."

"We'll pray," Nana said. "God will take care of her. Elizaveta? Do you have any requests?"

"*Sí*, for Louisa," Elizaveta said. Then she explained to me, "Louisa is one of my hairdressers. She missed work twice this week, and when she did come in, she was a mess. Doug thinks she's on meth, but I can't imagine that's true."

"Doug would know," Carmen said.

Nana leaned close to me and said, "Elizaveta's husband is a pharmacist."

"If Doug had seen her and said so, I would believe him," Elizaveta said. "But he's just guessing based on what I've told him. I don't want to fire her—she's lovely—but something is definitely going on."

"God knows," Nana said. "We will pray. Isabella? Do you want to add a prayer request?"

So many, but few I would share in this crowd. "Just that I can keep up with school and my new job."

"Are you brave enough to pray out loud?" Nana asked. "We usually pray for the person on our right. So you would pray for Carmen's grandbaby."

"I'll pray," I said, looking to Carmen. "Her name was Carrie?"

"Good memory!" Carmen said.

We prayed, then Nana started the Bible study video. This study would last six weeks. There was homework to complete during the week to give us something to do each day, then when we got together on Saturdays, we would watch the video and discuss it and the homework.

I expected the first lesson to start with the story of David and Goliath, but it started before that, when Samuel anointed young David as king, chosen over all his brothers. In the very next verses, King Saul wanted someone who could play music for him when he was feeling tormented. Some of his servants recommended the son of Jesse of Bethlehem who could play the lyre and sing, and Saul sent for David. Then the Bible described David as a brave man and a warrior.

The speaker in the video found it significant that a man after God's own heart would be so multifaceted. David wasn't only a warrior who could kill the giant Goliath with a sling and a stone, as he would in the very next chapter. He was also a musician and a songwriter. David's character had a balance of hardness and softness. He was both courageous and sensitive. The speaker believed that people need both. To have too much of one and little or none of the other makes a person unbalanced.

It occurred to me that I was unbalanced at the moment. To cope with the aftereffects of Zac and the Dropbox scandal, I had focused on being strong. So much so that I had pushed aside my best trait: kindness. Before Zac, my whole world revolved around being cheerful and making people happy. Nowadays, I lived for self-protection alone. I didn't like the realization that I had lost part of myself, especially when I'd been so determined to find the real me. A turtle with its head in its shell would rarely succeed at making friends or loving others. I wanted to trust God to protect me so I could go back to my old ways of loving people.

That felt scary, but it also seemed right. I decided I would make cupcakes for someone this afternoon. Who might God put in my path today?

—⋙—

After Bible study, I headed over to Grounds and Rounds to meet Zoe. After seeing her with Cody the last two weeks, it was weird to see her sitting alone. Since I changed the time of our meeting to four because of Bible study, I had no way of knowing whether Cody had met with Zoe earlier in the day.

"Hey," I said, falling into the seat.

"No drink today?" she asked me.

"I had coffee at Nana's house."

"Did you enjoy the Bible study?"

"I did. I mean, it was a little awkward here and there. They do prayer requests at the beginning, and everyone takes turns praying for someone else. I had to pray for a lady I didn't really know, so that was weird."

"But you'll get to know her, won't you?"

"Sure! I already know she has four kids and twelve grandkids, one of whom is a one-year-old baby who has pneumonia. That's who I prayed for. Also, her husband is a school bus driver. There were three ladies there besides me and Nana. They're Nana's friends. Two of them are grandmas."

"What is the Bible study about?"

"David. Today's study was good, but I don't really like David. Grown-up David, anyway. He was all right before he started piling on the wives."

Zoe chuckled. "There's a lot to learn from David. He's a great model of redemption for us all."

"Yeah," I said, though I had no idea what she meant.

Zoe and I talked about my new job and how things were going at school. She urged me to find a time to talk with Shay.

"Shouldn't the person who started the fight apologize first?" I asked.

"That would be nice," Zoe said, "but it doesn't always happen that way. James 4:10 tells us to humble ourselves in the sight of the Lord and He will lift us up. No one is perfect. We all need forgiveness from God and from others, too. If you love Shay, you could be the one to reach out first."

I didn't bother to say that Shay had been sending me pictures and videos of her pets and had tried to talk to me a few times at school, or that I had perfected the art of ditching her. I also didn't tell Zoe that the girls were trying to get us all together so we could fix things between us. "I can't be around someone who I know is looking at porn," I said.

"Why not?" Zoe asked.

"In the Bible, Paul says not to associate with sinners."

"Yes, but I don't think this situation is quite what Paul meant. Do you think Shay would look at pornography with you around or try to get you to look at it with her?"

"No," I said.

"Do you have proof that Shay is still looking at porn? It could be that she's stopped."

I didn't like how Zoe was so good at poking holes in my logic, so I said nothing.

"You won't know if you don't talk to her," Zoe added.

"I'll pray about it," I said.

—⁓—

As I rode my bike home from Grounds and Rounds, I thought about Shay. Zoe wanted me to talk to her. Tessa and Amelia did too. I wanted Shay to apologize to me, but when she'd tried to talk to me at school, I avoided her. How could Shay apologize if I wouldn't let her?

Why wasn't I letting her talk to me?

Because I was angry. Because she had gone looking for the very thing that had hurt me and the other Dropbox girls. Sometimes I felt guilty about Shay's problem. If I had done a better job of explaining how I felt, Shay might never have looked for naked pictures online.

But then I would get mad at myself because this wasn't my fault. Shay had made her own choices. So had Zac. I had been a victim. Jenna, Fatima, Dee, Corinna, and Selena had been victims too. And there were so many more victims out there who'd gone through so much worse.

Porn normalized the objectification of women. It desensitized our culture to all kinds of immodesty and promoted promiscuity. Girls were kidnapped, trafficked, and forced to pose naked, forced to create videos, forced to become prostitutes, forced to have babies that were sold to unknowing, desperate would-be mothers. There was terrible darkness in the world. It was enough to swallow me in despair on behalf of those girls.

And Shay had gone looking for it. Was it my job to educate her about the harms of pornography? Could I speak about such things without getting angry or spiraling into shame? And if I managed to, would Shay even listen?

I didn't know.

The truth was, I didn't want to know. I was weary of all this. Every time it came up again, I felt anxious and angry, like I was in the middle of the Dropbox scandal all over again. Life was easier for me when I avoided the topic.

That's why I was avoiding Shay. Because it made life easier for me.

The realization felt awful, but it also felt justified. I was protecting myself. I had to. I was the only one who ever truly could.

At home, I pulled out ingredients to make a batch of chocolate cupcakes. God hadn't put anyone on my mind, though I hadn't really asked or tried to listen. My prayers lately were more like rants that went one way. I figured I should probably go feed Mrs. Kirby's animals. Maybe I would think of someone who needed cupcakes while I was over there.

I glanced out the window of the study, but I couldn't tell if Cody had been there or not. We only mowed our lawn once a month, so the super-short grass at Mrs. Kirby's place wasn't giving anything away.

I decided to go for it. As always, I started in Mrs. Kirby's house, feeding Oliver and Jack, her two Maine coon cats. Oliver was fluffy and gray and slightly smaller than his brother Jack, who was brown and orange and weighed twenty pounds. Once the cats were fed, I moved out to take care of the chickens. Harland almost got out, but I caught her halfway through the door and tucked her under my arm.

"Harland, this has got to stop," I said. "I know you like to run wild, but it is just not safe to do that in our neighborhood. What if Dan Nichols ran you over with his car? He always drives so fast! Or what if Mr. Nereuta's German shepherd tried to eat you? Mrs. Kirby would be heartbroken."

I lifted the chicken up toward my face and nuzzled my cheek against her silky feathers. "Let's make a pact. When I open the door to come in and get the eggs, you stay put. Is that clear?"

I stepped inside the coop and latched the door before setting down Harland. I gathered the eggs in a basket to take home. Part of the pay for taking care of the chickens was that we got to keep the eggs. With that done, I grabbed the chicken feed. I was dumping it into the trough when I heard the gate squeak. My arms prickled. I turned, and sure enough, here came Cody Nichols.

"Hey," he said, grinning while he carried an empty lawn mower bag toward me.

I frowned at the bag. "How long have you been here?" I asked.

"A half hour. I'm just about done."

Stars! I hoped he hadn't heard me talking to Harland. "I didn't hear the lawn mower."

"It stalled. I think it needs a new filter for the carburetor."

I could come up with no response to mechanical words, so I just stared.

"What time do you usually feed the animals?" he asked.

"I don't know," I said. "Whenever I remember to?"

He dropped the lawn mower bag beside the mower, which was sitting in plain sight between the back porch and the chicken coop. How had I missed that?

"Well, I've been trying to come over here when you do," Cody said, "but I haven't been able to figure out the right time. Now I know why."

Heat warmed my cheeks. I couldn't believe Cody wanted to spend more time with me. I felt like we were together practically all day at school.

"I feed them before school," I said, "and I've been coming in the afternoon right after school. But sometimes I have to watch Bash and can't get over here until later."

Sure, Izzy. Blame your family.

I suddenly realized Cody and I were staring at each other, so I finished filling the chicken trough, then put the feed bag away in the shed. When I came back out, Cody was on one knee, hooking the empty lawn mower bag back to the mower.

"Did you see Zoe today?" I asked, suddenly emboldened by his friendliness.

He looked up at me, his eyes wide. "Yeah, why?"

"Just wondering. I had to change the time I meet with her because I'm going to a Bible study at my Nana's house, so . . ." I trailed off, summoning the courage to ask what I'd been dying to know ever since I first saw him sitting with my youth leader. I walked to the house, turned on the hose, and pulled it off the wall mount, dragging it back toward the chicken coop. With my back to Cody, I went for it. "Why do you meet with her so much?"

Silence.

I should have expected that. I truly was the nosiest human alive. I poked the nozzle through the chain-link fence and squeezed the handle. Water shot into the tray, and one of the chickens came running.

"My parents wanted me to talk with somebody," Cody said. "Because of the Dropbox thing."

Shock nearly rendered me faint. I released the handle and spun around. "You paid to look at pictures?"

His eyes bulged as he furiously shook his head. "No!" he said. "No, no, no." He sighed and fell back onto the freshly mowed grass, wrapping his arms around his knees. He averted his gaze from mine, now intently studying a rogue dandelion that had somehow survived his daily shearing.

"You don't have to tell me," I said. "It was rude of me to ask."

"I don't mind," he said softly, but his tone sure sounded like he wasn't eager to spill the beans. "The thing is, lately I've been struggling with anger toward Dan for his part in the whole mess. What he did not only ruined our family's reputation, but people at school assume I was part of it too." He blinked, and when he opened his eyes again, he was looking at me. "And I wasn't. I promise."

The immense relief and surprise of his confession drew goose-bumps along my arms. I shivered, then said, "I'm still mad too—at how people think that picture of me was real."

"It's all so twisted," Cody said. "I just . . . Dan knew better. Dad taught us about this stuff."

"I feel that way about Shay," I said. "She knows better too. And even though she's not looking at pictures of people we know, it still feels like a betrayal to me."

Cody's pale eyebrows knit over his eyes. "Shay looks at porn?"

I winced. "Probably shouldn't have told you that. It just feels like she's no different from all those boys at school."

"It's a little different," Cody said. "I mean, she's not paying someone at school to look at pictures of her classmates, right?"

I scowled so hard my vision blurred. "No, but even pictures on the internet are of someone out there, someone alive in this world. A lot of times they're people who were trafficked or coerced by a loved one to do something they don't want to do."

Cody nodded, pensive as he picked the dandelion and twirled it. "My parents think Zoe can help me work through my anger at Dan, but it's hard to forgive him when he won't apologize and keeps digging in his heels about how he didn't do anything wrong."

This reminded me so much of waiting for an apology from Shay. I sank to my knees on the grass in front of Cody, still holding the hose in one hand. "I don't think God is going to forgive them until they admit what they did is wrong and try to make amends. Isn't that one of the twelve steps for healing addictions?"

Cody shrugged. "I don't know. It would be easier to forgive Dan if he weren't such a jerk all the time. He keeps wearing my socks but not putting them in the laundry after he wears them. I swear, every time I open my sock drawer, it's empty."

"Rude!" I said, trying not to smile as I pictured a barefoot Cody searching his house for socks. "Well, Shay hasn't said a thing to me about this. She keeps trying to talk about her pets, but I just can't pretend nothing is wrong. Until she is ready to apologize, I don't want to talk to her about anything."

We exchanged vulnerable smirks. How weird that Cody and I had this in common. It changed everything.

"It's nice to be able to talk to someone who understands all this," I said.

"It is," Cody said. "How about you and I work on Mrs. Kirby's chores at the same time each night so we can check in and see how we're both doing? You know, so if my brother steals my socks again, I can grouch about it to you."

"And I can tell you if Shay texts me adorable pictures of her cat."

Cody laughed so loudly, the chickens scrambled.

"I'm serious," I said. "She is crossing a line with those. Animals are adorable, and they should not be used for nefarious purposes."

Cody was gazing at me with the goofiest grin on his face. He kicked his shoe gently against mine. "So, what time do we work?"

No more avoiding Cody? Was that wise? I no longer cared. "After you're done with work at Paprika's?"

He thought for a moment. "Can you do seven thirty on weekdays and five o'clock on weekends?"

"Sure," I said, admiring the way his raised brow pinched three little wrinkles on his forehead.

Cody and I finished our chores. By the time I got back to the kitchen and saw the cupcake ingredients I'd left sitting out on the counter, I realized Cody was the only person on my mind. I wasn't sure I should make Cody cupcakes, though. He didn't need cheering up, and I felt like giving him cupcakes after the talk we had today might send the wrong signal. I decided to make a batch for my family. With Cody, I would tread carefully.

Chapter

12

SUNDAY MORNING AT CHURCH, my mood was more upbeat than it had been in a long time. Cody was quickly proving himself an exception to my assumption that all boys were going to rip out my heart and use it as a temporary rug.

I found Tessa in the teen section and sat down in the vacant seat beside her. "No Lauren today?"

"She went to Ohio for the weekend to visit family," Tessa said. "I need to talk to you about something."

"What's up?" I asked.

"Don't get mad. Please just listen first. Okay?"

Whenever people say *Don't get mad*, you know they're about to say something that will make staying calm extremely difficult. "Is this about Shay?" I asked.

"Yes, but not how you think."

Ugh. Be the Black Panther. Be the Black Panther. "Oh-kayyyy . . ."

"I've been inviting Shay to church for a while now," Tessa said.

"Yesterday, she asked me to stop inviting her. She said she'd like to come, but she knows you'll be here, and she doesn't want to make you uncomfortable."

This annoyed me on several levels. First, it annoyed me that Shay knew I was angry with her and didn't care enough to apologize or try to fix things. Second, it hurt my feelings that Tessa was putting this on me. I knew exactly what she was going to ask, and it wasn't fair. "So, you want me to say I don't mind if Shay comes to church," I said.

"Well, yes. I know you two are having trouble, but church is for everyone. Isn't her relationship with God more important than anything?"

"Apparently," I said.

"Izzy . . . don't be like that."

"I'm not trying to be mean," I said. "It just feels like lately everyone's feelings rank higher than mine. And since I'm bad at sticking up for myself, no one ever knows how upset I am about anything. Which I suppose is my fault, but our church is one place I know I belong. It's my safe place. But you're right. Church *is* for everyone. Especially someone who doesn't have a church family. Especially for someone addicted to porn."

"Izzy, we don't know that Shay is addicted."

"So, sure," I said, filled with way too much energy that was shooting out my mouth without a filter. "Invite Shay. I'll just start sitting with my family. It's fine. I'm already helping with the nursery on Wednesday nights." I stood up.

Tessa reached out and grabbed my hand. "Please don't go."

Tears had filled my eyes as I stood there, so hurt and angry and guilty. How could I behave like this when Shay needed a church home too?

"Why the tears?" Tessa asked.

I looked down at her, and the movement flushed the tears from my eyes. They fell in huge drops down my face. "I feel like I'm losing all my friends. I feel like you chose Shay over me. No one cares how I feel. No one cares that I'm still hurt."

"How, though? How did we hurt you?"

"None of you thought about me when we did Operation Encouragement for the girls."

"That's not true," Tessa said. "I asked you about it, and you said you were fine."

"You asked me if I was okay about the *Peter Pan* flyer, and I thought I had to be fine because my picture wasn't real. What right did I have to complain compared to the other girls? But I wasn't fine. I was hurt. Then we did Operation Encouragement, and no one wrote me any notes. No one prayed for me. And if I hadn't invited myself, none of you would have thought to include me in the talk with Zoe."

"I'm sorry," Tessa said. "I guess I just don't understand how you feel."

"Exactly. No one understands. And I'm tired of it."

"Help me understand."

"I'm a Dropbox girl, Tessa! It might not have been a real picture of me on Snapchat and the Dropbox server, but it feels like it was. When I walk through the halls at school, people stare. And boys still make rude comments about it."

"But it wasn't you."

"That doesn't matter. People think it was, and it humiliated me. It . . . Zoe says it might have left scars. PTSD, she suggested."

"Oh, Izzy. I'm so sorry. I had no idea."

My voice was getting squeaky, so I sat down beside Tessa, where I wouldn't make such a scene. "School is hard for me already because of all that," I said softly, "but now you and Amelia sit with Shay. So I don't have a place to eat where I'm not afraid. Cody has been very nice, but there are a lot of boys at his table. It's scary to sit there. I just know they're all thinking about the picture every time they see me."

"I'm sure that's not true."

I shrugged. "Who can know? But I have to sit with them because I can't sit with Shay." I sniffled and wiped a tear off my cheek. "Church isn't like that, though. I can sit with my family and be just fine. While it's not as fun as sitting with you, I know my family isn't thinking about the picture. So invite Shay to church, Tessa. Tell her not to worry. Tell her I said it's okay." I swallowed, then squawked out, "Okay?"

Tessa leaned over and hugged me the way I hugged people in happier times, nearly cracking a rib. "I love you, Izzy. You're amazing."

"I love you too," I said, knowing I had just given up the one time I got to see Tessa alone regularly each week. It hurt. It felt like I was losing her forever. Maybe I was. But it was the right thing to do. *Right, God? The Black Panther way?*

"Tessa, please don't tell the others what I said. Promise me?"

She pulled back from our hug. "I'm sure they'd want to know."

"It's my decision," I said, "and I just want it left alone."

On Labor Day, because of the holiday, Cody and I were both working from eleven to seven. Since we had the same shift, rather than ride my bike, I went with Cody in his car. I was used to riding with Claire in her little truck, so when I sank down into the passenger's seat of Cody's Acura, it felt way too low to the ground, like I was sitting on the road. A black tree-shaped air freshener hanging from the rearview mirror filled the car with a masculine, citrusy evergreen scent. The combination of that overpowering scent and the way the soft, charcoal-colored leather seats vibrated tickled my nose.

"It's so rumbly," I said.

Cody grinned my way and shifted into reverse. "That's how I like it."

"You're a car dork."

"And proud of it."

Now out on the street, Cody shifted into first gear, and we shot away. Before the stop sign at the end of our street, he shifted three more times and then slowed to a stop. Then he looked both ways and took off, shifting through the gears again.

I scratched my itching nose. "Is it hard to drive a stick shift?"

"Nope," he said. "Makes me feel like a race car driver."

I chuckled. "I have a feeling you'd be a good race car driver."

"I totally would. Chase Elliott's got nothing on me."

It took Cody only five minutes to drive us to the store, a trip that took me twenty minutes on my bike. We walked to the break room and put on our aprons. Mr. Bellanger found us there.

"Good morning, you two," he said. "Ready for a busy day?"

"We were born ready," Cody said.

"Cody's car has given him a confident new outlook on life," I said.

"Nothing wrong with that," Mr. Bellanger said. "It's been slow these past few weeks, so we could really use a big sales day to help us with next month's rent."

"You pay rent?" I asked.

"We certainly do."

"Do you mind telling me how much?" Cody asked. "I'd like to start a sporting goods store someday, so I'm curious how all this works."

"We pay thirty-six hundred a month to our landlord," Mr. Bellanger said.

"Ouch!" Cody said. "That's more than my parents pay for their monthly house mortgage."

"The downtown retail area is pretty expensive," Mr. Bellanger said.

"You know how much your parents' house payment costs?" I asked.

"I think it's close to a thousand dollars," Cody said. "They say it's not going to be paid off for another six years."

I just stared at him. I had no idea what my parents paid every month.

"Dad and I took a Dave Ramsey course," Cody said. "I learned a lot."

"Your dad is a wise man," Mr. Bellanger said. "Cody, why don't you prep the second register? I'll be out in just a minute. Izzy, come with me. I've got some boxes for you to unload." He started walking away before he finished his sentence. I grinned at Cody and chased after my boss. In the stockroom, he showed me several boxes of freight that held autumn-colored dinnerware.

"Over this next week, after you unload freight, I'd like you to start swapping out the front window displays," he said. "I doubt you'll have time today, but the rest of the week should be quiet. I thought you might enjoy working on the displays."

"I would love to!"

Mr. Bellanger showed me which items he wanted in the window display and said I was free to incorporate anything in the store that I felt matched. "The idea is to create a display that brings people inside to take a closer look."

"Gotcha," I said.

Mr. Bellanger left me to it. I had opened three boxes and just figured out where I was going to put the merchandise when Mr. Bellanger called me out to help at the counter. He had a meeting and needed me to work the second register.

From 11:16 until 11:53, Cody and I didn't stop for a moment. I don't know where the people came from, but the store was packed with customers. I wasn't as fast as Cody, and I had to ask him questions during almost every sale I rang up, but I hung in there and kept saying, "Next customer, please," every time I finished a sale.

There were still customers shopping in the store when our line vanished, but with no one to ring up, I looked at Cody and said, "Now what?"

He reached under the counter and took a drink from his water bottle. "Get a drink. Take a deep breath. The lull won't last."

He was right. I had just returned from the break room with a water bottle of my own when I found Cody ringing up a sale, with two more people standing in line. I lifted the counter leaf to let myself in, then waved the next customer over.

"I can help you right here," I said.

The day flew by, and before I knew it, Mr. Bellanger came out to replace me so I could take my lunch break. Mamá had packed me some leftover enchiladas, so I warmed them in the break room microwave and ate by myself. It felt kind of lonely, but after the steady stream of customers, it was also kind of nice to just sit, rest, and not have to think.

When I was done, Cody took his lunch break. I didn't think it was possible, but the afternoon was even busier than the morning had been. Several times we got so backed up that Mr. Bellanger came out and took over my register because I was too slow. At those times, he asked me to bag the purchases he and Cody rang up. Even with the three of us, it was still constantly busy.

Around six, things started to slow down. This gave Cody some time to reshelve the pile of returns, exchanges, and items customers had changed their minds about at the last minute. While he was out on the floor, Tessa's stepmom, Rebecca, came in with baby Logan in his stroller. I watched her push him around the store and wondered if she would recognize me. Logan eventually got fussy, and Rebecca parked the stroller by the door and carried Logan around on her hip.

She came to the register with a set of Pyrex food storage containers with colored lids. She set them down, then lifted her purse from the shoulder opposite the arm holding Logan and set it on the counter as well.

"Hello," I said, smiling at Logan. "Will this be all for you today?"

"Yes," Rebecca said, finally glancing up when Logan giggled at me. Her head tipped a bit to the side. "You're Tessa's friend."

"Yes, I'm Izzy," I said. "How is Logan today?"

"Good at the moment, though he's been a little grouchy. I think he has some teeth coming in, and that doesn't feel too good, does it?" She had started out talking to me but ended up talking to Logan in a silly baby voice.

"Oh man," I said to Logan. "You'll be glad when they come, though. Then you can eat apples and cheese and lots of yummy things."

Logan reached for me, so I gave him a high five.

"How much are these?" Rebecca asked, patting the Pyrex containers.

Right. I had a job to do, and it wasn't playing with the customer's baby. I rang up the purchase. "Twenty-four dollars and ninety-eight cents," I said.

"That's fine." Rebecca zipped open her purse and, with one hand, removed her wallet. She passed me a Visa card, and I finished the sale. "I'm going to put him in the stroller," she said, leaving her purse on the counter.

I bagged her containers. Once she had Logan buckled into the stroller, she pushed him over to the counter to collect her things.

"Have a nice day," I told them as she started for the door.

Rebecca smiled back at me. "You too."

Satisfied, I panned the store, looking to see how many customers were still in here. My gaze landed on Cody—leaning against the wall, arms crossed, and watching me with a smile on his face.

"What?" I said.

"Just admiring my coworker's people skills," he said.

Stars, I didn't need Cody admiring me, did I? I thought I should say something nice back, so I settled on "I learned from the best."

Chapter
13

"Who's ready to get down to business today?" Mr. Federici asked casually from the back of the room. I guessed it was time to start our big group project. He'd mentioned it a few times over the last couple of weeks.

The class quieted as we all turned and focused on him. He was sitting on the edge of his desk, one leg on the floor, the other bent over the edge, his foot swinging slowly.

"Today you're going to start your group project. You're going to create a business model. I want to know what you're going to sell, where you're going to get it or make it, who you're going to sell it to, and how you're going to sell it and deliver it. That's it. But I want a plan, and I want you to think of all the loose ends. When you're done, you're going to present to the class. If you think you're ready to present, come get me, and I'll take a look. If I think you're ready, you'll present. If not, you'll keep working. You can work in groups of two or three. No groups of four or more, or there won't be enough work for everyone to do. Capiche?"

"Capiche," we all said.

"All right then," he said. "Get to work."

Cody turned to me. "Want to be partners?"

Did I? "You have an idea for a business?"

"Not really. I'm a little intimidated to try pitching a sporting goods store to Federici. I think the town might have enough stores that sell sporting goods."

"What about a mobile cupcake store?" I asked.

"Mobile how?"

"I've been thinking about how much it costs Mr. Bellanger to rent the retail space for Paprika's each month, and it's scary. I doubt I'd ever be able to afford to start my own store at those prices. I'd have to save up for years, and I just don't think I could sell enough cupcakes to justify the monthly expense. But if I converted a motor home into a mobile kitchen, the overhead wouldn't be nearly as expensive. Plus, I wouldn't be chained to the store like the Bellangers, who can hardly take a day off for a holiday, let alone a family vacation. As long as I had a place to park the motor home, I could be open or closed whenever I wanted."

Cody's face lit up. "That's brilliant," he said, holding up his hand. "Cupcake store?"

I slapped him a high five. "Cupcake store."

He slid his desk beside mine, and I couldn't help but notice his fresh boy smell. What made him smell so nice? Shampoo? Soap? Cologne? Someone should start making candles of that scent.

We brainstormed a quick list of up-front costs and recurring monthly expenses. Cody opened his computer and looked up the prices of motor homes, and we quickly realized we didn't want to buy one of those. What we wanted to purchase was a food truck, and while they weren't as pricey as motor homes, they weren't cheap, either. We might as well be buying a condo.

"Maybe we should sell only at local events and fairs for the first few years to save some capital," I suggested.

"In reality, yes," Cody said. "But this is a project, so we can dream and pretend we already did that. Let's say we've spent the last five years selling cupcakes at local events and catering parties. We did it out of our house."

"Our house?"

He waved his hand no. "*Your* house. So our expenses were much lower, and we were able to save up to purchase a used food truck. The cheapest one I can find is around forty grand, but there are also food trailers, and they're half that."

"So we'd need a truck to pull it," I said.

Cody grinned. "Turns out we already have one."

"You already have what?" Mr. Federici said, stopping beside Cody's desk.

"A Ford F-150," Cody said. "It's what I drive in our hypothetical future business arrangement, so I can use it to transport our food trailer."

"Nice try, Mr. Nichols," Mr. Federici said. "In real life, yes, you can use your personal property in your business. For the purposes of this assignment, however, I want you to know your full costs, and I want your business plan to allow for every single one. What does a Ford F-150 cost?"

"Too much," Cody said, grimacing.

Mr. Federici laughed and tapped his finger on Cody's notebook. "Write it down, Mr. Nichols. Let's find out exactly what this dream business will cost the two of you."

As Mr. Federici wandered over to Ryan and Luke, Cody shot me a look. "A used truck and a used food trailer will cost us about as much as a used food truck. So we might as well just buy a used food truck."

"I don't think so," I said. "I think a food trailer is better."

"How come?" Cody asked.

"Well, if the engine in a food truck breaks down, we don't work," I said. "But if a truck's engine breaks down, we can borrow or rent a truck to complete any events we have on the calendar while we get the truck fixed. Also, if we were far from home, at the state fair or something, I like the idea of parking the food trailer at the venue and using the vehicle to drive around town or to and from the hotel, or to get more supplies if we need them."

"Yeah," Cody said. "Great points. Let's price out a food trailer and a good truck."

"Does it have to be a Ford whatever you said?"

"Nooo," Cody said slowly, "but I'd like it to be."

I chuckled. "I'm the baker," I said. "I know nothing about vehicles, so I bow to your expertise in the area of transportation."

We quickly realized that buying a truck and a food trailer would cost us more up-front money than renting a space like Paprika's for a full year. That made us pause and rethink my idea of a mobile cupcake store. We'd have remodeling expenses for either type of space too, but we both still liked how a mobile business wouldn't tie us to a strict retail schedule. It took us the rest of class, but we were able to make a quick five-year financial statement for a retail version of our business as well as a mobile one. We could pay off our debt and make a profit after only two years in the mobile store, whereas the retail location's expenses would continue annually.

That settled it. "Mobile cupcake store!" I said, putting up my hand.

Cody slapped me a high five. "Mobile cupcake store!"

I smiled at the idea of this being a real business that I owned. "Now we just have to decide what kinds of cupcakes to sell."

Cody and I talked about cupcakes all through lunch. We'd decided to play with my idea of naming cupcakes after musicals. So far we had a Dough-Re-Mi cookie dough cupcake in honor of *The Sound of Music*, a Flying Monkey Bread cupcake inspired by *Wicked*, a *Little Shop of Horrors* Feed Me Seymour zucchini cupcake with cream cheese icing, and a Legally Blondie cupcake that tasted like a blondie cookie.

We were still debating our menu when we walked into creative writing class.

"Ten recipes will be enough to start," I told him. "We don't want to have too many choices. Plus, once I see a master list of ingredients for all those recipes, I'll be able to brainstorm a few more. But no more than twelve."

"We should make an Elvis cupcake," Cody said.

"Elvis? Is there an Elvis musical?" I asked.

"Well, I guess he's just a musician. But I bet there's been a musical about him," Cody said. "He liked peanut butter and banana sandwiches. I think the cupcake should have chocolate frosting."

The boy made a good point. "That's a tasty combination," I said, writing it down the moment I found my seat.

"What are you guys talking about?" Tessa asked.

"Mobile cupcake store," I said.

"Mobile cupcake store!" Cody yelled, raising his hand.

I slapped him another high five. "It's our project for business class. We have to start a pretend company."

"And you chose a cupcake store," Shay said. "That's perfect!"

"A mobile one," Cody clarified. "A food trailer."

"You're okay with a cupcake store?" Tessa asked Cody.

"Why not?" he said. "I like cupcakes. Ooh! How about a Spamilton cupcake? Because of *Hamilton*."

I wrinkled my nose. "The cupcake is made of Spam?"

"Can you make that taste good?" Cody asked.

"I don't know if anything can make Spam taste good. I think we should stick with dessert cupcakes for a few years. For *Hamilton*, it might be better to do something like a Lafayette Gingerbread."

"You're going to make musical-themed cupcakes?" Amelia asked eagerly.

"Not actually bake them," I said. "Though that might be a good idea for our presentation."

"You could make me an Elvis cupcake," Cody said.

"Good afternoon, everyone," Mrs. Lopez said. "Please get into your small groups. Your assignment is on the whiteboard."

Cody and I shifted our desks as we did every time we had small group in creative writing class. After the first time we circled into groups, Mrs. Lopez had decreed we stay in those groups for the entirety of the project, which meant I was stuck in the same group as Shay. So far, Cody had been the perfect buffer, though.

Once my desk was in place, I read the assignment Mrs. Lopez had written on the whiteboard.

1. Based on what you've learned in previous discussions, write a short introduction paragraph about the person directly across the circle from you. (Every group should have even numbers. If there are any odd-numbered groups today, write about the person on your left.)

2. Take turns reading your paragraph aloud. Ask the person you wrote about if they feel you've written an accurate introduction. Ask your group for their feedback as well. If there is any criticism, note suggested changes, consider them, and revise your paragraph.

3. Turn in your written paragraph by the end of the day.

I examined the circle we were sitting in. Today, Shay sat across from me.

Oh, come on!

I wanted to ask Cody to switch seats, but that would be rude and not at all like the Black Panther. Maybe if Shay and I went last, we'd run out of time. I glanced at Tessa. She had already written four lines about Cody, who was busy scribbling words about Tessa. Even Shay was writing.

Sighing, I opened my notebook to a blank page and read the first item on the board again. An introduction paragraph. Here we go.

I remembered Shay saying she was loved, so I started with that, hoping it would soften anything angry that might spill onto my page.

When it came time to present, Tessa said, "Who wants to go first?"

"I will," Cody said. "*Tessa Hart is a girl with just that—a lot of heart. She is kind and smart. She's an award-winning swimmer, a good friend, and an excellent big sister. She even tries things she knows she'll hate and is a good sport about it. For example, last year she took a drama class even though she doesn't like being on a stage. She performed in two different plays and did a fantastic job. Tessa also has a deep faith in God, which guides everything she does and serves as a compass for her life when hard times come. She's the kind of person you want on your team: loyal, honest, and hardworking.*"

Tessa's mouth gaped. "Oh my goodness! That was so sweet. Thank you."

"You're a good creative writer," Shay said to Cody.

Cody shrugged as we stared at him. "It's all true, so it wasn't really that creative. Any feedback?"

We shook our heads.

"Okay then," Tessa said, "I might as well go next." She cleared her throat. "*An antelope can sustain its running speed far longer than a cheetah. They are lean and tall and fierce when defending their habitat and herd. That is how I picture Cody Nichols. He is always active—running, playing sports, working, volunteering at school. He is tireless and loyal and fierce when he needs to be. Most of all, he is dependable, which is a deeply admirable trait.*" Tessa folded her arms and leaned back in her seat. "That's all I wrote. Any comments?"

I watched Cody, amused by the funny expression on his face.

"I thought it was nice," Shay said. "Antelopes are all those things."

"I'm an antelope," Cody said, as if suddenly realizing this about himself after years of wondering.

I burst into laughter.

"I'd rather be a cheetah," he said.

Tessa lifted her hands and dropped them. "I watched a documentary about antelopes at my dad's house the other day," she said. "The comparison came into my head and just wouldn't leave."

"I'm cheetah food," Cody said, which made me laugh harder. Tessa and Shay joined in.

"Do you want me to rewrite it with you as a cheetah?" Tessa asked.

"If the same things are true of cheetahs, then yes," Cody said.

Tessa smiled and rolled her eyes. "Fine. I'll make the edit."

Cody beamed. "Thank you!" Then he leaned close to me and said, "I'm a cheetah."

I chuckled but quickly fell into an awkward silence as Shay and I regarded each other.

"You want to go next?" Shay asked.

"No, you go," I said.

"Okay." Shay flipped over a sheet of paper on her desk. "*Izzy Valadez is really nice. I like hanging out with her. She is usually all smiles and bounces around like a Pomeranian, full of energy and fun.*"

Okay, comparing me to a Pomeranian was the sweetest, and I fought the urge to smile.

Shay went on. "*She can bake sweets better than the ones they serve at Grounds and Rounds.*"

Cody gasped, glanced at me, and scribbled something onto his paper.

Shay looked at Cody, hesitated until he stopped writing, and then continued reading. *"She spends a lot of time with her family and likes to watch TV, musicals, and superhero shows. She sings, acts, takes great photographs, and is the most talented person I know. She also loves animals but can't have any because her brother is allergic. I used to joke that she probably wouldn't be friends with me if I didn't have a dog and a cat. She has always been a pretty forgiving person, and I hope that doesn't change."*

My head tingled as anger flushed up to my brain. Shay just *had* to use this assignment to sneak in something about our fight. "What you don't seem to get is that I would be happy to forgive you if you would just apologize."

Shay's eyes widened, and her cheeks flushed. "Apologize for what?"

"You know what."

"Hey." Tessa reached out and grabbed Shay's and my hands. "Let's not talk about this here, okay?"

I bit the inside of my cheek, frustrated and embarrassed to have said anything at all. Why couldn't I keep my big mouth shut? "I have a critique," I said, wanting to say that I didn't care that she owned a dog and a cat, that I still wasn't her friend. I wasn't brave enough to say that, though, especially in front of Cody, so I said, "I see myself as more of a pug than a Pomeranian."

"Sure, with your face all wrinkled up like that," Shay said.

My jaw dropped.

"Cody wrote something down!" Tessa yelled, again grabbing our hands and shaking them. "Did you have some feedback for Shay, Cody?" She gave him a desperate look, like she was trying to hint that he'd better do something to defuse the situation.

"No," he said. "But Shay did give me an idea for our Federici project. We could sell cupcakes to other businesses. Coffee shops like Grounds and Rounds."

"That *is* a good idea," I said, then added a stiff "Thanks, Shay."

"No problem," she said to her desk.

Tessa took a deep breath. "Izzy? It's your turn."

The group seemed nervous, probably wondering what jab at Shay I had hidden in my paragraph. The thing was, I hadn't written anything mean or a word that even alluded to our fight. I had tried to keep my paragraph as generic and truthful as possible.

"*Shay is loved*," I read. "*She works at Booked Up. She works at Second Chance Farm. She takes care of Stanley and Matilda. She*"— and here I changed the word *is* to—"*used to be steady and unchanging with her love of Earl Grey tea, her cowboy boots and Carhartt jacket, her ponytail, and her sack lunches filled with a peanut butter sandwich, an apple, and carrot sticks.*" At the end, I had written *Shay is loved* again as kind of a bookend, but since I was still annoyed and had no interest in doing the right thing, I said, "But these days she might be spending too much time online."

Tessa exhaled and rubbed her hands over her face. I avoided all eye contact and ripped the page from my notebook. Before anyone could say anything, I got up from my chair and turned in the page to Mrs. Lopez.

—⁓—

After school, I rode my bike to Paprika's. The tires crunched over yellowed leaves on the sidewalk. Fall had come early this year, and many of the leaves were falling before turning deep red, brown, or orange. Papi said it was because the trees hadn't gotten enough rain all summer, so they were too weak to hold on to their leaves. This made me think about how weak I was when it came to Shay. I felt guilty for losing my temper in front of Cody, who I knew would say nothing about it, and Tessa, who would likely confront me the first chance she got. More than anything, it annoyed me that Shay didn't see that she had any reason to apologize. It was just further proof that no one really understood what I'd been through. It made me feel very alone.

Being at the store helped because it took my mind off my problems. We were so busy that when Cody came in to relieve me after practice, Mr. Bellanger asked if I could work another hour. I texted Mamá, who said it was fine, then found myself back-to-back with Cody in the island, each manning our own register. His hair was damp from having showered after cross-country practice, which made his clean boy smell stronger than normal. I tried not to let it distract me while I helped the customers, but his presence made me feel like I was being watched. Or maybe it was just my body trying to alert me that a boy was standing right behind me.

I hadn't forgotten.

Cody had promised to work later than usual too, so I told him I wasn't going to wait for him to feed Mrs. Kirby's animals.

"Good call," he said. "Harland would bite you for sure if you made her wait that long."

I wasn't sure about that, but I wasn't going to risk finding out. At 7:55, Mrs. Bellanger came in and relieved me. Cody was in the middle of helping a customer, but he did yell out "Bye, Izzy!" as I made my way toward the back room.

"Bye," I said, reluctant to leave.

I rode my bike home, a journey that seemed even farther after such a long day, as Papi had predicted. I left my bike out front and ran next door to feed Mrs. Kirby's animals. The chickens were extra loud, letting me know they didn't like waiting so long for dinner.

"I'm sorry!" I said. "The store was busy tonight, and Mr. Bellanger needed me to stay until his wife could come in."

The chickens were too hungry to hold a grudge and instantly started devouring their feed. Hungry myself, I made quick work of my chores, then headed back to my own yard. I punched the code for the garage keyless lock to put away my bike, and there I found Papi, Leo, and Sebastian crowded around the open hood of the Mustang. This seemed strange to me, as Sebastian had a pretty strict self-imposed eight o'clock bedtime.

"Working late on the car?" I asked.

"*Sí*, Isabella Valadez," Sebastian said. "We have a new radiator."

"But isn't it time for you-know-who to go to bed?" I asked.

"The girls needed some privacy," Papi said.

"Mamá and Claire are fighting again," Leo said.

"It is very loud in the house," Sebastian said.

"He's right," Leo said. "You might want to hang out here with us for a while."

"No way," I said. "I'm too hungry." I opened the interior door as quietly as I could and crept toward the kitchen. Sure enough, the argument was in full swing.

"I've told you over and over, that's not how it works," Claire said.

"Then show me," Mamá said. "Look it up so I can see it."

"I'm not going to sit here looking up scholarships with you watching over my shoulder."

"Why not? You want me to stop asking about it. Show me so I can see the deadlines for myself."

At the counter, I set down my backpack. Mamá and Claire were in the living room. Claire stood on one side of the sofa, Mamá on the other. I opened the refrigerator as quietly as I could.

"Mamá, I love you," Claire said, now pacing in front of the mounted TV, "but this isn't about you. I'm asking you to trust me to apply for scholarships. It's only September. There is plenty of time, and a lot of them haven't even opened yet."

"You could be writing essays now," Mamá said.

"Not until I know the prompts."

"Did you at least get your applications done?"

I pulled out a pot of macaroni and cheese and set it on the counter. I added some to a bowl and put it in the microwave.

"Two of them, yes," Claire said. "I'm still waiting for the letter of recommendation from Mr. Lucas."

"Did you remind him you needed it?"

"*Sí*, Mamá. He will get it to me when he can."

"I'll give him a call tomorrow," Mamá said.

Claire glanced at me. I rolled my eyes about the same time the microwave beeped. This caught Mamá's attention.

"How was your day, Isabella?" Mamá asked.

"Good," I said. "It was nice to get a few more hours at work."

"You should be looking at colleges too, *mija*."

I still hadn't decided if I even wanted to go to college, which wasn't really a discussion in this house. Mamá wanted all her children to have a bachelor's degree. "We've started talking about it in homeroom," I told her, digging a spoon into my macaroni dinner.

"What have you been talking about?" Claire asked.

"Oh, just which schools we're interested in," I said. "What we'd like to study. Which AP classes will give us college credit."

As I answered, Claire crept slowly toward the stairs. Oh, no. She wasn't going to push Mamá off on me.

"You've done a great job of choosing AP classes," I said, putting the pot of cold macaroni back into the fridge. "How many college credits do you have already, Claire?"

My sister, who had both feet on the stairs, turned, one hand gripping the railing. "I don't know. Several."

"How many?" Mamá asked.

"Uh . . . it depends on the college," Claire said. "I have twelve from last year, and if I pass all the tests this year . . . Let me think."

As Claire tallied AP credits in her head, I grabbed my bowl of mac and slipped back into the garage to join the boys. It was much safer out there.

Chapter
14

SATURDAY AT NANA'S, I was sitting in the living room listening to Elizaveta share the latest drama with her unreliable employee when my phone sang, *"We love you, Miss Hannigan!"*

The ladies laughed—all but Nana, who said, "Put it on silent, please, Isabella."

I pulled out my phone, turned the sound off, and saw a text from Cody. Since Nana hadn't started the Bible study yet, I figured I had time to read it.

Cody: Have you been to Mrs. Kirby's house already?

I texted back: Yes.

Cody: :-/

Cody: Want to go on a run with me?

There had been an away cross-country meet today.

Me: Didn't you run all day?

Cody: Yes, which is why I need to run again later. Don't want to get stiff.

Me: Well, I don't run. Unless there's a fire. Or a puppy in the road.

Cody: A walk then. We could talk about the project. I have some ideas I want to run past you.

Me: Can't you run them past me Monday at school?

Cody: I suppose I cooouuuuulllddddddd . . .

Cody: But then I'd have to wait until then. And I really want to tell you about them.

Me: I'm not home right now. At Bible study.

Cody: I'm not home now either. Still at the meet. Can I come by later?

Erg. Did I want to see Cody? Yes. All the time. So was it wise to agree to see him outside school and at Paprika's and in Mrs. Kirby's yard? Probably not.

Me: Bible study starting. I'll check with parents and text you later. Bye!

My parents always told me to use them as an excuse if I ever needed one. I'd found them quite handy with Cody these past few weeks. Before Cody had a chance to respond, I put my phone away.

We began Bible study with prayer. Elizaveta was on my right. I prayed for her employee Raquel, who was often late and had some concerning relationship problems. I couldn't help but think I was wise to keep boys at a distance. Raquel was an adult, and look at the trouble she was having!

Today, our video teacher had us read 1 Samuel 17, which was the story of David and Goliath. She centered her points on the scene where King Saul dresses young David in his own armor. But David tells the king, "I cannot go in these because I am not used to them."

After the video, we discussed the topic as a group.

"I think many people do the opposite of what David did," Carmen said. "We surround ourselves with unnecessary things or habits that we think will protect us, but it's just an excuse not to trust God."

"My neighbor recently installed a new security system for her house that has video cameras," Elizaveta said, "so she can see who is outside."

"Oh, I like those," Felisa said. "I've been wanting one for a while."

"Well, now that my neighbor has them," Elizaveta said, "she just sits at her computer, watching the camera feeds. No one has rung the bell, but she's watching, just in case."

"What a waste of time," Felisa said. "I have too much to do."

"That's the point I was trying to make," Carmen said. "Sometimes we set out to do something good, but all the bells and whistles we add do us less good. David knew right away that Saul's armor, which might have protected his body, wasn't going to let God use him to his full abilities, so he took it off. To the king and the other warriors, he likely looked vulnerable and foolish, but David knew he had God on his side. He trusted God with his life."

It occurred to me that I was doing something similar with Cody to what Elizaveta's neighbor had done with her security system. I kept looking for ways to protect myself from Cody when God had clearly put him in my life this year. Were my attempts to put distance between us just me wearing armor too clunky to navigate? If I put down all that armor, would God keep me safe?

That was the wrong question. I knew God didn't promise that we wouldn't have trouble in our lives. And sometimes we chose trouble, like I did with Zac. I also knew God had promised not to leave us.

Although I had been easing up on my illogical boundaries, I was still punishing Cody for Zac's sins. And that wasn't fair. Even more than that, I'd been using my hurt and shame over what happened with Zac as an excuse not to trust God. Instead, I'd made up a list of rules to protect myself, rules I continually broke when I wanted to and invoked whenever I got scared again. *Cody must think I'm crazy to be so hot and cold.*

David was not afraid to fight Goliath, because he knew God was bigger than Goliath. He did not waver. He did not doubt. He was completely certain of his faith.

I needed to measure the size of my obstacles against the size of my God.

I didn't have to seek out girlfriend status with Cody, but I could allow myself to like him and spend time with him and see where it led. I could still have boundaries to make sure things stayed wholesome and safe, but I was done trying to fight my growing feelings for that boy. He was too amazing a person to brush aside.

The moment Bible study ended, I texted him back.

Me: Okay, I can walk tonight. What time will you be home?

He didn't answer right away, so I rode my bike to Grounds and Rounds for my meeting with Zoe. I told her about my revelation today in Bible study, and that I had agreed to go on a walk with Cody tonight.

"I'm proud of you," Zoe said. "This is a big step."

"I'm still worried it will somehow ruin everything."

"It's okay to be friends with Cody," Zoe said. "Just because you like him doesn't mean you have to date him."

"All I want is to be friends," I said, hoping that saying the words out loud to Zoe would help me convince myself that they were true.

"I think that's wise," Zoe said.

"What if he wants something different?"

"Don't worry about that right now," Zoe said. "Until he says or does something that makes it clear he wants something different, just enjoy his friendship. Don't sabotage your friendship by acting on your fear of things that might happen. Wait until they happen to worry. Because you know what? They might never happen—at least not the way you're imagining they might."

I left Grounds and Rounds with Zoe's outlook giving me courage for what lay ahead.

Before I got on my bike, I checked my phone. Cody had texted back.

Cody: Not sure. I'll text when I know.

Well, that was clear as mud. I rode my bike home, but I wasn't sure if I should wait for Cody before I started my chores at Mrs. Kirby's house. Mamá's car was in the garage, though, so I figured she was likely in the kitchen, making dinner. I didn't want to talk to her, so I headed over to Mrs. Kirby's and fed the animals. I was on my way back when Cody texted again.

Cody: Just got back to the school. See you in ten?

Ten minutes? Stars!

I ran the rest of the way to my house. I opened the front door quietly. Thankfully, I didn't see Mamá anywhere. I rushed up the stairs and started tearing through my drawers, looking for something cute to wear.

It wasn't until I'd pulled out most of my leggings that I stopped myself. Why should I care how I looked? I wasn't trying to impress Cody.

Still, I glanced in the mirror on the back of my door. My shirt had flour on it from making cookies for Bible study this morning, and bits of chicken feed and feathers peppered my leggings.

More people than Cody might see me walking out on the road. I should at least look presentable.

I dug out a fresh pair of leggings, changed my shirt, and put my hair in a ponytail—not that I would be running. I was waffling over adding some mascara when I heard the doorbell ring.

No mascara, then.

I ran down the stairs and found Mamá standing there with the door open, one hand on the knob. Cody stood on the front step, hands in his pockets and chatting freely about Riku, the foreign exchange student his family had hosted last year.

"Well, next time you talk to him, tell him we miss him," Mamá said. "Sebastian, especially."

"I will," Cody said. "I have his address, if you think Sebastian might like to write to him."

"That's very thoughtful," Mamá said. "I'll ask him and let you know." She turned to me, and her friendly demeanor faded. "Dinner is at six. Don't be late."

"I won't," I said, and slipped out of the house.

"Hey." Cody's smile lit up his face. Magic. What a smile like that could do, even to someone already as adorable as Cody Nichols. He was wearing a cobalt-blue long-sleeved Northside High Basketball T-shirt and jeans. I'd never seen anyone look more like a homegrown superhero boy than Cody.

Then he said, "Did you feed the cats and chickens already?" Which is what all superheroes talk about.

"Yeah," I said. "I hadn't heard from you, so I figured I'd get it out of the way."

"That was smart," he said. "Coach won't let us have our phones during the meet. We get them on the bus there and back and can check them on breaks."

When we reached the end of the driveway, Cody's arm brushed against mine and roused the Team Cody butterflies that had been dormant since my Zac phase. That pleasant sensation was followed by a pang of fear, but I reminded myself that Zoe had encouraged me to explore my friendship with this boy.

"How was your meet?" I asked.

"Good. We came in second. I ran my fastest ever at 16:48.74."

"Awesome!" I held out my fist, and he tapped his against mine. "Honestly, though, I know nothing about cross-country. How far do you run?"

"We run a 5K, which is a little over three miles."

Stars, that was far. "And I'm assuming sixteen-something is a really good time?"

"Eh . . ." He tipped his head from side to side. "It's a really good time for me, but I'm far from the best runner on A Team. Anything under twenty minutes is a respectable time. If you want to compete at state, you pretty much have to be sub-seventeen. Last year's state champion ran a 15:40. That's more than a minute faster than me."

Our arms brushed again. We were walking really close to each other.

"Well, your time sounds amazing," I said. "I doubt I could run it in thirty minutes."

"It takes a lot of training."

"And you do a lot of that."

"I've been running cross-country since junior high, but I'm an athlete. I'm happiest doing something active. Where are you happiest?"

I forced my thoughts away from the fact that our arms were constantly touching now. "Either in the kitchen or on a stage."

He nodded. "I can see that. You were a great Lost Boy."

I turned to grin up at him, and my arm felt chilled apart from his. "You saw *Peter Pan*?"

"I went with Alex."

"Tessa and I were both Lost Boys."

"Yeah, but I could tell you wanted to be there and she didn't."

"You're very perceptive." Tessa hated drama and had taken the part only because her grade was based on participation.

Cody and I continued walking, settling close to each other again. Was this friendship? It felt like more. It felt dangerous, but in a good way.

The same had been true of my feelings for Zac in the beginning. The mere thought of Zac brought a shiver of revulsion over me and caused me to step away from Cody. I reminded myself of the things Zoe had said. Right now, I was just friends with Cody. We still had two years of high school, and then who knew where we'd end up?

"Do you know what you want to do after high school?" I asked.

"I have an idea, but it keeps changing."

"Will you tell me?"

"I kind of already did. I've been thinking about starting a sporting goods store, but the things I've been learning at Paprika's and in Federici's class have really shaken up that plan. In a good way, though."

"You have a different plan now?"

"Not a plan, really, but ideas. Part of me thinks it would be wise to go to college and earn a business degree so I could get a better day job and save up money to invest in a business. Another part of me says college is a waste of time if I just want to run my own store. Mr. Bellanger didn't go to college. He just learned on the job. I'm already kind of doing that at his store. So that makes me think I'd be wasting money going to college—money I could use to invest in my own business, you know?"

"I don't think there's one right path," I said. "You could get to the same goal either way."

"Exactly. Which leaves me kind of stuck in a place of indecision, and I hate that. I like weighing my options and choosing the one that fits me best, but these both feel like good options."

"You don't have to decide right now," I said.

"No," he said. "But it bothers me not to know. I just keep, uh, praying about it." His cheeks flushed adorably.

"That's a good idea," I said.

Somehow the magnets in our arms had brought us back together, and for the briefest moment, the backs of his fingers brushed against mine.

The butterflies in my stomach flew like acrobats. "I like your shirt," I said.

"It's just our basketball shirt from last year."

"It's the color," I said. "I've noticed you wear a lot of that color."

"It's our school color."

I smiled, thinking I should tell him what the color always reminded me of, but I stopped myself, worried it would sound silly—or worse, like flirting.

"What?" he asked, grinning back at me.

Then the words were spilling out of my uncontrolled mouth. "You make me think of Captain America."

"Me? The Cap?"

"Sure," I said. "You're always wearing blue or red."

"Red is my favorite color," he said. "I like Captain America. Being compared to him is much better than being compared to an antelope."

We laughed, and when a car turned at the end of the road and headed toward us, Cody tucked his arm around my waist and drew me to the side of the road. He let go right after, but just that little bit of touch was like going over the crest of a roller coaster.

This was more than friendship. I didn't feel this way about Alex or Michael.

At the stop sign, we turned around to head back. Cody asked if I'd seen the newest Marvel movie, which started a discussion about the franchise that could have lasted us weeks if I had let it. However, when we were almost back to my house, it occurred to me that Cody hadn't told me what he had wanted to talk about. "So, what's this incredible idea for the Federici project?"

"Oh!" He clapped his hands. "I think we should market the mobile cupcake store to schools and churches for special events. We could either charge people directly or charge a flat fee for a certain number of cupcakes. Like if a church had a special event, they might say, 'We expect about two hundred attendees,' so we'd be sure to prepare two hundred cupcakes, or something like that."

"I like it!" I said. "How weird would it be if I actually started a cupcake food truck someday?"

"Not weird at all," Cody said. "I think you'd be great at it."

Not going to lie. I kind of liked the sound of Cody telling me I was great.

"I still think we need to add the idea I got from Shay," he said. "Imagine having a standing order from Grounds and Rounds every week for a dozen cupcakes."

"I would hope they'd order more than a dozen a week," I said.

"Three dozen?"

I nodded. "That sounds better."

He bumped his shoulder against mine. "I'm sorry that creative writing class got awkward on Friday."

"Yeah, I'll be glad when this whole 'Who Am I?' assignment is over. Then we can write about things that interest us."

"And Tessa can write about antelopes," Cody said.

I giggled.

He held out his hands to the side. "Seriously, when you look at me, do you see an antelope or a cheetah?"

"Definitely a cheetah."

"Thank you," he said, bumping his shoulder against mine again. "Captain America is a cheetah. The Silver Surfer is an antelope."

"I completely agree." We were now standing awkwardly in my driveway. I checked my phone. It was 5:54. "I have to go in for dinner," I said.

"Hug?" he asked, holding out one arm.

"Hug," I said.

He moved in close, his arms sliding snugly around my waist. My arms went around his waist as well, and I buried my face in his shoulder. He felt firm, as opposed to the softness of Papi and Mamá, but not as skinny as Sebastian. He squeezed gently, just long enough that I could hear his breathing and inhale his fresh Cody smell. I squeezed back.

Some people are natural huggers, like they're not afraid to let people close and risk being vulnerable. Hugs from people like this are like being wrapped in pure love and acceptance. These were the kinds of hugs I always tried to give, but it was rare to be on the receiving end of one.

Cody let go, and a tender expression crossed his face. It was a look I'd never seen him wear. A little lost, a little longing, and a little cautious, too.

Then he reached out and gently patted my arm. "See you tomorrow."

"Bye," I said, watching him go.

He looked back three times before I lost sight of him.

As I went inside to dinner, I knew something had changed. And on the very day Zoe had encouraged us toward friendship. I didn't know what friendship with Cody should look like, but I certainly wasn't going to hide from it anymore.

Chapter

15

SUNDAY MORNING AT CHURCH, I spotted Shay sitting with Tessa in the teen section, so I sat with my family.

"What are you doing?" Claire said. "You never sit with us."

And Claire never sat in the teen section, claiming no one paid attention over there. "So?"

"*¡Apúrate!*" Mamá said, shooing me away. "Church is about to start."

"I'm sitting here today," I said.

"With us?" Papi said, incredulous.

"You don't want me to?" I asked.

Papi wrapped his arm around my shoulder. "We always want you, *mija*. Is something wrong with your friends?"

I shrugged. "I'm sure we'll work it out soon."

Papi squeezed me against his side. "Pray about it," he said. "I'll pray too."

"*Gracias*, Papi."

Today, Pastor Brad preached a message about brokenness. He spoke about how, a long time ago, broken people weren't allowed into the Jewish synagogues. Yet Jesus not only healed the broken, He came to die for them too.

"We are all broken," Pastor Brad said. "Yet Christ's body was broken for us so we could be forgiven of our brokenness, our sin."

As he led us into prayer, I thought about what Papi had said—that I should pray about what was wrong between Shay and me. I had been venting to God about it for a long time, but today I decided to give the whole problem over to God. Only He could mend what was broken.

Jesus, please help Shay get free from porn. And please help me to know how to talk to her again. It would be great if she would apologize to me. But if she never will, please give me the wisdom to know what to say and the strength to say it, because I don't know what to say, and whenever I'm around her, I'm just so angry I can't think straight. I know You can fix this, but I also know You need us to be willing. I'm willing. I want to be, anyway. Please help me know the good I need to do, and help me do it. Amen.

After church, I texted Cody to tell him what time I'd be at Mrs. Kirby's house. When I got there, he had already arrived. The trees in Mrs. Kirby's backyard had dumped their leaves early too, covering the backyard with crispy yellow foliage. Cody had raked a huge portion of them into a pile.

"Hey," he said, smiling when I walked through the side gate. "How was church?"

"Good," I said, making my way toward him. "How about yours?" Cody went to a different church than my family.

"Inspiring," he said, leaning on the end of his rake. "Pastor

Tom has been doing a series about how to live in God's will rather than our own so He can work in us and through us."

"That does sound inspiring," I said, stopping just in front of his pile of leaves.

"What did your pastor talk about?" he asked.

"Today he was talking about how we're all broken. He started by talking about physically broken people, but eventually he talked about how we're all sinners."

"And need Jesus," Cody said.

I smiled. "Pretty much."

"That's cool."

"Yeah, it was." It was also cool that I was talking to a boy about God. I had thought Zac was a Christian because he'd gone to church a few times with his dad, but Zac and I had never talked about God or sermons or Jesus. I liked that I could talk to Cody about these things. It seemed an important, even vital, part of a friendship.

I toed the leaves in Cody's pile. "Bet raking leaves wasn't something you thought you'd be doing in September."

"Yeah, not this early. It's weird." He flicked the bottom of his rake forward, sending a flurry of leaves against my legs.

"Hey now," I said. "You'd better watch it."

"Or what?" he asked.

"Or this." I kicked my shoe through his pile, thinking I would send a gust of leaves all over him. A single leaf fluttered up out of the pile, then drifted right back to the same place it had been before my attack.

"Wow," Cody said, smirking at the leaf. "That was terrifying."

I crouched and used both hands to scoop leaves over him.

"Whoa!" he said, ducking out of the way. "Careful! You're going to make a mess." Yet he shoveled another rakeful of leaves my way. This time the leaves reached my head, and I turned away to avoid getting any in my face. As soon as they fell, I went after him, shoveling up handfuls of leaves and throwing them like snowballs. They didn't fly like snowballs, of course. They had no momentum at all. This meant I needed to get closer to my target.

Cody laughed as I chased him around the yard, trying to drop leaves on his head. I managed to stick a fistful down the back of his shirt, but that only made him come after me—and his hands were bigger. Soon we both had our hair, hoods, and necklines stuffed with scratchy leaves. We were laughing so hard that I could barely breathe. We finally collapsed on our backs in what was left of Cody's original leaf pile.

Cody pulled his phone out from his back pocket and held it up, flipping the camera to take a selfie of us.

I rolled aside. "What are you doing?"

"Taking a picture?"

I propped myself up on one elbow and shook my head. "No pictures."

His brow quirked. "Why not?"

"I don't want anyone taking pictures of me."

He put his phone away and pushed himself to sitting, propping his elbows on his knees. "Okay."

I could tell my answer confused him. "It's just . . . after the whole Dropbox thing, I don't do pictures or social media or anything like that. I just don't trust it."

"Oh."

I could almost see his thoughts whirring. I waited for him to say he understood, but it was taking him longer to get there than it should.

"Look," he said, swallowing in a way that made him look guilty. "I promise not to take any pictures of you . . . from today on." He fell silent. Too silent.

"What's wrong?" I asked.

He winced. "When was the last time you went on Instagram?"

"I don't know. A few weeks?"

"Ah. That explains the lack of engagement." He rubbed the back of his neck. "Look, I posted some pictures of you on my Instagram. Two, actually. I tagged you. But you didn't see them, apparently."

I paled, my eyes losing focus as I considered this confession.

"No, no," he said, hands raised in defense. "It's nothing bad. Look." He pulled out his phone. "I'll show you." A few swipes, and he handed me the phone, open to his Instagram page. "See?"

I sat up and inspected his Instagram account. The first was a picture of my profile as I held Harland, looking into the chicken coop. It was the day I had lectured the pesky chicken to stay put. Cody must have heard me. Stars! How embarrassing. Yet he had somehow made the picture look artistic. The caption talked about how he and I were doing chores for a neighbor and how nice it was to have company when you worked.

It was actually really sweet. Had I seen this post a year ago, I would have swooned and shared it with all my friends and told my stuffed animals all about the cute boy who had taken a picture of me and written nice things.

The second was a picture of me behind the counter at Paprika's, beaming at a customer holding a baby. You could only see the customer's back, but I recognized Rebecca and the top of baby Logan's head. I looked pretty. Cody had caught me with the biggest smile on my face. Babies had a way of making me deliriously joyful. The caption read *A happy heart makes the face cheerful.* —*Proverbs 15:13*.

Cody had taken these two pictures of me without my knowledge. How many more had he taken? I couldn't decide if I was touched or terrified. The mixed signals my body threw off weren't helping. Why my hormones couldn't listen to reason, I would never understand.

Clearly this boy liked me—I couldn't comprehend why—but

I liked him too. I had always liked him. The question was, what to do about it?

"I'm really sorry, Isabella," Cody said, melting the frigid parts of me by saying my full name. "Do you want me to delete the posts? I'll do it right now."

I reached over and gripped his wrist, which sent tingles all up my arm. "No," I said, fear and joy warring within me. "It's okay. Just don't post more. Okay?"

He nodded, and his gaze dropped to my hand, his dark lashes casting shadows on his peachy cheeks. Then he looked up, pulled a leaf from my hair, and smiled. When he looked into my eyes again, my stomach twisted a thrilling warning. If I stayed here, I just might get kissed. Last year I would have wanted nothing more in the world. Not so today. I dropped my hand and stood up, running my fingers through my hair to dislodge any other rogue leaves.

Yesterday I thought I was ready for whatever my friendship with Cody might morph into, but now that the potential was here for the taking, I was no longer sure of anything.

—⁓—

Monday morning, Amelia was waiting for me when Cody and I got to US History. Cody sat with Jeremy and Alex, and Amelia followed me to our usual seats in the front of the room.

"I've been wanting to talk to you," she said. "I'm frustrated that the four of us never hang out anymore. When was the last time we all got together?"

Like I could forget. "The trail ride," I said.

"That was well over a month ago. You need to get over this. Don't you know that if you don't forgive Shay, God won't forgive you?"

My eyes smarted at Amelia's sudden attack. "What did *I* do?"

"You're withholding forgiveness. That's a sin."

"Good morning," Mr. Lucas said. He walked to the front of the classroom, looking trendy in his sporty Northside Robotics jacket and slacks. "Today we are going to continue our examination of the American dream versus the American reality. What does it mean to be an American?"

Around me, hands shot into the air. I still felt wounded from Amelia's judgy words.

"Jeremy?" Mr. Lucas said.

"Yeah, I think that being an American is about being proud of my country and defending our rights to freedom."

"Ellie, will you write responses on the whiteboard, please?" Mr. Lucas said. "Just one-word summaries will do."

As Ellie got up and wrote *freedom* and *proud* on the board, Amelia passed me a note. I opened it and read her sloppy handwriting: *So? Are you going to forgive Shay?*

I set my jaw, annoyed. I scribbled my answer beneath her question: *I'm more than happy to forgive her, but she never asked.*

"Yes, Cody," Mr. Lucas said.

"To me," Cody said, "being an American means having the freedom to choose my education, worship God the way I want to worship, read the books I want to read, watch media I want to watch, travel freely without restrictions, choose a career that interests me, vote in elections when I'm old enough, run for office if I want to, have my own bank account and save money, own a home someday, and have the right to privacy in that home. All of that without influence from the government or military or cancel culture."

A few people clapped. On the board, under *freedom*, Ellie added a list of the topics Cody had mentioned. She also wrote *independence* and *democracy*. I beamed at that adorable boy. What a smarty-pants. He could run for office. *Cody for President!*

"Hey," Jeremy said. "That's basically what I said."

"Yeah, but I said it better," Cody replied.

As the class chuckled, Amelia passed the note back to me.
She shouldn't have to. You're her friend.

I wrote: *And she was my friend. Why do I have to make the first move? She was the one looking at porn. Not me.*

"Melissa, go ahead," Mr. Lucas said.

"I think being an American is caring about the good of our country and our citizens. Caring about our core values of life, liberty, and the pursuit of happiness. But it doesn't mean I agree with everything the government does, because sometimes the government does crazy things."

Amelia's note came back: *You're being extremely judgmental. We all sin, you know.*

Oh, I knew all about that. I thought about writing the word *Pharisee* on the paper but managed to refrain. When I didn't write back, Amelia gestured for me to pass her the note. I did. She scribbled something down and handed it back.

Just do it, Izzy. It would fix everything.

"Izzy and Amelia, put the note away," Mr. Lucas said.

I shoved it into my binder, cheeks flaming as I imagined all the scenes I'd watched on TV or in movies where the teacher read the note aloud to the class. I didn't think Mr. Lucas would do that, but I wasn't about to take the risk.

After class, though, Amelia picked up right where she'd left off.

"Well?" she said. "Are you going to forgive her so we can all get back to normal?"

Cody was waiting for me outside, but I waved him ahead and drew Amelia over to an alcove where I hoped we wouldn't be overheard. Frustrated to have been bullied into this conversation, I tried to keep my voice just above a whisper, but I could hear the anger adding an edge to my tone. "You have no idea what you're talking about. You have no idea what I've been through. You guys all banded together to help the other Dropbox girls and completely ignored me."

"What?" Amelia said, her green eyes wide.

"You think life is easy for me? Every time someone looks at me, I just know they're picturing me without clothes. While I've been practicing having more faith in people—trying to convince myself that maybe they aren't thinking about that at all—some guy will say something nasty that proves me wrong."

"Is that why you don't want anyone taking pictures of you?" Amelia asked.

"Duh," I said. "Was that really a mystery?"

"A little. I thought it was just because you were mad at Shay. Why didn't you say something?"

"Honestly? I didn't think there was room in our friendship for that kind of honesty. You all expect me to be over this by now. You expect me to always be smiling and delivering cupcakes and hugs. You expect me to forgive Shay, even though she's part of the problem. No one wants to see Izzy breaking down."

"We all have hard times," Amelia said, "but we have to do the right thing. Shay needs—"

"Shay needs help," I snapped. "The Bible says we shouldn't associate with people who call themselves believers yet sin in such ways. I read it in 1 Corinthians. I wrote it right here." I pulled up my notebook and showed her. "So until Shay gets help, I can't be her friend. And I'm certainly not going to be the one who goes out of my way to make her feel better for contributing to the very thing that ruined my life."

I stormed off and headed to Chemistry, but I knew Amelia, my lab partner, would be right behind me.

I managed to make it through Chemistry with no more heated talk with Amelia, which freed me to run off to business class with my safe partner Cody, who understood what it meant to have people and their porn addictions mess you over.

By the time I fell into my seat next to Cody and listened to him prattle on about his idea for Officer Krupcakes from *West*

Side Story, I just felt weary. Why couldn't I get past this thing with Shay? Would it truly haunt me forever?

"I love Officer Krupcakes," I said. "What should they taste like?"

"He's a cop," Cody said. "So I'm thinking coffee-flavored cupcakes with some vanilla frosting on top, then one of those mini crumble donuts stuck on top."

My problems with Shay faded in a heartbeat. "Yasss," I said. "That's so fun!"

"Today your business must have a name," Mr. Federici said. He was sitting at his desk with a vacant expression in his eyes, looking like he had better things to do than teach us about business. "I'll be coming around shortly to make sure you have created a name."

Ack. That's something Cody and I had been putting off.

"Any ideas?" he asked me.

"Something to do with sugar," I said.

"The Sweet Spot," Cody said. "The Sweet Life. The Sweet Tooth."

"Wow. You're good at this." Maybe naming our business wouldn't be as hard as I thought. "Ooh! What about Sugar Rush, since we'd rush to the scene of anyone needing cupcakes?"

He grinned. "I like that one. It's going at the top of the list." He put it in all caps at the top of a clean sheet of notebook paper. "What about something to do with baking, like Bake It Easy or Bake My Day?"

"Bake Me Happy?"

"Yeah!" Cody wrote them down.

"Maybe it should say cupcakes in the title somewhere," I said. "Like Cupcakes on the Go or Cupcakes to Go or Cupcake Road."

Cody wrote them down, then said, "Cupcakes on Wheels. The Cupcake Tour."

"Cupcake Caboose," I added.

"That could be fun. Design the food trailer to look like a train caboose?"

"Maybe," I said. "What about Cupcake Cart?"

"The Cupcake Wagon."

An idea popped into my head, and I couldn't help grinning as I suggested it. "Cupcake Cubby."

"No. Veto," Cody said, pouting. "No former nicknames in the title."

"Cubby Cakes?" I said.

That one got a tiny grin. "Okay, that one's cute, but still no."

"Aww," I said. "What about something for people who love cupcakes, like Cupcake Love?"

"Love on Wheels," he said. "Oh!" He grinned, nodding. "Love at First Bite."

"I like that one," I said. "Circle it."

Cody wrote it down and circled it. "How about a name that speaks to our level of service? Cupcake Pros."

"That's fun. Or Cupcake Masters."

"Master," Cody said. "There's no plural here. You're the master baker. The Cupcake Whisperer. The Cupcake Queen. Hey, those aren't bad." He added them to the list.

I wrinkled my nose. "I'd rather it be about the cupcakes than me."

"What about drawing on your heritage? Any Spanish words or phrases that might be fun? Cupcake Amigos?"

I chuckled. "There's not really a perfect translation for *cupcake*. They're kind of an American thing. For the Crazy Cupcake, maybe El Pastelito Loco or El Quequito Loco. I remember a restaurant in Mexico called Boca Loca, which means Crazy Mouth. Uh . . . Maybe Ay Ay! Cupcakes."

"What does *ay* mean?" Cody asked.

"A lot of things. It can mean 'Oh!' or 'Ouch!' or 'Oh dear!' or 'OMG!'"

"Those aren't my favorite," Cody said. "How do you say Isabella's Cupcakes in Spanish?"

"Pastelitos de Isabella, I guess." I studied Cody's list, trying to think of something that might be fun in Spanish. "El Sabor Dulce would mean The Sweet Taste. Camino de Pastelito for Cupcake Road. Camino de Dulzura for Road of Sweetness."

"I think we have some good ones here," Cody said. "I still like Love at First Bite the best, though I'm not sure people would know it was a cupcake store just from the name."

"You could say the same thing about McDonald's."

"Maybe not the *same* thing," Cody said. "McDonald's does have eighty years of advertising and word-of-mouth recognition behind it. But if we had excellent customer service and a delicious product, I bet we could build a name for ourselves in, say, half that."

"Ha ha. So what you're saying is, if we choose a nonobvious cupcake name, we're going to have to talk about that in our presentation."

"I think so. Otherwise Mr. Federici will ask us if we thought about it."

"Okay, let's go with Love at First Bite," I said, liking our business more and more every day.

In creative writing class, the first people who had completed their dioramas were presenting. Lauren had made a box almost exactly like Mrs. Lopez's example. She talked about basketball and being the middle of five sisters. A guy named Rick made a poster with pictures of himself on motorcycles and ATVs, and even driving a race car. He wanted to be a NASCAR driver, and apparently his uncle drove a race car at a local course already, so he felt like he was on the right track.

I groaned inside when Mrs. Lopez called Amelia to present.

After our little talk, I so didn't want to hear what she had to say about discovering herself. She had made a collage on a poster board. The background had nine of her school pictures over the years in big squares, like the start of *The Brady Bunch*, though the picture for this year was a black-and-white headshot. In between all the pictures, she had glued dozens of smaller images from different points in her life, mostly her singing onstage at church. Some were pictures from One Acts or school plays or her summer camp job. There was a photo of the four of us in the One Act we did last fall.

"I am a thespian," Amelia said. "In part, the stage defines me, yet as I play each role or complete each job, I become my character or role. Therefore, I am versatile. That's why I didn't put a stiff backing on my poster. I wanted it to be able to bend."

She wiggled the poster to show us that it was flexible.

"A versatile actor is defined differently by each role they play. But an actor alone does not make a successful performance. Not even when it's a one-man show. The best plays and musicals are made up of a company of production staff, cast, and crew. Each member is essential to the success of the show. I have served as a stage manager as well as acted. That is why I didn't define myself as only an actor. I have been on both sides of the stage. I'm versatile in that, too."

I was both proud of Amelia's presentation and exasperated by it. She had made a beautiful collage, and her speech about theater was inspiring. While she did have a picture of her family on the board, which she referred to only by saying that a thespian needed a strong support system, she didn't define herself by anything but theater. What about the words *friend* or *sibling* or *Christian*? She was those things as well. It was weird that she neglected them.

Though I couldn't talk. I hadn't even started my diorama yet, and I didn't have much more time to procrastinate.

—∞—

Tonight, my Bible study homework was on 1 Samuel 20, which talked about the friendship between David and Jonathan. I admired how they were able to be honest with one another and still be friends. I wished I could do that. I had tried to be honest today with Amelia, but it had been more of a freak-out confession. And I hadn't even bothered to try with Shay. I didn't know how. It all felt too personal, and I didn't think Shay would understand.

Still, I was moved by this section of Scripture and by the corresponding verses they had us read in Ecclesiastes 4. The passage read, "Two are better than one, because they have a good return for their labor: If either of them falls down, one can help the other up. But pity anyone who falls and has no one to help them up." On the surface, one would think Shay was the one with the problem. She had fallen into sin. What a sad pity. Yet Shay had Tessa and Amelia to help her up. I had no one.

To be fair, that was my fault. I hadn't been honest with my friends about how much I was struggling, so how could they know I needed help? Jonathan and David had been honest with each other, and that was what made their friendship work.

Sure, Shay had kept secrets from us about what she'd been reading and looking at online, but if Amelia's reaction to my confession was proof, I had kept secrets as well.

Chapter
16

THE VERY NEXT DAY, Shay gave her creative writing presentation. She had made her diorama in a shoebox. Covering the back of her box were pictures of a grassy field. In front of that, she had pasted six images onto bent pipe cleaners that made them stand up like traffic signs.

"The pictures in this box define who I am," she said, wringing her hands together. "This first one is of my parents. They both died, but I'm part of them, and I really admire who they were. Um, next are my grandparents. I lived with them for a while. This is my aunt Laura, who I live with now. She owns Booked Up, which is a bookstore downtown."

A girl named Maggie gasped. "Oh, I love that place!"

Shay smiled, but it quickly faded as she got back to her project. "Next, I have a picture of a horse. This isn't a horse I know, but it symbolizes my love of horses and what I want to do with my life."

"Which is?" Mrs. Lopez asked.

Shay scratched her ear. "Uh, be a professional horse trainer," she said.

Mrs. Lopez smiled and nodded. "Wonderful, go ahead and continue."

"Okay, so next is a picture of my pets. This is, uh, Stanley and Matilda. Stanley is a greyhound."

As Shay went on about the accident that nearly took Stanley's leg, my gaze locked on the last picture in Shay's box. It was the very same picture Amelia had on her poster—the one of us from the fall One Act play. Only Shay had cut me out of it. There were only three people in her picture.

I can't explain why I suddenly cared, but seeing me literally cut off from my squad hurt. My eyes flooded with tears. I tried to choke back the actual crying, but I was failing miserably.

"And these are my friends," Shay said. "We had to be in a play, which is not something I ever want to do again. But I chose this picture because they make me brave. That's all."

She glanced at Tessa, smiled, and grinned bigger at Amelia, who was clapping silently. Then her gaze panned over to me, and her smile vanished.

I dropped my head, looking at my desk. Two huge teardrops fell onto my open notebook, blurring the blue lines on my notebook paper.

"Thank you, Shay," Mrs. Lopez said.

Three more students presented, but I barely paid attention. From the fuzzy edge of my vision, I could see Shay shooting me furtive glances. I pretended she wasn't there. If she could cut me out of her life, I could do the same.

When the bell finally rang, I jumped up from my desk, ready to flee to the restroom. Obstacle Number One: Cody Nichols standing in my way.

His brows knit over his eyes. "What's wrong?"

"Tell you later," I said. "I just need to get out of here."

"Okay," he said, then like some kind of Mr. Darcy from *Pride and Prejudice*, he offered me his arm.

Desperate, I grabbed it with both hands and let him tow me out of the classroom, which brought us to Obstacle Number Two: Shay, standing in the middle of the exit.

"Izzy," she said.

"Excuse me," I said, practically strangling Cody's arm. "We'd like to pass by."

"I can see you're upset," Shay said.

I didn't want to talk to her. Not here. Not with an audience watching. "You cut me out of the picture," I said, my voice a squeaky whine.

"I was trying to honor your wishes," Shay said. "You didn't want us to use any pictures of you."

This threw a warm blanket over me drowning in my cold misery. "I didn't want any pictures posted *online*," I said.

"I tried to tell her." Amelia appeared at Shay's side, her arms folded. "Tessa and I both used pictures of you, and you didn't care, did you?" she asked.

"No," I said, suddenly unsure that I had a right to be upset about this.

"I'm sorry," Shay said. "I just didn't want to risk doing anything to make you angry. I guess I screwed that up big time."

I opened my mouth to respond, but all I could do was shake my head. "I gotta go." And this time, I pulled Cody away. I didn't take us toward the multipurpose room where Drama II was held. I led us toward where Cody had Graphic Design over in the art wing.

"You going to be okay?" he asked.

I realized I was still squeezing his arm, so I let go and gestured to his rumpled sleeve. "Sorry."

He shrugged it off. "No worries."

We stood outside the door to his classroom while kids flowed around us. "I have to fix it," I said.

His lips twisted as he seemed to think for a moment. "Want me to pray for you?"

I nodded, thinking it would be nice to have someone else praying about this besides my papi and my own pathetic attempts. What I hadn't expected was for Cody to pull me into a one-armed hug and pray for me—right there in the hallway outside the graphic arts classroom.

"Jesus, please comfort Izzy," Cody said. "She's hurting and needs Your touch. Please heal her relationship with Shay. You know this is hard for Izzy, but You also know she loves Shay very much. Please heal the brokenness between them. Help Izzy know what to do to fix this. Give her the words. Give her peace to get through the rest of this day. And if I can help her in any way, please give Izzy the courage to ask me. Bless my very good friend. Amen."

He squeezed, rubbed his hand along my arm, then stepped away, watching me. "I'll see you later at the store, okay? And we're still going to get together tomorrow to work on Love at First Bite?"

I had pretty much turned into a gummy bear, which made me a jellied statue. I somehow managed to nod.

"Okay, see you then." Cody grinned and entered his class.

I inched my way toward the multipurpose room, simply stunned. The words of Cody's nearly-fully-answered-already prayer ran through my mind. God had used that boy's words to give me peace, to shock me right out of my misery and self-loathing. I'd never heard a boy pray like that. The way he kept saying *please* . . . Ahh. Stars, there was no one like Cody Nichols. I didn't think my heart would be content to remain in the friend zone for long. Yet at the same time, I felt especially lucky to be there.

I managed to survive Drama II by warning Amelia that if she said one word to me about Shay, I was dropping the class.

Choir, however, was a lovely way to end the day with a slate of friends who knew nothing about my current problems. Usually, it felt nice to have a class without Cody, since it gave my traitorous heart a break from the total confusion the boy put me through. But today that thought seemed fairly blasphemous after Cody's kindness.

I couldn't wait to see him at the end of my shift at Paprika's, but when the time came, Mr. Bellanger came out to relieve me.

"Cody's coach called for a longer practice, so he won't be here for another half hour at least. It's pretty slow, so you go ahead and take off. I'll cover until he gets here."

"Oh, thanks," I said, faking a smile I didn't feel. "Are you sure you wouldn't rather me stay until he gets here?"

"No, you go. It will save me a few bucks on your salary." He winked.

I clocked out and was outside unlocking my bike when a truck pulled up beside me.

"Need a ride?"

I looked up, surprised to see Daniel Nichols, one arm hanging out the driver's-side window of his retro baby-blue-and-white pickup truck, his vapid gaze locked on me. Someone sat in the cab beside him. A guy I didn't recognize. Both wore yellow Riverbend Country Club polos.

My heart lodged somewhere in my throat, and I struggled to form words. "No," I managed. "I'm good." I arced my leg over the bike and took off. Behind me, the truck's engine revved, which made my pulse skyrocket. I pedaled hard but had to slow at the four-way stop sign by the Grounds and Rounds coffee shop.

The truck rolled up beside me and honked. "Yo, Izzy. Wait up!" Daniel yelled.

I didn't wait up. I took off again, and when I looked back, the truck was following me!

Rather than taking Randal Street, which would lead to a long stretch of vulnerable country road, I passed it by and turned the other direction on Grant, heading deeper into the downtown area.

Tires squealed behind me. I glanced back and saw Daniel turn his truck to follow me. He flashed his lights.

I pedaled harder, briefly wondering if there was something wrong. Maybe a notebook was falling out of my backpack, or my tire was going flat.

But no. Daniel was playing, and I didn't think it was funny at all.

I rode straight to Tessa's house and leaped off my bike, which rolled to a crashing heap on the small lawn, its front wheel still spinning. I ran up to the front door and knocked. I glanced over my shoulder and heard the truck's engine rumbling the next block over.

The door opened. Tessa's mom stood there, looking comfy in a paint-spattered T-shirt and leggings. "Izzy, hello!" she said. "Tessa isn't home right now."

"That's okay, Miss Carrie. Can I come in?"

"Sure."

Only when I was safe inside the house with the door closed did I let down my guard. I started to cry.

"Sweetie, what's wrong?" Miss Carrie put her arm around me.

"Some boys were chasing me in their truck. I got scared and didn't know where to go."

"What! What boys?"

"Daniel Nichols and his friend."

"Of all the stupid things to do." Miss Carrie steered me to the couch in her living room and sat down beside me. "Would you like something to drink? I have iced tea and apple juice."

"Water?"

"Sure, I'll get you some water." She got up and disappeared through the arched entryway into the kitchen. This house was so small, I could still see her as she pulled a glass from a cupboard and filled it with water at the fridge. "I wish I could offer you something yummy to eat, but about the only time we have such treats is when you bring them over."

She returned and handed me the cool glass. I drank a big gulp and noticed my hand was shaking. I lowered the glass to my lap and held it steady with both hands.

"I'm sorry I haven't been baking," I said. "I haven't been myself lately. In a while, really."

"Change can be so difficult," Miss Carrie said. "But Tessa and I sure miss seeing you!"

"I miss you guys too," I said, sounding weepy. Oh, I was so sick and tired of weepy Izzy. I was not a depressed person! I was cheerful. I was fun. I was happy.

"You hang out as long as you like," Miss Carrie said. "But do let me know if you would like a ride or if you need me to call your parents or anything."

"I have a phone," I said. "I'll call my sister to come get me."

"While you do that, I'll just pop back into the kitchen to stir my soup. I was making myself some dinner when you knocked."

"Sorry!" I said. "I hope it didn't burn."

"Nope, it's just fine. You go ahead and make your phone call." She went back into the kitchen.

I called Claire, who was there to pick me up not ten minutes later. I hugged Miss Carrie goodbye, then Claire and I loaded my bike into the back of her truck and headed for home. As I was telling Claire what happened, I got a text from Tessa.

Tessa: Mom just called me. Are you okay?

Me: I'm fine. Glad your mom was home.

Tessa: I can't believe Daniel would do that. What is wrong with him?

Me: IDK

Tessa: I love you. I'm glad you're okay.

Me: Thanks. Love you too.

Claire wanted to tell our parents what happened, but I made her promise not to. I rarely ever saw Daniel Nichols. If Papi went over and spoke to his father, I was afraid Daniel would pick on me more or take it out on Cody. That was probably foolish, but I was tired of being a trouble magnet. I just wanted the trouble to go away.

I was supposed to go over to Cody's house this Saturday evening to finish up our business project. If Daniel was going to be home, I didn't want to go over there. How was I going to ask Cody about that without telling him what Daniel had done? One way or another, I knew it was going to make for an awkward conversation.

At Bible study on Saturday, we finally reached the part of David's story I had most dreaded: Bathsheba. How could a man after God's own heart do such a thing? Had he forgotten who he was? Had his kingly powers gone to his head? Too many material possessions? Too many servants? Perhaps he'd just gotten used to getting whatever he wanted whenever he wanted it. A common problem of the rich, famous, and powerful throughout history.

Stories like David's were, unfortunately, common these days too. Adultery and sexual immorality were rampant in society. The #MeToo movement had exposed the secret sins of many powerful and well-known individuals. When the Bible study teacher cautioned us not to be drawn into thinking David and Bathsheba's relationship was romantic, I laughed inside. No worry from me on that one. Yet David's choice to sleep with Bathsheba was not the worst thing he did, in my opinion. It was his decision to kill off Uriah, Bathsheba's husband—one of David's faithful mighty men—that I found especially deplorable. When we got to that part, I started crying. I was totally embarrassed, but how could a man who loved God do such a thing?

Nana pointed out that God said David was a man after his own heart back at the time when he had rebuked Saul—before David fought Goliath. Then Carmen said that David repented and got right with God again. She was certain we would study that part next week.

But none of that changed the horrible things David had done. Many women of the time—and many men, too—had been stoned to death for committing adultery. And if someone did such things today, he could be put in prison for murder.

All that to say, I left Bible study feeling grouchy. I went straight to meet Zoe, where I told her all about stupid King David and his selfish ways. But she started defending him, like Nana and Carmen, so I changed the subject before I started crying again.

I told her how Daniel Nichols had followed me in his truck and scared me half to death. This made Zoe angry, and she wanted me to tell my parents. I told her why I didn't want to.

"I don't know that he was really going to do anything to me," I said. "He didn't say anything mean or threatening."

"He followed you in a truck when you were riding a bike. He honked his horn at you and didn't stop chasing you until you lost him."

"But he might have had a good reason," I said. "I just don't want to make trouble between him and Cody."

"This has nothing to do with Cody," Zoe said.

"I don't think Daniel will see it that way."

Zoe pressed her lips together, and I bet she was thinking about all the things Cody had told her about his brother wearing his clothes and not being sorry about the Dropbox pictures.

"All right," she said finally, "but if you have any other run-ins with Daniel Nichols, no matter how insignificant you might think them, promise me you will call and tell me. And that you'll tell your parents."

"I promise," I said. Eager to change the subject, I blurted,

"Something happened with Shay this week." Then I told her about Shay cutting me out of her diorama, my reaction, and what Shay had said at the end of class. I also told her about Cody praying for me at school. Zoe seemed to think that all this was headed in a positive direction between both Shay and me and Cody and me. Zoe reminded me to practice perspective and said I could have used that to keep from being hurt when I first saw the picture on Shay's diorama.

"I would be happy to meet with you and Shay as a mediator," Zoe said, "if you want to talk out this conflict between you in a safe place."

It was actually a good idea. Having Zoe there might make the whole mess so much easier, but it also felt a bit like tattling to my mother. I wasn't sure I wanted to let a grown-up fix my problems. It felt like something I needed to figure out how to handle on my own.

"I'll think about it," I said.

—✺—

Shortly after I got home, I met Cody at Mrs. Kirby's house, which quickly lightened my mood. While we were doing our chores, I asked him if his brother would be home when I went over to work on our project.

"He's working until nine thirty tonight," Cody said. "They started Night Golf at the club, and he volunteered for the later shifts. He said the cooler people golf at night, so . . ." He shrugged.

I wrapped the water hose back around the reel attached to the house, relieved that I wasn't going to have to see Daniel tonight.

"Just so you know, Daniel doesn't have that picture of you anymore," Cody said. "The police took all his tech—his computer, his iPad, and his cell phone. And when they gave them back, Dad had them wiped and sold them. Daniel doesn't even have a phone right now. He can't as long as he lives with us."

That Cody might think my fear was Dropbox related had never occurred to me, but it made perfect sense. "That's good to know," I said. "Do you think that happened with all the guys who were charged?"

"Yes," Cody said. "Their parents all had their devices wiped or destroyed."

"Oh." This realization loosened something knotted inside me, and I suddenly couldn't wait to go over to Cody's house.

When we finished, we walked there together, side by side, down the middle of the road until the sound of a car made us turn. Mr. Nereuta, my neighbor from across the street, was home. He pulled his white Honda Accord into his driveway and waited as the garage door rumbled up. Cody waved at him, and Mr. Nereuta waved back.

We continued on to Cody's driveway, which was empty. His Acura sat on the street out front. We walked up the driveway and along the house to the front door.

"Are your parents home?" I asked.

"Nope," Cody said. "My mom is at her book club tonight. They always have dinner and go pretty late. And Dad went to a baseball game with a friend."

"Oh," I said as Cody opened the door, and we went inside.

I had been in Cody's entryway a few times, but never farther than that. I remembered there being sports equipment everywhere. But today, as he led me into the living room, there was no sign of it.

Cody gestured to a beige leather sectional and a dark wood coffee table that held a laptop and several notebooks. "I got us set up here, but we can go to your house, if you'd rather."

"No," I said. "This is great."

He shoved his hands into the front pockets of his jeans. "Do you want a tour?"

"Let's wait until we're done working," I said. "It'll be my reward."

"Don't know how rewarding it will be, but okay."

We hunkered down at the table and got to it. We not only had to turn in a completed business proposal next week, but we also had to present it live to the class. We'd put many hours into this project. Cody had written the executive summary, and I had completed the industry overview. We'd both spent a lot of time on the market analysis and competition report. Cody was still working on the sales and marketing plan and the management plan, while I had written the operating plan, which talked about the day-to-day business practices we expected to have.

What had really put us behind, however, was the financial plan. This included a projected income statement, a balance sheet, and a cash flow chart. Cody was stronger at math than I was, but this wasn't a favorite part of the assignment for either of us.

We worked until eight, which was when I had told Papi I'd start wrapping things up.

"How about that tour now?" I asked, curious to see the rest of Cody's house.

"Yeah, okay." Cody jumped up and headed for the stairs. I followed.

The layout of Cody's house was similar to ours, which made sense. They'd been built around the same time. The floor plan was reversed, though, and his parents' bedroom faced the street and side yard, while the master bedroom in my house faced Mrs. Kirby's house and the backyard.

I barely glanced into his brothers' rooms and was a little surprised to see posters of insects on the walls of Daniel's room.

"Bugs?" I asked.

"He wants to be an entomologist," Cody said. "We'll see if his gap year lasts one year or the rest of his life."

Science seemed like way too serious a field for a guy who chased girls around town in his truck to scare them. Unless he was just a sadist. I supposed an obsession with bugs might fit that theory.

The first thing I noticed about Cody's room was the patriotic color scheme. The walls were a slate blue. His bedding was red with red-and-white checkered sheets spilling out one side.

"Mm-hmm," I said, smirking. "Looks like Captain America's room."

Cody laughed. "Told you my favorite color was red."

Then I saw the poster. A single poster of Gal Gadot as Wonder Woman hanging on the wall at the foot of Cody's bed.

He caught me staring at it. "You like it? I prefer Marvel, honestly. About a month ago, this whole wall was posters, and all but this one were Marvel. I had one of Thor and one of the Black Panther and one of Captain America and one of Black Widow. It started to feel more like a movie theater than a bedroom, though, so I took the others down."

Staring at the poster made me feel cold. "And kept up this one."

He grinned. "Yeah. Wonder Woman is awesome."

"Don't you think she looks a little bit . . ." *Half-naked?* was what I wanted to say, but I settled on "sexy?"

"Uh . . ." Cody coughed, his cheeks flushing. He spun away from the poster and motioned to the bottom shelf of his bookcase, which was solid with the narrow white spines of comic books along with a white plastic tote. "I've always liked superheroes," he said. "I used to read the comics. I still have my collection of action figures in this container."

The question wasn't whether he liked superheroes and comic books. The question was why he chose *that* poster as the only one he left on his wall. Had I been wrong to start trusting Cody so much? Was this poster proof that he was just like every other boy? Obsessed with pictures of sexy women?

"I should get going," I said, wanting to escape the awkwardness I'd created.

"Yeah, okay. I'll walk you out."

Cody slipped into the hallway. I shot one last suspicious glance at Wonder Woman before following him. Cody was waiting at the top of the stairs. He smiled at me, then started down. He hadn't yet reached the middle landing where the stairs turned ninety degrees when he met someone coming up from below.

"What do we have here?" a guy said. "Cubby had a girl in his room?"

My body turned to ice. *Daniel.*

"Let us by," Cody said.

"Not until I see who you've got up there. Mom said you had a girlfriend, but I said, 'Not Cubby, Mom. Surely not Cubby.'" Daniel stepped up onto the landing with Cody, giving him a clear view of me on the stairs behind his little brother. "Oh!" A smile lit Daniel's face. Not a kind or friendly smile, but the kind a cat gives a mouse when he catches it in a corner. "Isabella Valadez. Nice choice, brother. She's got it all. I've seen it."

Cody pressed his hand against Daniel's chest. "Don't."

Daniel's brows tucked deep over his eyes. "Get your hand off me."

"Let us by," Cody said, pushing Daniel with his forearm. "Izzy needs to get home."

"Is this about the other day?" Daniel said. "Did she tattle on me?"

Cody frowned. "What are you talking about?"

Daniel's eyebrows popped into two high arches, and he met my gaze. "You didn't tell him."

"He followed me in his truck," I said, suddenly worried that keeping the secret had been the wrong thing to do. "I was on my bike after work. I rode to Tessa's and called Claire to come and get me."

"Why would you do that?" Cody asked Daniel.

"I just wanted to talk to her."

Cody leaned so close to his brother that it looked like their noses were touching. "Leave her alone."

"*Pfft.* That's it? That's all you got? A little growl? You want to defend your girl, put some muscle behind it." Daniel shoved Cody. "Like that."

"Stop," Cody said, hands raised, palms facing his brother.

"Stop what?" Daniel asked, forcing Cody against the wall. "This is what you wanted. Now your girl can go home. Go ahead, Isabella." He jerked his head for me to pass.

There wasn't a lot of space on the landing between the corner wall and Daniel's back. I glanced at Cody, who was watching me. They both were. Cody nodded for me to go.

"What are you waiting for, girl?" Daniel asked. "Don't want your papi to worry about his little *chica*."

My heart beat rapidly. I finally squeezed my hands into fists and went for it, slipping past Daniel and descending the rest of the stairs as fast as I could. At the bottom, I turned and glanced back up in time to see Cody push Daniel so hard his brother hit the wall and knocked down several family photos. Daniel's foot landed on the edge of the next step and slipped off, causing him to stumble. Cody reached for him, but Daniel fell, landing on his side, and slid shoulder first down the stairs. I backed up several steps to get out of the way as he spilled onto the wood floor of the entryway.

Cody rushed downstairs and crouched beside his brother. "Dan, you okay?"

Daniel lay there for a moment, eyes closed.

Please, God, let him be okay.

Cody nudged his shoulder. "Dan?"

Daniel sprang onto Cody, his face a mask of determination. They rolled over the entryway floor for a moment, then somehow popped to their feet. That's when the fists started flying.

I had never seen Cody look like that before. There really was a cheetah inside him, and right now, it was angry enough to rip apart his prey. But Daniel was a cheetah too, and I was worried they might kill each other.

"Stop it!" I yelled.

They paid no attention to me.

The fight drifted into the living room, and they knocked over a table, breaking a lamp. That was my cue to leave. I grabbed my bag and ran home, trying to decide if it was okay to leave them like that or if I should call the police.

"Mamá? Papi!" I yelled as I entered the house. Where was everyone? I found Papi in the garage, head tucked under the hood of his Mustang. "Papi!"

He straightened, his face etched with concern. *"¿Estas bien, mija?"*

"Cody and Daniel are fighting," I said. "Like punching each other and wrecking their house."

Papi pressed the garage door opener, and the door began to rumble. "Stay here," he told me, ducking under the edge the moment the door was high enough.

I scrambled after him, following to the end of our driveway. I stood there watching him sprint down the road to Cody's house in the cul-de-sac until he disappeared through the front door.

Both of those boys were in far better shape than my papi. Taller, too. If the Nichols boys were cheetahs, my papi was Mrs. Kirby's Maine coon cat Jack.

God, keep Papi safe.

"What's wrong, *mija?*"

I turned at the sound of Mamá's voice. She stood on the porch.

"Cody and Daniel started fighting," I said. "Papi went over to stop them."

"Is that all?" Claire said, stepping out to join Mamá. "I thought someone had gotten hurt."

"I'm sure someone did," I said. "They were punching each other."

Sebastian exited the garage in his pajamas, toothbrush in hand. "I will stop the bad guys, Isabella Valadez," he said, starting across the lawn.

Oh no. We all knew better than to use violent words around Sebastian. "They're not bad guys, Bash," I said. "They're just having a difference of opinion."

Sebastian did not stop.

Mamá ran ahead of him and pretended to trip, sprawling onto the grassy lawn. "Oh!" she cried. "Oh, I fell!"

"Mamá!" I said, catching on. "Sebastian! Help me check on Mamá. She fell!"

My brother ran with me to Mamá's side.

"Are you hurt, Josephina Valadez?" he asked.

Mamá sat up, fanning her face. "I'm all right."

That was good enough for Sebastian, who popped back to his feet and started for the driveway. "Now I will help Dañel Valadez," he said.

"Actually, Bash," I said as I jumped to my feet, "before Papi left, he told me he needed your help over here." I ran to the trash cans, scrambling for something to say that would draw him in. "The sinister squirrels have been at it again. They've been getting into the trash cans and making a huge mess. Papi needs someone strong enough to find some big rocks to put on the lids to keep those pesky menaces out!"

Sebastian stopped and regarded the trash cans. Had I captured the heart of the superhero inside him?

"Papi said you could do it better than me and Claire, since you're so strong," I added.

"Sí, Isabella Valadez. I can do it." Sebastian went straight for the decorative rocks Mamá had bought to edge the driveway. Worried, I glanced at Mamá, but she nodded her consent. The rocks could be put back. It was more important to keep Sebastian here and away from fist-fighting brothers.

Claire and I cheered Sebastian's efforts to protect our trash from the sinister squirrels. The moment I saw Papi walking back from the Nichols house, I ran and met him in the street.

"What happened?" I asked. "Are they okay?"

"They're fine," Papi said. "It's over. What is your brother doing outside?"

I filled him in on the sinister squirrels.

"Let me get Sebastian to bed, then you and I need to talk," Papi said.

My heart sank. Talks with Papi about boys rarely went well.

"¡Ay! Sebastian!" Papi said as we walked up the driveway. "Eres muy fuerte, mijo."

—⁓—

Once Sebastian was tucked in, Papi stopped by my bedroom. "Waiting up for me, I see," he said.

"As if I could sleep when you said we needed to talk."

He chuckled. "You're not in trouble. But Cody seemed pretty worried that his brother has been bothering you. Has he?"

I shook my head. "Not really."

Papi shot me a look. "Isabella . . ."

"Okay, once." I told him about Daniel following me after work.

"Hmm," Papi said. "I don't like that at all, but it seemed like maybe there was something more to make Cody so angry."

"Well, he doesn't get along with Daniel," I said. "He's mad about Daniel's part in the Dropbox thing. Daniel knows that and picks on Cody on purpose. Steals his socks. Dumb stuff like that." I considered telling Papi that Cody had been meeting with Zoe to work through his anger toward his brother, but that seemed private.

"It can be hard having brothers," Papi said. "Add trouble like that Dropbox case . . ." He shook his head. "I don't want you going over there again wh—"

"Oh, Papi, no."

He lifted his hand between us. "I wasn't finished, mija. I don't want you going over there again *when* no adults are home. Is that clear?"

That I was happy to agree to. "Yes, Papi." I got up and hugged him good night.

—m—

When I checked my phone, I had three texts from Cody.

Cody: Sorry about what happened with Daniel.

Cody: Sorry I lost my temper. I tried not to but . . .

Cody: He makes it really hard. ☹

He certainly did.

I felt like I should text back, but I didn't know what to say. The messages were readable on my home screen without my needing to actually open them, which meant they wouldn't show as read on Cody's phone.

"Mom said you had a girlfriend." That's what Daniel said. Had Cody told his mom I was his girlfriend? I didn't feel comfortable with that, especially when he'd never said anything of the sort to me.

And that poster of Wonder Woman . . . That had weirded me out. Wonder Woman was awesome. That wasn't the concern. It just bothered me that Cody woke up to Gal Gadot in that skimpy outfit every morning. It felt . . . dangerous somehow. Daniel had been part of the Dropbox scandal. Cody was his brother. They shared the same blood. Perhaps it was only a matter of time until Cody went down the same path.

My gaze flicked to my poster of Captain Marvel. Her uniform was skintight too—they all were—but at least she was covered. There was no skin showing.

Next to Captain Marvel hung my new poster of Captain America. He stood front and center, the rest of the cast smaller and distant behind him. His costume was fitted as well. Was I being hypocritical to judge Cody for the superhero he put on his wall when I had some of my own? All I knew was how it felt to see that poster of Wonder Woman, her bare arms and legs, her cleavage, that look in her eyes.

I had been far too careless with Cody. What did I really know about him? If tonight was any indication, not enough. I could still hear the sounds of his fist smacking his brother's face. I never would have imagined him capable of such violence.

I had let down my guard with Cody Nichols, and already I had fallen into the same pattern as with Zac—trusting a guy I didn't really know.

No matter how much I wished it, Cody Nichols was not who I thought he was.

Chapter
17

I COULDN'T GO TO SCHOOL ON MONDAY. I just couldn't.

I lived with a doctor, so faking illness was not something I'd ever gotten away with. I knew enough to get myself sent home, though. So when I got to school, I went straight to the nurse's office, clutching my stomach.

I found Michael Torres already there, waiting.

"You sick?" he asked.

I nodded. "Stomach."

"Don't give it to me. We have a cross-country meet on Saturday."

"Why are you here?" I asked.

"Low blood sugar," he said. "I thought I had a pack of Skittles in my locker, but it's gone. I don't have anything less than a ten in my wallet, and the cafeteria is already closed from breakfast. Mrs. Heinz always has something."

"Are you diabetic?"

"Mm-hmm," he said. "Type one. I manage it fine on my own usually."

The door opened, and a boy I didn't recognize came out, followed by Mrs. Heinz, the school nurse.

"Low blood sugar?" she asked Michael.

"Just a bit. I had some Skittles in my locker, but I must have run out. Thought you might have some."

"Let me check." She retreated into her office, and Michael stepped into the doorway. A moment later, Mrs. Heinz returned with a roll of Life Savers. "This is all I have. I'll pick up some more after school."

"Thanks, Mrs. Heinz," Michael said, walking away. "Bye, Izzy. *Que estés bien.*"

Mrs. Heinz turned her attention on me. "You all right?"

"I threw up." It was a lie, and I begged God's forgiveness the moment I said it. I doubted He was impressed since I had no intention of ending my deceit anytime soon.

"Oh, honey. Sit down, and I'll call your mother to come pick you up."

"My father," I said as I sat on the paper-covered cot, hand still cradling my perfectly fine stomach. "He works from home and is the one to come get me." He was also the one who wouldn't question my illness, especially if I mentioned the word *menstruation.*

An hour later, I lay tucked in my bed, lights out, staring at my Captain Marvel poster.

"I know," I said aloud. "I'm a coward." But I couldn't face Cody or Shay or Amelia or Tessa. It was all too much. I just needed some time.

"We love you, Miss Hannigan!"

I pulled out my cell phone, which I'd tucked under my pillow.

Cody: Are you okay? Missed you in class.

Cody: Worried about you.

Cody: I'm sorry for everything.

Ugh. This boy. What to do about him?

My phone burst into song, making me jump. The lyrics of "I Feel Pretty" from *West Side Story* blared out from the tiny speakers as Mamá's face filled the screen, the critical expression in her eyes convicting me.

I let it go to voicemail.

Mamá called again.

Then she texted.

Mamá: Answer your phone, mija.

Mamá: Call me back.

I heard footsteps on the stairs. Papi coming to check on me, no doubt per Mamá's command. I silenced my phone, crammed it back under my pillow, and pulled the blankets over my head. My door creaked open, and I tried to make my breathing even so Papi would think I was asleep.

"Isabella?" he said.

Please go away, please go away!

Thankfully, Papi left without making me talk to Mamá.

Under my head and pillow, my phone vibrated. I pulled it out.

Amelia: Where r u? What happened?

Tessa: Amelia says you're sick. Apparently, Michael saw you at the nurse's office. You okay?

Shay: Hope you feel better soon, Izzy!

Cody: Mr. Federici is out today too. No one to play questions with. ☹

Cody: You ever play questions?

Claire: Amelia said you're sick. Did you go home?

Mamá: Call me when you wake up.

Ugh.

I was starting to think playing sick was far more trouble than it was worth. I waited a few hours before calling Mamá. I told her I was feeling better and suspected food poisoning, maybe from one of Mrs. Kirby's chicken eggs, which put Mamá on a salmonella scare that I was barely able to deflect by swearing I had no fever. Mamá still made me go find her thermometer and take my temperature before she finally let it go.

I came downstairs for lunch and ate with Papi. Since it was already after creative writing class, I offered to go back to school for fifth and sixth periods, but Papi said that seemed silly. But he did say I could go to work if I was sure I was okay. I assured him and finally left my house by three o'clock.

Things were slow at Paprika's, which gave me time to finish my fall window display. I gathered several wicker baskets, which I lined with orange and brown cloth napkins and filled with artificial pumpkins, squash, wheat, and sunflowers. I set out a table setting of fall-patterned dinnerware and placed a large orange candle inside a fall wreath as a centerpiece. I also arranged some white CorningWare to balance out all the color. I was just adding the Mr. and Mrs. Turkey cookie jars, because they were just too cute, when the bell over the door jingled and Tessa, Amelia, and Shay came in.

Why would they come into my work when they knew I was sick? I stifled my frustration and was grateful to see a customer approaching the counter. I hurried over and rang them up, watching the girls linger near the display of fall cookie cutters. The way Amelia was gesturing between Shay and me made me think she was trying to get Shay to say something.

Maybe this was it. Maybe Shay would finally apologize and tell me she had gotten help for her addiction. Then I could forgive her, and we could go back to how things were before.

I rang up two more customers before the store emptied out and the girls approached the register.

"You look fine to me," Amelia said, arms folded.

Nothing like starting a conversation with a little accusation. "I think it was just food poisoning," I said.

"Ooh, that's unpleasant," Tessa said.

"Izzy, I want to apologize," Shay said.

Finally! "Oh?"

"It was wrong of me to cut you out of the picture on my creative writing project. I should have asked you if it was okay to use that picture. I didn't mean to hurt your feelings, and I'm sorry. You are one of my best friends, and I miss you."

Okay, not what I expected her to say, but it was a good first step. "I understand why you did it," I said. "You were just trying to do what I asked, and I appreciate that."

"Okay!" Amelia said. "So now can we all go back to normal? Finally?"

I frowned at Shay. "Are you done?"

"Done what?" she asked.

"Apologizing."

"I think . . ."

Shay glanced at Tessa, who said, "We're all sorry we didn't support you better through the Dropbox thing. We didn't know how hard that was for you, and I'm sad we missed a chance to love and help you."

"Yes," Amelia said, as if she had just remembered her line. "I was so overwhelmed with helping Ms. Larkin that I neglected everything else, including you. I'm sorry."

"I'm sorry too," Shay said. "To be honest, I found the whole situation weird and didn't really know how to deal with it or be there for you."

That hit me wrong. I mean, it wasn't surprising to hear Shay say something like that, but the fact that she had been looking at porn and reading trashy novels was the exact same kind of weird, in my opinion. "I guess that means you've stopped looking at porn?"

"Oh," Shay said. "I'm at, uh"—she glanced at Tessa—"thirteen days?"

"And counting," Tessa said, nodding.

"That's it?" I didn't need to be getting an A in Algebra II to do that math. "But that's only a little under two weeks," I said.

"Shay's been doing really well," Tessa said. "She just had one teensy relapse."

"I had to start my count over," Shay said. "Before the tenth, I was at twenty-six days. It's harder than I thought it would be to stop."

That made no sense. "It's not hard at all," I said. "You just don't do it."

"Hey," Amelia said. "There's no judgment here."

"But there has to be!" I said. "What kind of friends would we be if we said nothing?"

"That's not what's been happening, Izzy," Tessa said. "If you'd been around, you'd know."

I clutched my hair, trying not to lose my temper. "I can't be around that. I can't."

"As usual, you're missing the point and making this all about you," Amelia said. "Shay wanted to apologize to you, but Tessa and I do really need to talk to you."

"Yeah, no judgment," Tessa said. "But we do want to talk."

I felt like I was falling. "About what?"

"We're tired of you being a jerk, that's what," Amelia said.

I couldn't believe this. "*I'm* a jerk?"

"Yes!" Amelia said.

I looked to Tessa, who shrugged one shoulder and said, "Sometimes."

"The problem isn't me," I yelled. "Porn is evil. It's wrong. And it ruins lives."

The door opened, and Cody entered, dressed in a T-shirt and sweats.

"Hey," he said to the girls.

Good. Someone who would take my side. "Cody agrees with me," I said. "He thinks what Shay's doing is wrong too."

The store got very quiet.

Shay spoke in a small voice. "You told Cody?"

Tessa and Amelia looked to Cody, who shifted uncomfortably.

Tension still anchored us girls. Cody wisely kept his mouth shut, but the way he shoved his hands into his pockets somehow made him look suspect.

"Izzy!" Tessa said. "Why would you tell Cody?"

Shay strode out of the store, slipping past Cody, who practically lunged out of her way.

"Shay, wait!" Tessa ran after her.

Amelia stalked toward the door, but her eyes, narrowed to slits, were focused on me. "How could you do that to her?"

The bell on the door dinged as Amelia exited the store, leaving Cody and me alone.

"You okay?" he asked.

"No," I said. "I'm very much not."

"What happened?"

My hands were tingling, and I was struggling to breathe. "They hate me," I said.

"I'm sure that's not true," Cody said.

"Yes, it is!"

Cody pursed his lips. "I'm going to get my apron."

He slipped around the edge of the store to the back. I checked the time. It was five o'clock. I could go home now.

I pulled off my apron, folded back the counter, and walked out of the register area. I met Cody in the back of the store, coming out of the break room. He looked worried, his forehead all crumpled as he tied his apron behind his back.

"You're feeling . . . You were sick?"

"I'm fine," I said, my cracking voice proof of the opposite.

"Listen, about last night, I—"

"It's fine, Cody. I have to go." I stepped past him into the break room, clocked out, and hung my apron on the hook. When I came back out, Cody was still standing there, looking like a kid who had dropped his ice cream in the dirt.

"See you later," I said, wanting to keep from escalating the damage in at least one of my fractured friendships.

"Yeah, okay," he said. "Bye, Isabella."

Ugh. He just had to use my full name. I tried not to let that mend anything broken between us.

I had never told him how much I liked it when he called me Isabella, but I figured guys had a sixth sense about how to wrap girls around their fingers. I wasn't going to fall for it.

I went straight home and fed Mrs. Kirby's animals to be sure I wouldn't see Cody later. The next morning, when I went to feed them before school, Cody was sitting on Mrs. Kirby's back porch step.

"What are you doing here?" I asked.

"Waiting for you."

"Why?"

"I need to talk to you."

I went to the shed and pulled out the bag of chicken feed. "And you couldn't wait until school?"

"No," he said. "I know you're going through a hard time, and I want to be there for you. But it just really seems like you don't want any help."

At the door of the chicken coop, I dropped the bag of feed by my feet so I could open the door. I twisted the latch. "I don't."

"Okay, so . . . . Listen, I don't want to bother you, or anything like that. We just need to get through Federici's project next week, and then I'll find somewhere else to sit in business class. And algebra. And creative writing."

I stopped fumbling with the chicken coop door and stared at him, confused. "You don't want to sit by me in school anymore?"

"Not if you don't want me to."

"I want you to."

"You do." His forehead crumpled. He stood and then paced over to the chicken coop and back, hands on his hips. "Look, I'd like to be honest here."

"I would appreciate that."

He chuckled. "I seriously doubt that, but okay."

Across the street, Mr. Nereuta's garage door started to rise, which sounded extra loud on this quiet morning.

"I'm tired of your whole back-and-forth, yin-yang thing," Cody said. "You're nice to me. We laugh and have fun. And then you avoid me and act like you don't want to talk to me. Or you get angry over the strangest things. I feel like I can't trust you to be, well . . . you."

"*You* can't trust *me*?" I said, suddenly livid. "I'm not the one secretly taking pictures of someone and posting them online without permission."

His posture wilted. "I said I was sorry for that, and I offered to delete them."

"And I'm not the one throwing punches at my brother or hanging pictures of half-naked women on my bedroom wall."

Cody's eyes widened. "I . . . that's not fair," he whispered.

"I just bet you lied about never looking at the Dropbox pictures too. Admit it. I dare you."

His peachy cheeks had turned pink now. "What I admit is that I was very wrong about you."

"Oh? How so?"

"I thought you were kind and thoughtful, but you're so caught up in blaming everyone else for their mistakes, you can't even see your own."

The words hurt and shocked me, but before I had a chance to respond, the chicken coop door flew open, and Harland barreled out, right between Cody and me.

"Harland, no!" I yelled, chasing after her.

But the chicken was on a mission to run as fast and as far as possible. She headed for the street, right where Mr. Nereuta's car was backing out of his driveway.

"Stop!" I screamed, sprinting toward the chicken, but it was too late. The white Honda Accord rolled out of the driveway and turned right just as Harland disappeared behind the wheels.

A small thud caused Mr. Nereuta to hit the brakes.

"No!" I circled the back of the car and saw Harland lying on the asphalt. "Oh, Harland, no." I dropped to my knees beside the bird, tears blurring my vision.

"Is she okay?" Cody asked, kneeling beside me.

I stroked the chicken's salt-and-pepper-colored feathers. "I don't know."

"Izzy! Did I hit you?" Mr. Nereuta asked. "I didn't see anyone behind me."

"It's one of Mrs. Kirby's chickens," Cody said.

"What happened?" Claire asked, jogging toward us from our driveway.

Mr. Nereuta walked toward her. "I ran over one of the chickens," he said. "I didn't see it."

Harland twitched, then made a funny sound.

Cody and I looked at each other.

"I'll take her to the vet," Cody said.

"I'll come with you," I said.

"No, you won't," Claire said, "unless you want Mamá to kill you after yesterday."

I sighed. She was right. "I can't come," I said.

Cody scooped up the chicken. "It's all right. I've got her."

"I'll drive you over there," Mr. Nereuta said, opening his passenger-side door. Cody slid into the seat.

"Text me when you know anything," I said as Mr. Nereuta climbed into the driver's seat.

Cody nodded, and Mr. Nereuta sped away.

"Go back and check the gate," Claire said, "then we've got to go, or we'll be late."

I took a deep breath and ran back toward Mrs. Kirby's house, trying not to cry.

Chapter

18

HARLAND WAS OKAY. That was the good news. She'd just been stunned. Cody and Mr. Nereuta had put her back in the chicken coop where she couldn't escape.

The bad news? Everything else in my life sucked.

The next few days were miserable. I did my best to drift through Tuesday and Wednesday at school. Cody and I had enough to do on our project to keep us both busy independently, so we were able to work without speaking to each other much. At lunch, I went outside and sat with Hyun Ki and Lilliesha, but they were talking about makeup and K-pop bands, neither of which interested me in the slightest.

I was all alone, and I had no one to blame but myself. How had I gotten here? I tried to look back and see all the places I'd gone wrong, but it was hard to see past my own pain.

Friday in Creative Writing, Tessa presented her diorama. She had cut off one side of a cereal box, laid it flat, and covered the open top with blue cellophane. She'd run three pieces of yarn down the length, creating four swimming lanes. In them, different words and images had been taped to toothpicks like cupcake toppers, and Tessa had stabbed them through the cellophane so they stood up in the "water."

"I'm a swimmer," Tessa said, "so I felt this image best represents who I am and how I see the world. I sometimes feel like my life is fractured into lanes. Some lanes I made myself, and others were made for me. Some lanes I feel comfortable in, and others, not so much."

She frowned at her project, like she couldn't decide if she liked it or not. "At first, I wanted to compartmentalize all the bad stuff into one lane, but then I realized that's not how life works. Most of the time—not always, but most of the time—the bad things that happen to us come from good things.

"I made four lanes, mostly because that's all that fit on the box. I have a lane for family, a lane for friends, a lane for school, and a lane for my interests and things like that. In my family lane, I have my parents and grandparents, plus my stepmom and half brother. Last year, my dad left us and eventually got remarried to Rebecca. And they had a baby, Logan, my half brother. I love my dad, but what he did really hurt my mom and me. But now Logan exists, and I can't imagine the world without him. That's kind of what I meant when I said sometimes good things are bad and bad things are good. It's hard."

She pointed to the fourth lane. "Over here I have my interests, which are church, swimming, my car, and our new house. This big question mark is my future career, because I still don't really know what that will be. Lane three has a picture for all my classes and for Drama, not because I liked it but because I tried it. And lane two is for my friends. Each picture represents someone important to me." She touched the head of each person in the photos as she said their names. "Mackenzie, April, Alex, Cody, Abraham, Shay, Amelia, and this cupcake is Izzy." She looked up and smiled at me. "When you spend a lot of time with your family and friends, inevitably you're going to have times when you disagree and hurt each other. But I don't think that means you should give up on them.

"So that's who I am. A swimmer, making my way through life one lap at a time. Sometimes the water is nice, sometimes it's deep, and sometimes there's a strong undertow threatening to drag me down. But I just remember what I've been taught and who I trust, and I keep swimming. Thank you."

I applauded along with the class, grateful that Tessa had included me in cupcake form. Jonathan went next. He had made a giant book with pages for different parts of his life. He talked mostly about being a fan of Star Trek and Star Wars as well as his interest in writing science fiction novels.

When he was done, Mrs. Lopez said, "Cody Nichols?"

Cody approached Mrs. Lopez's desk. From behind it, he retrieved a cardboard box that said *CorningWare* on the side. I smiled, knowing he must have grabbed it from work before doing the recycling.

"I'm not as creative as the rest of you," he said, holding the box in front of him. It was filled with toy figures. "So . . . well . . . I like toys."

The class laughed.

"I'll just explain what's in the box. I don't play football, but this figurine is Tim Tebow when he played for the Denver Broncos."

"Go Broncos!" Jeremy said.

Cody laughed along with the class. "Tim represents my love of sports and the fact that I'm also a Christian. Those two things are big parts of my life. The baby Jesus in the manger represents Jesus. I borrowed that from my mom's Nativity set." He winced. "I hope she won't mind. Um, Mr. and Mrs. Incredible represent my parents and the life they've given me and my brothers. I'm fortunate to have such great parents. Um, the Sam and Dean Winchester characters represent my brothers because they're both awesome and intimidating, and sometimes one of them is super annoying." He chuckled. "But they're my brothers, so I love them anyway.

"The, um, Captain America represents my pastor because he's an amazing person, and I just, I don't know, kind of want to be like him someday. This Willy Wonka guy, he represents Mr. Bellanger, who owns Paprika's. I work there, and I've learned a ton from Mr. Bellanger about how to run a business. Oh, this little blue Hot Wheels represents my car. It's a Corvette instead of an Acura, but you get the picture. I love my car. Um, then I have a few other action figures over here to represent my friends. I've got Superman for Alex Hastings."

The class cheered, and Jeremy yelled, "Yee-ah, Alex!"

"Iron Man for Jeremy Jenkins," Cody said, and when the class cheered, Jeremy jumped to his feet and flexed his muscles.

"Sit down, Jeremy," Mrs. Lopez said.

Once Jeremy was back in his seat and the class had quieted, Cody said the next two action figures quickly. "Michael Torres is the Black Panther, and Trevor Mercado is Thor."

The class cheered so loudly that Cody started to laugh. "Okay, stop," he said. "I'm almost done. These last two are . . . Tessa Hart, I didn't have an Aquagirl, so you're Aquaman. And Wonder Woman is, um, Izzy Valadez."

Those brown eyes flicked my way for a half second. "That's it. That's all about me," he said, holding out his hands and taking a dramatic bow as the class applauded.

I stared at Cody as he put his project back behind Mrs. Lopez's desk and sat down by Jeremy. He didn't look at me again.

I was Wonder Woman? Is that why he had her poster on his wall?

What did *that* mean?

When I finally stopped staring and turned my attention toward the front of the class, I found Tessa, Amelia, and Shay watching me. I'm sure they were all thinking the same thing: *Izzy is Wonder Woman?*

—⁓—

At Saturday's Bible study at Nana's house, we had reached my favorite part of King David's story: Nathan.

I liked Nathan. He was super clever. I mean, he worked for King David, a warrior. You wouldn't want to get on King David's bad side. Yet Nathan had heard about all the bad stuff David had done, and there came a point when he could remain silent no longer. God was calling him to speak up. He found a clever way to confront the king without pointing the finger outright. He used a story. A story about a rich man taking and killing a poor man's only lamb, which David related to since he used to be a shepherd. The story Nathan told so enraged King David that he was ready to kill the man who had done such a thing.

Then Nathan said, "You are the man."

Classic burn. David was caught. Fully exposed. And there was nothing he could do but fall on his face before God, confess all he had done, and repent.

As Carmen, Elizaveta, Felisa, and my nana started to talk about the incredible depths of David's redemption, a horrifying possibility came to mind.

Was I like King David?

I mean, of course I wasn't a king or a man or an Israelite. I had no spouse or army or mighty men to boss around. But I had betrayed people. I had lied to get what I wanted. And now my sins were staring me in the face. David had been left with no choice but to depend on God. None of his kingly wealth or power could help him out of the hole he'd dug. When it came down to it, David repented and made peace with God. He humbled himself. He did the right thing. Finally.

That was what made him a man after God's own heart.

If I was like David, I might have some repenting of my own to do.

—⟋⟍—

Earlier in the week, I had texted Zoe to ask if we could meet somewhere besides Grounds and Rounds. With everything that had happened, I just didn't want to meet in the public space of a coffee shop. Zoe told me to come to her apartment instead. I had been there a few times before when she'd hosted a girls' Bible study, so I rode over after I left Nana's.

So much had happened in the past week. I told her about Cody's Wonder Woman poster, Daniel and the fight he got into with Cody, the girls ambushing me at Paprika's, Shay's porn relapse, and their accusation that I was the one with the problem. I told her about Cody accusing me of playing games with him and saying I had a problem with pointing the finger at everyone's problems rather than dealing with my own.

"Oh, sweetie," Zoe said. "I'm so sorry. I knew this was hard for you, but I had no idea you were carrying this much weight."

Instantly, I felt better. Just telling someone and having them respond with compassion helped—until she said, "I'm going to ask you something, and it might be a little awkward. Would that be okay?"

I leaned back in my chair, curious yet extremely wary. "I guess."

"Have your parents talked to you about the purposes sex serves in marriage?"

Tingles shot up my arms. Wow. This was *not* happening. "Are you kidding?"

"No, I want to know what you think. Is sex wrong?"

I cringed. "Sometimes?"

"When?"

"When you're not married. When it's rape or coerced, like with victims of trafficking."

"Okay, then when is it right? What purpose do you think it serves in marriage?"

I rolled my eyes. "Do we have to do this? I've taken health class already."

"Humor me, please, Izzy. This is important."

"It's for making babies," I said.

"That's it?"

I shrugged, so mortified I could barely breathe. I was so glad we were not at Grounds and Rounds.

"It's for more than that, Izzy. God designed sex to be a holy union, to bring joy to couples in the bond of marriage. The Bible says that the man and his wife were both naked and not ashamed. It says they became one flesh. And God said it was very good."

I wrinkled my nose. "This is not really what I wanted to talk about today," I said.

"Oh, I know it. But honey, we need to talk about this. The truth is, God made us sexual creatures with a longing for physical and emotional intimacy. For those who choose it, marriage is the place to find that intimacy. Girl-crazy boys and boy-crazy girls . . . whether they know it or not, they're reaching for true intimacy. Our culture is constantly promoting its version of sexuality instead of joy, oneness, and commitment. The world tells us to chase promiscuity and lust and profanity. Those boys and girls who took pictures of themselves and passed them around—they were reaching for the right thing in the wrong way. That doesn't make those people evil. Just broken and drawn to sin. You and I know there's a dark side to chasing that sort of thing."

"I never chased it, though," I said. "I didn't want to be part of it at all."

"I know. I'm sorry Zac forced that upon you."

I nodded, tears falling.

"I have a verse for you." Zoe lifted a Bible off her shelf and flipped through it. "In Song of Songs chapter 8, verse 4, it says, 'Daughters of Jerusalem, I charge you: Do not arouse or awaken love until it so desires.'" She set the Bible in front of me and turned it around so I could see the verse for myself. "What do you think that means?"

I thought about it, and heavy despair filled my chest. "The daughters aren't ready to know such things until they're married?"

"Something like that. Izzy, I think you've developed wrong thinking about sex. Any feelings that remind you of what you felt with Zac—both good and bad—you're vilifying them all. Let's see if you can learn to separate the two. It's okay to be attracted to a boy. It's even okay to long for physical touch or sex, but it's important to manage those longings. Bottom line? It's okay to like Cody."

I shook my head. "I don't really know him."

"Yes, you do. You're just afraid. There's a big difference. You've been telling me this for weeks—that you're afraid dating Cody might ruin your friendship with him. There is nothing wrong with that fear, as long as you don't imagine things that aren't there and convict Cody for things he hasn't done or aren't really wrong. Like having a poster of Wonder Woman."

"You don't think it's wrong for a guy to have a sexy poster on his wall?"

Zoe shrugged. "Maybe. I guess I don't know why Cody has that poster."

"I think it could mean that he really wants to look at porn. What if the Wonder Woman poster is, like, a gateway to Cody looking at porn?"

"There is a big difference between a Wonder Woman poster and porn, Izzy. I understand what you are saying, but your concerns are coming from a place of fear."

Tears filled my eyes. "But he might do those things. We can't know for sure."

"No, we can't. But guess what? No one is perfect. Even if you simply remain friends with Cody, he might do something that hurts you. Friends do that, you know. When you spend a lot of time with people, you'll get a little bruised knocking into each another every now and then. That's life. We don't live in a bubble."

"I wish we did."

"Do you remember how happy you were last spring after the hard talk you had with your parents?"

That was after they had found out about the fake picture on my Snapchat and the nude photo Zac had sent me. "I felt very relieved."

"You were grounded from your phone indefinitely, yet you were practically skipping."

"Because we got the evidence we needed against Zac," I said.

"Yes, that was a big part of it," Zoe said. "My point is, reconciliation is a beautiful thing. You had been holding a lot of hurt and fear and anger inside, and once your parents knew about it, you felt lighter. In fact, I think you felt closer to them. Would you agree?"

I nodded. "Because my secret was out in the open. I could talk to them about Zac. And I even told them how I felt about having to watch Sebastian all the time."

"The truth will set you free, Izzy. Rather than accuse Cody of something nefarious with his Wonder Woman poster, why not tell him how seeing that poster made you feel?"

"It sounds so judgmental," I said.

"If it came across that way when you talked to him about it before, maybe you need to apologize for that."

Ugh. I did need to apologize. It was going to be so hard!

"Remember, you can't control how Cody receives what you say," Zoe said. "But if you're honest about where you were wrong, and you share honestly how you feel, I don't think he'll be upset. I think it will help him understand."

"Maybe."

"You could also ask him what Daniel meant by the girlfriend comment. But you have to be ready for answers you might not like."

"What do you mean?"

"Cody might say you're silly for worrying about his poster. He might say he did tell his mom you're his girlfriend. He might tell you he wants you to be his girlfriend. You won't know until you ask him. Promise me you'll think about it."

"Okay."

"Now let's talk about Shay." Zoe reached toward her bookshelf and drew out a thin book. "I would like you to read this. It's a part psychology, part self-help book that dives into the impact of adverse childhood experiences on an individual's life. Adverse childhood experiences are traumatic events that happened during childhood, and they can affect how a person responds to stress in their life. Reading this book might help grow empathy in you toward Shay."

"Her parents died," I said. "And before that, when she was just a baby, her mom left her dad."

"Yes," Zoe said, "and any *one* of those is very difficult for a child to experience. Shay is your friend, isn't she?"

I nodded.

"And you want to keep her as a friend?"

I frowned, nervous about being honest, but Zoe always said she wanted honesty from me. "As long as she gets help."

"Interesting. What did Jesus say to the sinners He met in the Bible?"

"He said to go and leave your life of sin."

"Okay . . . but He also forgave them before they could even ask. How many times did He tell us to forgive those who hurt us?"

I remembered a Bible verse about that. "Seventy times seven?"

"Yes! And sometimes it takes us that many times to forgive and forgive again because someone really hurt us—and even though we forgave them, the pain keeps coming back. But it's not our job to judge anyone. That's God's job. It's God's job to keep tabs on Shay's sin and Daniel's sin and Cody's sin. That responsibility is impossible for you."

I squeezed my hands together, feeling like I was being chastened. "I just feel like if I only surround myself with good people—people I can trust—then I won't get hurt again."

"That is a brilliant plan, but it doesn't work so well, does it?"

My laugh came out dry, and I coughed. "No."

"The responsibility to keep tabs on the sin of everyone we know—it's too much for us to carry," Zoe said. "It makes life heavy. And it makes us judgy and self-righteous. We spend all our time thinking we're better than others, and we forget to examine our own behavior. God wants us to love people and forgive them when necessary. He will do the hard work of judgment. So let me ask you, Izzy, what matters more to you: holding on to Shay's sin, or holding on to her?"

My eyes blurred. I knew I *should* say that Shay mattered more, but I'd been acting like Shay's sin mattered more. Zoe was right, though. It was all connected to my own fears. Fear that Shay was just like Zac, or that if she continued down the path she was on, she soon would be. But maybe Shay was only trying to fill the holes in her life with the wrong things. If I honestly thought about it, I really wasn't all that different from her. My hormones never listened to reason. Maybe no one's did.

"Shay matters more," I said, ashamed that I had been such a poor friend.

"Good! But it seems like lately you've been gripping her sin so tightly that you've let her friendship go. You've always been a great hugger, Izzy. How about you try to let go of Shay's sin, and grab hold of Shay again?"

"I didn't think that's what I was doing," I said. "I was just so mad that she would look at that stuff."

"Oh, honey, I know it. Did you tell her that's how you felt?"

I shook my head. "No."

"How about you try telling her? As children of God, we should be open not only to God's love and blessings, but to correction as well. We need to listen and check ourselves when we fall out of line."

"Maybe I deserved it," I said over my tears. "I have been something of a jerk."

"I think you've been doing the best you could, Izzy. I know it's been very hard for you. I also know you hold your feelings close and are vulnerable with very few people. There's nothing wrong with that in theory, but it's a good idea to have a few friends you're brutally honest with."

"I told Tessa," I said. "And I told Amelia, too, about how much it hurt to be left out of Operation Encouragement."

"Good," Zoe said. "What did they say?"

"They were both nice."

"Did it help them understand you better?"

I nodded. "I think so."

"I want you to be able to understand Shay better, but she might not be able to put her feelings into words you'll understand. That's why I think reading this book will help you."

"Okay," I said, gripping the paperback tightly.

"Remember what 1 Corinthians chapter 13 says about love?"

"It never fails."

"True! It does say that. It also says that love keeps no record of wrongs. Even if there are seventy times seven wrongs. God will judge. That's His job. Leave that messy, hard stuff to Him, and you focus on loving your friend. God is not depending on you to fix Shay. Trust her and her problems to Him. He is more than capable of helping her through everything, but it's going to happen on His timeline, not yours."

"Okay," I said.

Zoe prayed for me, then I rode my bike home, thinking about everything we had discussed. It was all so much. How could I possibly fix everything? I had made so many mistakes. Zoe had said I needed to ask God to help me and not be afraid.

Easier said than done.

When I got home, I wanted to read the book Zoe had loaned me, but I just felt too numb. I needed some time to think.

Unfortunately, I walked into what sounded like a fight. At first, I thought Mamá and Claire were at it again, then I realized it wasn't really a fight. Mamá was cooking in the kitchen, and she was on speakerphone with Abuelita. Those two couldn't talk without it sounding like an argument. By the look of the ingredients on the counter, Mamá was making *chiles rellenos*.

"No," Mamá said. "It could be reflux disease or a peptic ulcer. It might even be stomach cancer. She needs to be seen."

"I told her she needs to try some broth," Abuelita said. "Get some food down."

"*¡Má!* It's not about eating. If she's feeling full all the time, there is something else wrong. Tell your friend to go to urgent care right away."

"Urgent care costs too much," Abuelita said. "Her insurance won't cover it."

"You called for my medical advice, and that's my advice."

"All doctors want people to go to emergency so they can charge huge bills."

"*¡Má!* That's not true. I want your friend to get help before things get worse." Mamá noticed me and waved. "*Hola, mija.* Má, Isabella just got home."

"*Hola*, Isabella!" Abuelita said.

"Hi, Abuelita," I said.

"Tell your mother she needs to get back her job at the clinic," Abuelita said. "That money could help pay for your driving school. You need to get your driver's license. It's dangerous riding your bike all over town—a young girl like you."

I opened my mouth to reply but could think of nothing to say.

Mamá waved her hand at me. "We already have the money set aside for Izzy's driving lessons, Má, and I'm not going back to the clinic. It was too much time away from home."

"You need to put your family first," Abuelita said. "If Dañel won't get a better job, you need to pick up the slack."

Mamá rolled her eyes at me. "My sauce is about to boil over, Má. I've got to go."

"Okay, *hasta luego, muñequita*," Abuelita said.

"*¡Nos vemos, cuídese!*" Mamá hung up and smiled at me. "To my mother, the best way to put your family first is to make a lot of money. Your Papi and I have decided being present is just as important, maybe more so."

I gave Mamá a hug and a kiss on the cheek. "I'm glad you're home more," I said. "Need some help?"

"*Sí*, thank you. You want to make the filling or cut the rest of the chilies?"

"Filling," I said.

While Mamá and I made dinner, I thought about the conversation I'd overheard. It was nothing new. Abuelita always criticized Mamá, and Mamá ignored her and did her own thing. It was the same with Mamá and Claire, though. Could it be that I had been doing the same thing to my friends? Clearly, criticism was in my blood. It occurred to me that discovering the real Isabella Valadez wasn't only about discovering the positive things or even the obvious ones. I needed to understand my weaknesses as well.

After dinner, I pulled out my diorama poster for Creative

Writing and started ripping off some of what I'd already glued in place. I took off so much that I decided to start from scratch.

I thought about all I had been through recently and realized I had been miserable because I chose to be miserable. Cody was right. I had pointed an accusing finger at everyone but myself. I judged Shay for her problems when I was guilty of my own sins. I made an unfair assumption about Cody because I was afraid. I might not have sinned as grievously as King David, but I had done my fair share of manipulation.

Like King David, I needed to confess and repent. I stopped working on my poster and prayed right there on the floor of my bedroom. I asked God to forgive me for letting fear overwhelm me to the point of not trusting Him. I asked for forgiveness for judging my friends and for gossiping to Cody about Shay. I prayed longer than I ever had before because I had a lot to say, but in the end, I felt free. For the first time in a long time, I wasn't afraid.

Grateful, I went back to working on my poster. It occurred to me that there was another thing I'd learned from King David: I needed to return to a balance of being strong and kind. I'd realized that a while ago, but I hadn't understood just how skewed my behavior had been. My version of kindness lately had been items on a to-do list motivated by works, not love. I wanted to go back to my old ways of loving people. But that would mean choosing to trust God to protect me even when I was afraid and to help me if I got hurt.

Also, it would mean choosing love over fear. Love of God, love of Shay, and love—*like?*—of Cody.

It was more than that, though. Loving people well also meant having grace for them. I needed to extend grace to my parents, my sister, my brothers, Shay, Cody, and even Daniel and Zac. I didn't do *alone* well, but if I didn't learn how to forgive people even when I couldn't understand them, I had a feeling I was going to remain alone for a very long time.

Chapter
19

I DIDN'T LIKE BEING AT CHURCH ON SUNDAY. I sat with my parents, but I knew Tessa and Shay would be there and could see me from the back. I felt like a bug under a microscope, though since I never looked at where they usually sat, I had no evidence that they were even at church, let alone looking at me. I kept my eyes on the floor and the stage, and I didn't relax until we were in the car on the way to eat lunch with Nana and Tata.

I thought over what I could possibly do to try to fix things with my friends. An apology was a must, but I felt like I needed to go bigger. Make some kind of grand gesture like they did in the movies. It might be too late, but I had to try.

When my worrisome thoughts began to drive me crazy, I picked up the book Zoe had loaned me and read about adverse childhood experiences.

I had no idea.

I could never understand what Shay had gone through, but I

now had an idea of what kinds of scars came with surviving traumatic events. Shay struggled with anger. That same emotion now
came upon me quickly too. I hated feeling out of control, but I
didn't know how to stop it. How did Shay do so well controlling
her anger?

I thought about the stories told in Zoe's book and what I knew
of Shay's life. Shay was a good person who had made some poor
choices. From what she had said in Paprika's, though, she was
working on her problem; she'd gone almost two weeks without
looking at porn. I didn't understand why she wanted to look at it
in the first place, but I could see how it might help for us to celebrate her small victories. The last thing she needed from a friend
was the kind of judgment she got from her grandmother. That
self-righteous criticism ran in my family too. I hated that I had
treated Shay in such a way, and I wanted to break myself of the
habit so I wouldn't end up nagging everyone I knew in the style
of Mamá or Abuelita.

Maybe I should start counting the days I went without assuming the worst of anyone. Stars. That might be hard. Really hard.

I tossed the book aside and checked the clock on the wall. It
was two thirty. That was plenty of time to make some cupcakes
and a house call.

—⟋⟋⟍—

I shouldered slowly through the front door of Booked Up, the
store owned by Laura, Shay's aunt, clutching my plate of cupcakes.
The smell of French roast coffee and old books greeted me like a
friend, and a pang of sorrow shot through me that it had been so
long since I'd been here.

Shay's tortoiseshell cat, Matilda, glanced up at me from her
spot on the leather chair beside the front window display. She
looked bored but meowed in greeting.

My heart stuttered at the sight of that animal. "Hey, Matilda," I said, moving my plate of cupcakes to one hand so I could reach down and pet her. Gah, I missed this cat!

Ginny stood behind the register, talking to a slender guy with multiple piercings—the bridge and nasallang ones looked rather painful. While the guy had Ginny beat in piercings, she was way ahead in the tattoo department with sleeves up both arms and a small one on the back of her neck.

At the sound of my voice, Ginny and the guy glanced my way.

"Hey, Izzy," Ginny said. "Those for me?"

"They're for Shay," I said, "but I suppose I could spare one." I set the plate on the counter and lifted the edge of the plastic wrap. Ginny snaked out a cupcake decorated to look like a cat's face. I glanced at the guy, whose eyes were feasting on my plate. "Or two," I added, grinning at him.

"Thanks," he said, grabbing one of the dog cupcakes. "These are epic."

"This is Brom," Ginny said. "He's a fan of the band."

Ginny played guitar in a rock band. "That's cool." I startled when something touched my foot. I glanced down, delighted to see Matilda rubbing against my leg. I crouched beside her, showering her with attention. "Do you know if Shay is home?" I asked Ginny.

"Not sure," Ginny mumbled through a full mouth. "Laura's in her office, though."

I gave Matilda one last pat, then stood and re-covered my plate of cupcakes, now two shy of a dozen. "I'll ask her," I said.

"Thanks for the snack," Brom said, toasting me with the remains of his cupcake.

"You bet," I said.

Laura's office was in the back. I found the door open and stepped inside, nervous. Laura was standing at a file cabinet, her back to me. The red streak in her wavy dark hair, and her skinny jeans and trendy boots, made her look every bit like she could be in Ginny's band.

"Laura?" I said. "Is Shay home?"

Laura spun around, a hand pressed to her chest. "Izzy! You scared me."

I winced. "Sorry."

Laura took in the plate of cupcakes in my hands, and her expression softened. "She is home. Do I need to come up there with you?"

Shame crept through me at the insinuation that Laura knew of the trouble between Shay and me. "I don't think so," I said. "But pray?"

Laura frowned, and I kicked myself when I remembered she was relatively new to church. *Duh, Izzy.* "You hungry?" I asked. Laura often forgot to eat when she got busy working. "They're chocolate."

"I'll take one," she said, circling the desk. "Oh, how cute." She took one of the dogs. "We've missed you around here, you know. No one else has dressed up to read to the kids."

"I could probably come on a Saturday morning," I said.

"That would be great," Laura said. "Readings are at ten or two."

"I can do ten," I said. "Sorry I've been . . . away."

"I'm just glad you're back."

"Me too," I said, though it wasn't really up to me.

I left Laura and made my way upstairs to the apartment above the store, where Shay and Laura lived. I knocked on the door, and inside, Stanley began barking. I heard his toenails clicking over the floor as he danced on the other side of the door, desperate to see who had come to call.

"Stanley, move." Shay's muffled voice sent my heart racing.

Please help us, I prayed. *Please help me.*

The door opened a crack, and Shay peered out. "Izzy."

"Hi," I said. "Can I come in? Please?"

"Okay."

And suddenly I was inside Shay's apartment, Stanley sniffing my leg, his tail tap, tap, tapping the wall as those big brown eyes stared up at me.

"Hi, Stanley," I said, then forced myself to stay on task. I turned to Shay and offered her the plate. "These are for you. They're chocolate. There were a dozen, but Laura, Ginny, and Brom each had one."

Shay took the plate from me. "Wow," she said. "They're really cute."

"They're supposed to be Stanley and Matilda, but it was harder than I thought to make brindle- and tortoiseshell-colored frostings."

Shay snickered at this, which I hoped was a good sign.

"Shay, I'm sorry," I said. "So sorry for so many things."

"I'm sorry too," she said.

Those words brought so much relief that tears blurred my eyes. "You are forgiven a hundred times," I said.

A small smile curled the corners of Shay's mouth. "You're forgiven too," she said.

I took a deep breath and exhaled. "Thank you," I said, grabbing her around the waist from the side. She lifted the plate of cupcakes out of the way and laughed as I squeezed.

"Can I put these down?" she asked.

I released her. "I suppose."

Shay headed into the kitchen. "I'm really working hard to stay away from all that stuff."

"That's really none of my business," I said as I followed her. "Do you remember when I came over on Christmas break and we talked about how difficult people sometimes don't know they're being difficult and unfair?"

"Your mom and my grandma," Shay said.

"Right," I said. "And, as it turns out, me."

Shay set the cupcakes on the counter. "You?"

"Yep. Nana had told me that Mamá was sometimes critical and controlling because she thought if she could make everything perfect, then life would be okay. After what happened with that fake picture of me, I tried really hard to keep anything dangerous away from me. Technology, Cody, you . . . All it did was hurt everyone, including me."

"I would never hurt you," Shay said. "Not on purpose, anyway."

"I know," I said. "Hey, you know how sometimes you get really angry and it's hard for you to calm down?"

Shay nodded.

"It's kind of like that for me when I see one of the boys who was part of the Dropbox scandal, or if someone says something about the fake picture. Just thinking about pornography makes me angry."

"So when you heard about what I had been doing, it made you angry?" Shay asked.

"Yeah," I said. "It felt like you had picked Zac's side. Silly, right? I made it all about me. I was being selfish."

"What changed your mind?"

"Cody called me on it. He's really smart." I needed to apologize to him, too.

A knock at the door turned our heads.

"Shay? It's us!" Tessa said through the door.

"The girls were coming over to watch a movie," Shay said, walking toward the door.

This was perfect! I would be able to apologize to them, too.

"What movie?" I asked.

"I don't know," Shay said. "It's Amelia's turn to pick, so probably a musical."

I steeled myself as Shay opened the door and Stanley loped over to greet the newcomers. Tessa took one look at me and squealed.

"Oh, I'm so glad to see you here!" she said, hugging me.

Amelia was not so generous. "You shouldn't have let her in until we got here, Shay."

"It's fine," Shay said.

"Amelia," I said over the top of Tessa's head. "I'm very sorry for everything. For being such a jerk. Tessa," I said into her hair, "you too. I'm sorry."

"I love you," Tessa said. "I'm so glad you and Shay are okay." She released me. "You are okay, right?"

I raised my eyebrows at Shay. "Are we?"

Shay smiled. "Yes, we're okay."

"Finally!" Amelia said. "Now, are we going to watch *The Greatest Showman* or what?"

I squealed. "Yes, please!"

"Izzy brought cupcakes," Shay said.

Tessa patted the bag slung over her shoulder. "I have the popcorn."

"Can we have a group hug first?" I asked.

"Absolutely!" Shay said.

We embraced each other, giggling madly, which made Stanley so excited that he jumped up to join in. This made us topple over onto the couch, laughing harder.

Thank You, Jesus, for my friends.

Together again. I was so, so grateful.

Now that things had been mended with my squad, I set my attention toward Cody Nichols. A Hollywood-worthy grand gesture was already forming in my mind. Since I'd always told Cody I hated running, I needed to do exactly that. I looked up several Bible verses about running races, thinking I might hide out and wait for him to pass by, then chase him down. I might not be able to catch him, though. He ran a lot faster than me.

Completely aware that I needed advice, I texted Tessa late Sunday night.

Me: Can you talk?

Tessa: Give me five, and I'll call you.

Four minutes later, my phone rang.

"What's up?" Tessa asked.

"I need to apologize to Cody," I said. "I have a plan, but I need to know roughly what time he'll run by Paprika's in the race on Tuesday. I thought you might be able to ask Alex?"

"I would be happy to ask Alex," Tessa said, "but first you have to tell me your plan."

"I was going to wait for him to run by, then run alongside him since he knows how much I hate any kind of cardio."

"Izzy, that's super sweet, but you can't run with a runner during a race. He'd be disqualified."

"Oh."

"And while he might not mind personally, he's the third best runner on A Team, so his getting disqualified would hurt their overall score. Then the rest of A Team would be mad. At you."

"Ah. Don't want that."

"No," Tessa said. "But you could try doing it tomorrow when they run their trial. Since they can't block off the road yet, they're not running to make good time so much as to get a feel for the chart of the race."

"Do you think Alex might know when they'd be running past Paprika's?"

"I'll ask him. He might be suspicious, and since I don't want to give you away, I might say I want to come out and wave. Is that okay?"

"That's fine," I said. "Alex seems really protective of Cody, so it's probably better if he doesn't know I'm involved."

"Believe it or not, Alex is rooting for you guys."

"Really?"

"Yep. But don't tell him I said that, or he'll just deny it." She paused. "This is so exciting. It's like something from a Hallmark movie. Or an eighties rom-com."

"That's the idea," I said. "I'm trying to make a grand gesture."

"It's going to work. Let me text Alex, and I'll let you know what he says."

Twenty minutes later, she texted me: He thinks they'll pass by anywhere between 3:15 and 3:30. It depends on how quickly the team gets dressed for practice.

Me: Thank you! I'll talk with Mr. Bellanger and see if he'll help me.

Tessa: Fingers crossed!

—m—

School on Monday was the best it had been in a while, save for the awkwardness with Cody. If he noticed my friendliness with Amelia in second and third hour, he didn't say anything. I was as kind and peppy as I could be in business class, but we still had a lot to do, and Cody gave my questions nothing more than short, polite answers.

I sat with my squad at lunch. I had been sitting with Lilliesha and Hyun Ki, so I doubted Cody missed me there. Creative Writing was just more presentations.

After school, when I got to work, I went straight to Mr. Bellanger's office.

He glanced up. "Izzy, how are you today?"

"Not the best, honestly. I need a favor and was hoping you could help me."

He got up and sat on the front edge of his desk. "I'll certainly try. What is it?"

"I hurt Cody's feelings, and I need to make it right. I was hoping I could clock out for about a half hour when he runs past the store."

Mr. Bellanger smiled. "You want him to see you cheering him on."

"Something like that, yeah."

"I thought the race was tomorrow."

"It is, but I don't want to risk getting him disqualified. So it would be better to do this on his practice run today."

"Not a problem. We'll make it happen. Any idea what time he'll be here?"

I winced. "Soon. We think between three fifteen and three thirty."

"Okay, let me see if Katie can work another half hour, and if not, I'll cover for you."

"Thank you!" I rushed forward and hugged the man. "Thank you so much."

He chuckled. "I can't have any trouble between my employees, now, can I?"

I shook my head. "No, sir."

Katie was happy to stay for another half hour, and I thanked her profusely.

"Cody is such a sweetie," she said. "I'm happy to help."

I paced at the window, tinkering with my display as I watched the road in the distance. According to Tessa, the runners would start at the school, head down Fifth, then take Cherry Street over to Main. They'd run through the entire downtown area, then take Spruce Street west. The race zigzagged around the police station and city hall before turning back toward the high school.

At 3:19, I saw them coming. There were about two dozen students in cross-country, which was broken into smaller teams. Alex was out front, followed by Michael. Cody was in third.

Just as he ran past, I sprinted out of the store. Only because of his measured pace was I able to catch up with him. As I came alongside, he glanced at me, then did a double take.

"What are you doing?" he asked.

I pumped my legs to keep pace beside him. "I need to talk to you."

"Izzy, now is not the time."

"But it is, because I wanted to say these things while I'm doing something hard. To show you that I would do hard things for you."

He smirked. "I'm not sure that makes sense, but I'm intrigued."

I panted to catch my breath. I could feel my body funneling energy where I suddenly needed it, but I didn't think my non-athletic self would be able to keep up such activity for long.

"It's just that I'm a little broken," I said.

"I know, Izzy."

"Please let me say this." I paused for a deep breath. "I was incredibly naive when I met Zac. At the time, I didn't think God would allow me . . . to meet someone bad for me."

So much panting already. Why was I so out of shape?

"And even though God sent plenty of warnings"—*inhale*—"I didn't want to listen." I stopped talking to just breathe for a few seconds, surprised by how hard my lungs were working.

"What I went through with Zac . . . scarred me pretty badly." Another pause. "So when you and I are just being friends . . . life is really good . . . but when I feel things about you . . . that are more than friendly . . . my instincts tell me to run. I'm about to get hurt again."

Now my emotions were growing big, which shortened my breath even more. "So I say, 'No, instincts . . . this time is different.' But my imagination has . . . always been . . . really out of control . . . and every time I feel . . . feelings for you that are more than friendship . . . I freak out and do . . . something completely irrational."

"You feel feelings for me?"

"Um, yeah." I tried to look at him but couldn't. "I swear . . .
I'm not trying to play games . . . or hurt you . . . I would never
do that. I'm just a little scared. I act super weird . . . because I'm
unconsciously . . . trying to protect myself . . . from getting hurt
again." I paused to catch my breath. "I'm sorry my fear hurt you."

He slowed to a stop. "Izzy, I would never intentionally—"

"No! You have to keep running." I grabbed his arm and ran,
pulling until he started jogging again. "I don't want you to get a
bad time because of me."

"It's just a run-through. It's fine."

"Well, I want to run it with you . . . for a while. It's a metaphor.
You know . . . how the Bible says to forget what's in the past"—
I gasped in a breath—"and look forward to what's ahead?" Two
breaths. "To press on with the race?"

Cody had to slow down to keep pace with me. We were barely
jogging now. Speed walkers pushing strollers could lap us.

"It's talking about eternal life with God," Cody said. "Not an
actual race."

"Right, but the Bible . . . also says . . . in Hebrews . . . that we
should throw off everything that hinders us . . ." *Oh, so hard to talk
and jog.* "And run the race of life . . . God marked out for us." *Deep
breath. Almost there.* "I just think I want to run my race with you."

Cody turned and jogged backward, looking me right in the
eyes. Gosh, he made sports look easy. "Even if we're just friends?"
he said.

The question set my cheeks on fire, but I was already about
to internally combust—could that really happen?—so I doubted
Cody would be able to tell the difference.

"Even if we're just friends," I said. "For now."

His eyebrows shot up, and he spun around, jogging alongside
me again. "For now?"

"Yeah," I said, then pushed hard to get my next words out in one breath. "I just think that being fast about things isn't the only way to win a race."

A slow smile grew on Cody's face. "That," he said as he reached down and squeezed my way-too-sweaty hand, "is one of the wisest things I've ever heard."

Chapter

20

ONE WOULD THINK I WAS DONE HAVING BIG DAYS, but Friday loomed ahead—the day of my business presentation with Cody and the last day of diorama presentations in Creative Writing.

I wasn't nearly as worried about our business presentation. We had worked hard and were ready. For my creative writing assignment, though, I'd stayed up until two thirty trying to complete it, which was why I felt overly tired the next morning. Thankfully, Claire had already agreed to drive me to school. I'd made three dozen cupcakes for Mr. Federici's class, and Ms. Larkin had promised I could keep them in her classroom as long as she got to sample the goods.

I wanted to surprise Mr. Federici. And Cody.

After Chemistry, Amelia helped me transport the cupcakes from the multipurpose room to our business classroom. She, too, was paid with a cupcake.

"Where's Cody?" she asked as we set the cupcake boxes on the back counter of the room.

Cody chose that moment to walk into class, carrying a box of his own.

"You made cupcakes?" he asked, his eyes wide as he took in my confection creations through the see-through lids.

"I did. What's that?" I asked, pointing at the box.

"A present," he said, setting it down beside the cupcakes. "Open it."

I ripped off the tape and pulled back the flaps. Inside was a toy motor home. Cody had painted it to look like our store. There were also colored printouts of cupcakes and the words *Love at First Bite*; the *o* in the word *Love* was a small cupcake. There were two dolls inside the motor home, a boy with blond hair and a Hispanic girl. Both were wearing stiff cotton T-shirts with the words *Love at First Bite* painted on the fronts.

"My mom made the shirts," he said, "but I did the rest. You like?"

I took out the boy doll. "Who is this?"

"Blaine, so says my cousin. This was all her stuff."

I laughed. "Blaine is a good likeness."

Cody wrinkled his nose. "I don't know . . . I think he looks too much like a surfer."

"Mr. Nichols and Ms. Valadez," Mr. Federici said from his desk. "If you're ready to present, why don't the two of you come to the front of the class and regale us with your business proposal."

"We're ready," I said.

Cody started the presentation by showing off the model of our store. Then I presented our industry overview and passed out our products to the class. I'd made eighteen of my Flying Monkey Bread cupcakes, inspired by *Wicked*, and eighteen of Cody's Elvis-themed Thank You Very Much cupcakes.

"There is no extra credit for bribery, Ms. Valadez," Mr. Federici said, biting into a Flying Monkey Bread cupcake. "Though you may very well have found your first loyal customer. This is excellent."

I beamed.

Cody then shared our executive summary and went over zoning regulations and availability of parking places, which was a problem for food trucks that made their living off trying to feed rush hour crowds each day. As a company focusing on invitations, that wasn't a concern for us.

I presented our staffing and operating plan, then Cody did the sales and marketing analysis and the competition report. We ended with our financial plan.

The class applauded.

"While this Elvis cupcake is excellent," Mr. Federici said, halfway finished with his second cupcake, "I think you'd be better off focusing your branding a little more, maybe by offering fewer cupcake options—fewer musicals and fewer songs. Your branding feels uncertain otherwise."

"True," I said. "We talked about that."

"All in all, you have a rather small profit margin," Mr. Federici added. "Have you considered the seasonal aspect of your business?"

"We have," I said. "We hope to offset that cost by catering Christmas parties."

"And with the steady income we derive from having stores like Booked Up and Grounds and Rounds carrying our product all year," Cody added.

"Very good," Mr. Federici said. "I'm curious, could either of you see yourself doing this as a career?"

"Absolutely," I said.

"Yes," Cody said. "I mean, as long as I could find someone to do the baking."

Mr. Federici finished his Elvis cupcake. "Seems like you've already found someone, Mr. Nichols. She makes a fine product and would most certainly generate some recurring revenue off me."

—ᴍᴠ—

When I walked into Creative Writing with Cody, I was feeling really good coming off our strong presentation in business class.

Two students went before Mrs. Lopez finally called my name.

I carried my final project to the front of the class and began to unfold it.

"My project is titled '¿Quién soy yo?'" I said. "This is Spanish for 'Who am I?' The title represents my Mexican heritage. I wanted something with many levels, and since I didn't want to tape together a bunch of boxes, I made this." I finished unfolding my giant fortune-teller game and tucked my palms inside so I could work the folds. Ms. Larkin had allowed me to use a large sheet of butcher paper from the art room, which was the only way I could have made such a huge one.

"My presentation has many layers because I am a complicated person," I said. "On the outside I have four different pictures. First, a drawing of me wearing my panda bear leggings and a Captain Marvel T-shirt, and my hair is down and blowing in the wind. This is how I see myself most days. This is how I want people to see me."

I turned to the second square. "This side has a cross, which represents my faith in Jesus. He died for my sins, and without Him, this fortune teller would be a crumpled-up mess." I turned to the third side. "This side is filled with all the things I love, like theater, singing, musicals, animals, baking, and cooking. There's a picture of a stage because I like performing. And I sprinkled glitter on there because life is better with a little sparkle." I turned the paper fortune teller one more time. "This fourth side is a grassy field of possibilities. This is the future, both here on earth and in heaven. This represents the vast potential of my life. Who but God can know what will happen?" I pushed the fortune teller tips together and held it up so the class could see all four tops.

"All this is what I experience and feel and show everyone on the outside."

Now I opened the fortune teller, baring the inside folds. "I keep many things inside me too. This first triangle has a wiggly face with big eyes. This represents the things I fear. All the little stick people in the second triangle are the people who are dear to me. My people. There are a lot of them."

I smiled, pleased with myself so far. "This red triangle represents a curtain concealing all the hopes and dreams that are too private for TikTok and Instagram. Some of this I share with those close to me. I've not been good about this, but I'm determined to improve. And the last triangle is covered in tinfoil. It's reflective, but I can't see myself clearly. Even though I know who I am on the outside, I sometimes look in a mirror like this, and culture and media tell me I'm not enough. Or sometimes I'm guarded, trying to hold myself back from being too much Izzy. Too wild. Too unbridled. Too silly. People are always watching. And I want them to like me."

I paused and looked around the room. I had the full attention of my classmates. They wanted to see the next layer. I opened it all the way, holding the big paper under my chin where I could see what I was describing. "Deep inside me is darkness. It's half black and half gray because some of it is a quiet refuge, the place I go inside to be alone or to spend time with God. It's also a place where I can hide and feel safe. The rest is shame and regret. Scars."

I flipped the paper around to show them the outside top squares. "I have the side of me that wants to do good and love my friends." I turned it back around. "Then I have the side that loves myself most and wants to be right or a superstar or the most beautiful girl in the world or the best actress. Sometimes this part of me is okay, but too often it can get ugly.

"I also make mistakes. I've been a bad friend. I've judged my friends and kept the truth from them. I've been so afraid of getting hurt that I justified my behavior by telling myself, 'This is necessary to be safe.' But I was wrong. It's okay to be afraid, but I need to be honest with my friends, even if that is scary, and even if they don't really understand."

I lifted the paper so that the image in the center would be easier to see. "In the middle of this dark background is Izzy. Some of you think you've seen her before, but you haven't. Still, some hard things happened to her, and this is where she lives, hidden in the darkness where no one can see her scars. There are names carved onto her body, things people have said that left a mark. Not good enough. Ugly. Stupid. Fat. Jerk. Worse names. Names I wrote in black crayon so no one could see how awful they are. Some names I might have earned with poor behavior. Some were flung by the careless cruelty of another. Some names I called myself."

I began to fold up my fortune teller. "All this is part of me, but I keep it where no one can see it. I keep those lies inside. That shame. That guilt. And I remind myself that Jesus died for it. He died to set me free. So I live my life as best I can. I'm a work in progress. The daughter of a King." I held the fortune teller closed again with carefree Izzy on the top, facing outward. "Thank you."

Saturday morning, I made my first social media post in a long time. I asked Claire to take a picture of me holding my fortune teller from Creative Writing, then I wrote a new "introduction" post that shared a condensed version of my "Who Am I?" presentation.

When I began my search for self, I was looking for externals like interests and personality quirks and even my culture to a small degree. Yet there is so much more to all of us than those things alone. A true search for self must dig deeper and face the ugliness inside as well as the good. A huge part of my identity is rooted in fear. I'm afraid of not measuring up to ideals set for me by my parents, my church, and society. That fear turned me into a people pleaser who takes on more than anyone ever asks of me. Then something happened that made me afraid to give my heart to a boy. I became so afraid that I pushed away my friends and ended up alone. In order to live my life again, I had to admit my fear and choose to trust God.

So now I know myself a lot better, my strengths and my weaknesses. I'm sure I will discover more things about myself as I grow older, but I hope that I will always remember to lean on God for the things I don't understand and always offer grace to others who are all doing the best they can.

I'm Isabella Valadez, and I'm a human who loves Jesus.

#whoami #quiénsoy #introductions #therealme #nicetomeetyou #gettingtoknowyou #hello

I tucked my phone into my back pocket and headed downstairs. Mrs. Kirby had gotten home two days ago, and she'd invited Cody and me over for dinner to thank us for taking such good care of her animals and yard while she was on her cruise.

So much had happened in the past eight months, but I finally knew who I was. Not only that, I knew who my friends were and what to do the next time I got hurt or hurt someone else. Because it was inevitable. I understood that now. No one is perfect.

I was also learning to be brave again and giving myself grace when that was hard. It would take time for me to get over the hurt of being betrayed by someone like Zac, but I was determined to do it, one day at a time.

Just as I stepped out onto the porch, my phone buzzed. I pulled it out and saw that an Instagram notification had popped up on my screen. I clicked on it.

codynichols liked your post.

I smiled, and as I returned the phone to my back pocket, I saw that very boy walking down the street toward me. He lifted a hand in greeting, and I waved back.

Maybe most important of all, I no longer minded being seen.

Appendix

You Can Be Set Free from Pornography Addiction

PORNOGRAPHY IS NOT A PROBLEM MERELY for teenage boys and men. The pornography industry targets teen girls with devastating effects. Pornography harms women and girls in several ways. It creates body image issues; it warps the perception of what constitutes a healthy relationship with a guy; it normalizes violent and reckless sexual behavior and desensitizes people to many forms of sexual abuse; and it can create problems with sexual addiction.

If you have fallen victim to the dangers of pornography, you are not alone—and there is help. Speak with a parent or a trusted counselor, and check out the following organizations for resources and tools to support you as you work to break free from pornography's trap.

Fight the New Drug: www.FightTheNewDrug.org
XXXchurch: www.XXXchurch.com
X3watch: www.X3watch.com
Covenant Eyes: www.CovenantEyes.com
Celebrate Recovery: www.CelebrateRecovery.com